The Tale of Genji

The Uji Chapters Part II

MURASAKI SHIKIBU

Translated by Kazuyuki Hijiya, Nahoko Toyota

YAMAGUCHI SHOTEN

I would like to dedicate this book to two individuals from Nada High School who opened up my eyes to the world of literature: Masami Katsuyama (a brilliant teacher of Japanese literature and later principal of the school) and Taihei Sumida (a boundlessly enthusiastic teacher of English).

と経ゆもるる橘の
小島の色は変らくは

橘の小島をそはうまる
う舟珠ゆき遣しくれぬ

Calligraphy by Houju Yasuda

書 安田 蓬樹

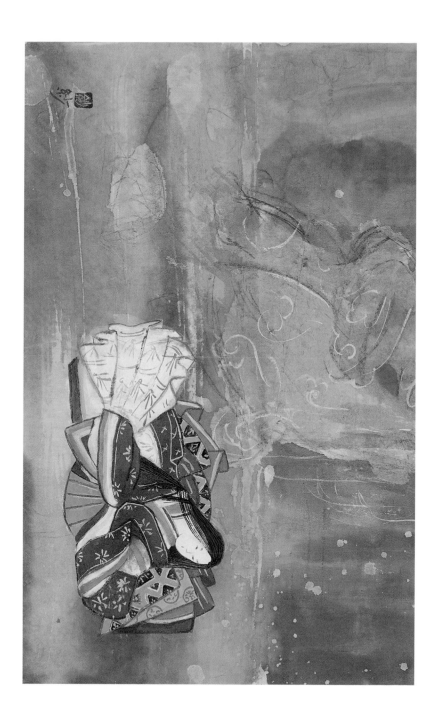

Courtesy of The Tale of Genji Museum (Uji City)

Courtesy of The Tale of Genji Museum (Uji City)

The Tale of Genji

The Uji Chapters Part II

CONTENTS

7. *A Drifting Boat 1*

8. *The Mayfly 85*

9. *Writing Practice 135*

10. *A Floating Bridge in a Dream 201*

Epilogue 219

7. A Drifting Boat

橘の小島きいろはかはらしをうりしてれね
うすく舟ぞゆくゑしられね

と経ゆくもうきむみより橘の小島のさきは契るくろは

A Drifting Boat

CHARACTERS

Ukifune (22), Prince Hachi's illegitimate daughter

Commander Kaoru (27), thought to be Genji's son
but actually the son of Kashiwagi

Prince Niou (28), son of the Emperor and the Akashi princess
and Genji's grandson

Lady Naka (27), Ukifune's half-sister and wife of Prince Niou

A young female servant of Lady Naka

Lady Shosho, Lady Naka's lady-in-waiting

Tokikata, Prince Niou's retainer

The Senior Secretary, secretary of the Ministry of Central Affairs
and Prince Niou's retainer

Nakanobu, father-in-law to the Senior Secretary
and Commander Kaoru's retainer

Ukon, Ukifune's lady-in-waiting

Jiju, Ukifune's lady-in-waiting

Ukifune's nurse

Lady Chujo, Ukifune's mother

Ben-no-Ama, a nun from Uji

Commander Kaoru's messenger

Prince Niou's messenger

Yugiri, the Minister of the Right

Prince Niou couldn't get the twilight liaison with the mysterious lady out of his mind. Memories of the evening he had spent with her remained firmly embedded in his heart. Although she was clearly not of noble status, he found her irresistibly charming. Since he had been intimate with many women, he found it far from fulfilling to have simply lain next to one another, and he became very eager to learn more about her. Lady Naka refused to discuss the matter with her husband, however, no matter how much he pressed her.

"Someone of your status needn't be jealous of such trivial things. You realize, of course, that this lady is of no consequence. Please don't disappoint me by acting so childishly, and kindly tell me what you know of her."

Every time he blamed her for something or talked down to her in this way, his words struck Lady Naka with such force that she sometimes thought about telling him the truth about Lady Ukifune. She ran over the situation in her mind:

"This lady may not be special to Prince Niou, but it seems that Commander Kaoru truly cares about her and keeps their relationship discreet, so as to protect her from the outside world. If I reveal the truth to my husband now, he will never let them be. It's not in his nature. Once he finds a woman attractive, no matter her social standing, he pursues her without hesitation. What is particularly surprising, and disturbing, are the lengths he will sometimes go to in order to become intimate with one of his conquests. It doesn't bother him in the least to visit disreputable areas where a lady he favors resides with her people, which is usually viewed as shameful behavior for someone of his standing. Considering his reckless nature and the fact that, in spite of his fickleness, he has been infatuated with the same lady for some months this time, I can definitively say that he must be so desperate for her by now that he will risk even ruining his reputation to have her as his own. Inevitably, he will hear about the relationship between Commander Kaoru and Lady Ukifune, which I am powerless to prevent. Since this will make it impossible for him to leave them alone, their relationship will end unhappily due to his meddling. Since Lady Ukifune is my half sister, if my husband ruins things as a result of my telling him the truth, people will gossip endlessly about us, and I will be shamed in society. I refuse to be the one blamed for such troubles."

Feeling put out by the tiresome situation, she didn't say a word and instead played the role of the jealous wife, for it seemed too bothersome to construct a convincing lie otherwise. As she intended, the Prince thought it was because of her jealousy toward his newest paramour that she refused to break her silence.

The Commander was taking things slowly, although he truly cared about Lady Ukifune, whom he was certain was pining away for him in Uji. Since he was a man of quite high standing in society, and there was no ready excuse for him to travel to Uji, there had been no real opportunity to visit. Feeling sorry for her, he suppressed his longings by trying to view things in a positive light.

"When things get sorted out, as they soon will, I will treat her in the manner she truly deserves. In the meantime, since I brought her to the house in Uji in an effort to establish a place of rest for myself, I should manufacture the need to take some extended business trips out that way whenever possible. It will provide me with a proper excuse to travel all the way to Uji and give us a chance to spend some time together. Sooner or later, I'll set her up in her own place somewhere quiet, so that we can continue our relationship far from people's notice. As time goes by, she will gradually settle into her new surroundings and I will be able to stay with her, all the while avoiding public reproach. If I make an obvious move now, however, the busybodies in society will try to find out everything about us, pestering me about what sort of woman she is or how long we've been together, which will annoy me to no end. Of course, another concern is how Lady Naka will react upon hearing about us. All I wanted to accomplish with Lady Ukifune was to keep the memory of Lady Okimi alive. I never intended to make Lady Naka mistakenly believe that I've forgotten the love of my life. I will send a message to Lady Naka, informing her that I am leaving Lady Ukifune in Uji for a while so as to maintain a strong connection with that area."

Thus, as was always the case with him, the Commander took as much time as possible to consider all the factors involved before making a move. After carefully weighing everything, he ordered that land be secretly arranged for, in order to build a new house in the capital of Kyoto in which he would eventually install Lady Ukifune.

More demands had been placed upon the Commander, not only because he had married a daughter of the Emperor but also by his new relationship with a half sister of his deceased lover, yet nothing had changed in his caring attitude toward Lady Naka. Although some people saw them together and suspected that they were having an affair, he was never shy about showing his true feelings towards her. Lady Naka herself was becoming mature enough to understand how men and women developed their relationships, and also how Commander Kaoru was as a person. She was very impressed by the fine example of a man he had become, one who truly cherished his lover even after her passing, regardless of how much time had elapsed. It seemed that the older he became, the more distinguished people found him. Every time she felt unsure about her own husband's feelings for her, she couldn't help comparing him with the Commander, thinking,

"How twisted life can become, moving in the least expected directions. In spite of what my sister had wished for me, I somehow ended up being married to such an amorous man, one who will never give me peace from worrying over his dalliances."

Nevertheless, it wasn't so easy to meet Commander Kaoru in person. It had been such a long time since they had lost Lady Okimi that some of Lady Naka's servants who were too new to the household to truly understand their connection were suspicious about what was going on between the two of them. If he had been just an ordinary man, it would have been normal for him to keep such an intimate connection with a longtime acquaintance, but since he was, in fact, part of the upper echelon of the government, one who had many responsibilities and constraints on his time, she had to feel somewhat uneasy about maintaining such a familiar relationship. It also bothered her that Prince Niou had always been unsure as to whether or not they were having an affair. For this reason, she could no longer feel fully comfortable spending time privately with the Commander, and her attitude toward him was becoming more and more distant. In contrast, Commander Kaoru's attitude hadn't changed in the least, and he stayed as close to her as he had always been. Prince Niou was viewed by many as a poor husband for his famously flirtatious behavior, but as his son, mothered by Lady Naka, grew up to be an adorable young boy, Prince Niou came to believe that this child would someday become his successor, and he treasured the boy so preciously that his flippant nature seemed to be slowly fading away. He treated Lady Naka with great respect not only because she was the mother of his favorite child but also because she was the person with whom he felt most comfortable, even more so than he did with his principal wife, Princess Roku. This permitted Lady Naka to feel more at ease than she had in the past.

A few days after New Year's Day, Prince Niou visited Nijo Palace to spend some time with his family. While he was playing with his son in the early afternoon, a young female servant burst into the room and presented something to Lady Naka. It was a beautiful letter wrapped with a fine, sheer paper and a small craftwork basket with an artificial pine branch tied to it. Another letter written on plain paper was included with the gifts.

"Who is that from?" he asked the girl.

"This was sent from Uji to one of the servants here, but the messenger could not locate the recipient and didn't know with whom he should leave it. Since I thought Lady Naka would be the one to read this, as is usually the case, I received it on her behalf."

The girl looked so happy to see such masterly crafts included in the gift, and continued chattering on quite restlessly, her facial expressions mirroring her excitement.

"I just realized that this basket is made of wires which were later painted. This pine branch looks so real too. They are so amazing!"

Upon seeing her lovely smile, the Prince also gently smiled and said,

"Then I'd like to take a look at them."

In fact, he suspected that they were from Kaoru. When he reached out his hand for the gift, including the letters, Lady Naka called out the young girl's name while exclaiming,

"The letter! We aren't supposed to open it."

Seeing her face instantly change hue, he became even more suspicious about the letter, imagining that Kaoru could have sent it anonymously. The fact that the gift was reportedly from Uji caused even more doubts to surface. Before he knew it, his hands reached out automatically to grab the letter and open it, but since it would damage Lady Naka's respectability in front of the others if things should turn out as he suspected, he managed to resist his impulse for a second and said,

"I'm going to open it. Or are you going to hold a grudge against me for this?"

It was quite obvious that he asked the question just to see how she would react. Sighing deeply, she calmly shook her head.

"This is not deserving of your attention. I have no idea why a man as great as yourself is so interested in women's private conversations. It's quite trifling."

As she didn't seem at all upset, he composed himself ever so slightly and said,

"So you mean that it's okay for me to read it, do you? I'm just curious to see how women talk to each other in letters."

He found youthful feminine writing in the letter, which read,

"The new year has already begun, yet we haven't written to you for months. In a sinister mountain village like this, the everlasting mist refuses to dissipate."

A few lines added at the end of the letter mentioned that the attached gifts were made for the son of Lady Naka and apologized for their simplicity. The message seemed not to have been written by one very nobly educated. As he had never seen the handwriting in the letter before, he also checked the other letter carefully, but it was clearly written by a female hand as well.

"A Happy New Year, madam. How are you? I hope all is well with you and yours. We are now staying at a very well-maintained house in Uji, which is most suitable for our lady. She actually finds it somewhat intimidating to live here, however, thinking that she doesn't deserve accommodations of such quality. I have suggested to her that she visit you once in a while rather than stay here all alone with her depressive thoughts, but she seems to be overly worried of stirring up any troubles to listen to me at all. Instead of paying you a visit to offer her New Year's greetings in person, she made a traditional charm hammer for the boy to protect him from bad spirits, hoping that Lady Naka and her beautiful son would take it out and look at it on occasion, although it would probably be better to do so while the boy's father is not around."

Prince Niou found that the expressions chosen by the author of the letter were quite negative and inauspicious for a New Year's message, which revealed the writer's lack of social graces. He couldn't grasp the entirety of the situation, no matter how many times his eyes ran over the lines of text.

"Now tell me. Who is it from?" the Prince asked.

"I don't really know, but I've heard that a daughter of a lady who once lived in Uji recently moved back there for some reason or other. She could be the one who sent it, I guess."

He wasn't convinced by Lady Naka's explanation and suspected that the sender was someone of higher status than simply a daughter of some servant. Upon recalling that she said in her letter that she had experienced some trouble in Nijo Palace and had expressed the need to avoid the Prince for some unknown but very strong reasons, he came to realize the identity of the mysterious letter writer. The charm hammer was also exceptionally beautiful and seemed to have been carefully crafted by someone free of responsibilities and other constraints.

The artificial pine branch was accompanied not only by imitation citrus fruit threaded onto its twigs, but also with a poem tied at its fork.

"まだ古りぬものにはあれど君がため

ふかき心にまつと知らなん

(Although this pine may appear immature, I trust you understand
it expresses my wish for the everlasting happiness and prosperity
of your little prince.)"

There was nothing impressive about the poem, but he couldn't tear his eyes from the words, wondering if the unforgettable young lady was, in fact, the sender.

"You should write back to her, since it would be impolite to do otherwise. I still don't understand why you hesitated to show it to me in the first place. What was it that made you feel so uncomfortable to do so? In any case, I have some business to attend to elsewhere."

Prince Niou stood up and left the room. Lady Naka immediately spoke to Lady Shosho in a hushed voice.

"This is no good. I cannot believe that that little girl received the package from Uji. Why didn't anyone take notice of that?"

Lady Shosho blamed the girl, saying,

"If we had noticed beforehand, we wouldn't have allowed her to enter your room. To be honest, that girl is always too obtrusive and acts without thinking. In my opinion, children should be quiet and well-behaved so that they will be well liked."

"You needn't be so harsh. It's unfair to get angry at someone's youth and inexperience," Lady Naka chided her.

The young servant in question had been brought to Nijo Palace last winter, where she had been spoiled by Prince Niou who very much adored her.

The Prince returned to his room and spent some time mulling over the situation.

"Having heard that Kaoru had been visiting the isolated mountain village of Uji for many years, and had even secretly stayed there for the night on several occasions, I had often wondered if he had lost his senses. Though it is honorable for him to treasure the memory of his deceased woman in the place where they spent so much time together, a nobleman such as himself sleeping alone in that ominous village seemed more than a bit odd. Now, however, I think I understand why he has been so keen to go there, even years after the death of Lady Okimi: He has been hiding the mysterious lady from Nijo Castle in Uji."

He remembered that his teacher of Chinese literature, a Senior Secretary of the Ministry of Central Affairs, was related to Kaoru, and so he summoned him immediately. Prince Niou ordered him to select some collections of old Chinese poems and stack them on his cabinet so that he could play a literary game with his fellows later. While the Senior Secretary was searching for appropriate poems for the game, Prince Niou asked him several questions to try to uncover some details about the lady whom Kaoru had likely hidden in Uji.

"Does Commander Kaoru still visit Uji village? Some say that he has built a magnificent temple there. Is that so?"

The Senior Secretary replied, without any sense of cautiousness,

"Yes, it is truly superb. It is said that he ordered the hall where the priests pray every day to be an especially solemn place. Since they finished its construction last autumn, Commander Kaoru has visited more often than ever before. Now this is only a rumor kept among some of his humble followers, but it seems that he is hiding a woman in the temple. According to what they say, he cares so deeply about this mystery woman that all the heads of his holdings in the surrounding area have come to the temple by his order to serve her. He even asks them to station night guards for her safety and takes secretive trips there as often as possible. Although it's a great honor to gain the favor of such a high-ranking nobleman, by now she must certainly be feeling at least somewhat unsafe to have stayed there so long by herself. This information reached my ear as recently as last December."

Prince Niou was pleased to hear what the man had to say and continued his line of questioning.

"Did they say exactly who it was that he was hiding? I remember hearing of a nun who has lived there for some time and I understand that Commander Kaoru sees her every time he visits. I wonder if this is who they have been talking about?"

The Senior Secretary answered unhesitatingly, wanting to gain his trust.

"The nun is said to live in a detached room, but the lady he cherishes lives in comfort in a newly-built house on the temple grounds with many beautiful female servants."

"Interesting. I wonder what he thought he was trying to accomplish by keeping the lady in Uji in such a manner? He is surely a man of his own mind, very distinct by nature from others. The Minister of the Right, Yugiri, has criticized him by saying that Commander Kaoru seemed to be too devoted to his religious life to judge whether it was appropriate or not to spend the night at some hidden temple in the mountains, with complete disregard for his responsibility as a highly-placed government official. I admit that I agreed with Yugiri because I too thought that there was no need to leave the capital and disappear so frequently, even in the name of religious services. Although the thought had crossed my mind as of late that the real reason could have had something to do with the lady he had lost years ago in Uji. See, who is dishonest now? Those who are respected the most for their high integrity usually appear trustworthy and forthright, but actually they are often the ones who get away with the most unimaginably scandalous things away from the public eye."

The Prince found the story very much amusing, although he tried not to let it show in his expression. The Senior Secretary knew quite well what was going on with Commander Kaoru because his father-in-law, who had served for many years as Commander Kaoru's head servant of the Uji house, had leaked the information back to him in private. Prince Niou speculated about what was going on behind his back.

"I have to make sure somehow that this lady is the one I've been searching for since our fateful encounter. Considering how carefully Kaoru has been treating this hidden lady, it's clear that she cannot be just any woman. Wait a moment, why is she on such intimate terms with my wife? Lady Naka must have known about this and collaborated to shelter this mystery lady at Kaoru's request."

The more he came to understand the circumstances surrounding the situation, the more irritated he became.

Prince Niou obsessed over this turn of events for days. After people had finished enjoying the traditional New Year's functions, the festival atmosphere was on the wane and everyone was settling back to their usual routines. While there was great intrigue over who would be appointed to which positions in the court of Kyoto, the Prince was quite indifferent towards such public concerns. All he could think of was when and how he could secretly travel to Uji to see the lady again. The Senior Secretary, a relative of Commander Kaoru, was making great efforts both day and night to gain the favor of Prince Niou and see his political ambitions rewarded through the Prince's support. Knowing how desperate the Secretary actually was, Prince Niou asked him for his assistance in a friendlier than usual manner.

"Will you do me the favor that I'm going to ask of you no matter how difficult it may seem?"

Upon hearing these words, the Secretary sat upright, struggling to imagine what would come out of the Prince's mouth.

"This is a somewhat delicate manner. You remember what we discussed the other day, you know, about the lady who lives in the Commander's newly-built temple in Uji? When you told me that story, it reminded me of a woman that I used to have a relationship with, but she went missing one day and her whereabouts have been unknown since. I realized that these two women have too many things in common to be different people. There is no way, however, that I can verify my suspicions. So I'm thinking of going there to have a peek in secret, so that my hunch can be proven true. Can you think of any way that I could accomplish this without anyone being the wiser?"

Although the Secretary was surprised by the complicity of the situation, he managed to respond,

"You'll find the distance itself not too great, although the journey involves traversing steep paths over the mountains. If you leave here early in the evening, you'll get to Uji around 10 p.m. or so. Make sure that you come back here by dawn the next morning. Then who would know that you have been away? Only some of your followers, but they wouldn't understand what was really going on anyway."

The Prince agreed.

"Indeed. I have been to Uji a few times, though it was a long time ago. I don't mind the steep climbs. What I'm afraid of is being later criticized for behaving inappropriately, given my position in the government. I don't care to be the subject of people's gossip."

Saying so, he fully understood that he was taking an unnecessary risk. His mind had already been made up, however, and the only path left for him then was to continue on, past the point of no return.

Prince Niou chose some of his closest men to accompany him, in addition to bringing the Senior Secretary as a guide. Many of these men had traveled with him to Uji several times before, but he also brought along a young chamberlain, who was a son of his nurse. The Commander's schedule had been checked carefully beforehand to make certain that he was unable to visit Uji in the coming days. Preparing for the secretive trip to Uji reminded him of the old days when he would travel there often to see Lady Naka. In those days, Kaoru was always at his side to support him in so many ways, and even kindly accompanied him to and from the mountain village. In spite of their long-term friendship and what Kaoru had done for him, he found himself attempting to steal Kaoru's secret lover away, which made him feel a little ashamed. An array of different thoughts passed through his mind. Since he couldn't go out in public without being recognized, it thrilled him greatly to wear simple clothes and travel on horseback, not in the customary carriage of a nobleman. His basic curiosity toward this sort of adventure was quite powerful. The deeper he went into the mountains, the more excited he became about meeting the lady. He managed to calm himself down, but his heart was beating so loudly, like waves crashing on the beach.

"I'm so nervous about how it is all going to play itself out. I cannot even imagine how disappointed I will be if I should end up going home without seeing her tonight. I may lose my mind."

While so many thoughts were ricocheting around his head, their carriage arrived at a temple located halfway to Uji. Here they switched to horseback and continued onward.

It was early in the evening when they finally arrived at the temple in Uji, not having taken as much time as anticipated because of the fast pace they had maintained throughout the journey. Having been briefed ahead of time by an informant who was very familiar with the layout of the place, the Senior Secretary guided them so as to avoid the night guards and reach the west side of the temple. Then the Senior Secretary entered by himself to scout inside the wall, breaking a portion of the latticework to gain entrance. Although he wasn't feeling particularly confident, since it was his first time to see the place with his own eyes, luckily there weren't many people about, and thus it was easy to approach the main house. Along with shafts of dim light trickling through gaps in the doors on the south side of the house, footsteps and the rustle of women's dresses could also be heard. He returned to where Prince Niou and his men were waiting.

"You can come in through here, but be cautious, because people are still awake inside."

He helped the Prince make his way in through the latticework and led him to the house, taking the safe route he had just discovered.

Prince Niou approached the main house and stepped quietly onto the porch. There was an opening between the lattice doors where a curtain fluttered gently in the breeze, the sound of which slightly startled him every time the wind picked up. Although the temple was newly built and very well designed, it appeared the construction was a bit rough and there were slight gaps between the doors. Nobody in the house seemed to care, however, thinking that there would be no one outside looking through them. The long, interior curtains which functioned as room partitions had also been pulled aside and hung on a bar set on the side wall. Inside the room, several female servants were sewing clothes near the light. A lovely young girl was sitting nearby, twining the threads for them with her hands. This girl was, without a doubt, the one he had seen the other day in Nijo Palace before he met the mysterious lady. He also recognized Ukon, one of the women sewing, who had introduced herself on that same day. He looked all around the room, feeling his heart beating ever harder. It was then that the lady he had been longing to see came into view. She was staring at a burning lamp at the front of the room with her head resting on her arm. Her eyes, as well as the beautiful curve formed by the hair covering her forehead expressed her natural elegance and youth. He also noticed a strong resemblance to his wife, but he was unable to pinpoint the features which stirred this feeling of recognition.

The female servant named Ukon spoke to the lady while trying to crease some fabric for clothing.

"Once you reach the temple, it will take you a while to return. The messenger said that his lord would visit here after the election of the capital's Governor at the beginning of next month, when this festive time of the year comes to an end. How did you word your reply to him?"

Lost in her thoughts, the lady didn't say a word or change her flint-like countenance.

"I'm just concerned because of how things have been these past few days. It will be a great inconvenience if he thinks that you have abandoned him as a show of your dissatisfaction," Ukon said.

Another servant who was sitting opposite her disagreed.

"We can avoid any trouble simply by writing him a letter saying that our lady has been to the temple for some particular reason. It is out of the question that she should disappear without giving him any advance notice. She can return soon after they pay homage at the temple, isn't that so my lady? Although you must be feeling lonely and restless here, you won't find any comfort at your parents' house. It will feel as if you are staying there as a guest. You have already grown accustomed to your life here, free of restraint."

A third lady became involved in the conversation.

"Nevertheless, I think the easiest and also the safest choice is to wait a little while longer until his next visit. Since he will welcome you to live in the capital at some point, at that time you can visit your mother as you like. Your mother must have been convinced somehow of this idea, suggested indiscreetly by your nurse. An ancient saying goes 'The more patient you are, the greater happiness you can gain in the end.' As far as I know, it has been and always will be true."

Ukon sympathized with her on getting at the nurse.

"We should have just stopped her from going to your mother's. How in the world do old people think of such meddlesome things?"

From the way she said it, it was obvious that she harbored some sort of hostility towards the nurse. Hearing it all from behind the doors, Prince Niou vaguely recalled that there had been an old lady who had very much annoyed him in Nijo Palace, although it seemed so long ago to feel like anything but a dream.

The private nature of the conversation made him feel even more ashamed to stand there listening.

"Don't you think that Lady Naka is one of the most blessed people in the world? While the Great Minister of the Right has added to his already considerable power and his daughter has become the first wife of Prince Niou, Lady Naka has come into the greatest favor of all the Prince's wives since giving birth to his son last year. She always maintains a moderate state of mind and treats her husband in such a gentle manner that he can easily relax around her. This must be due to the lack of pressure she feels with no nosy busybodies about."

"But honestly, now that our lady is in the Commander's favor, if he were to continue to cherish her, could anyone think of any reason our lady would be less worthy than even Lady Naka?"

Having listened to their conversation in silence, the lady slowly raised her head and said,

"Would you stop it? I don't mind if you compare me with anyone else, but not Lady Naka. Please refrain from mentioning anything about her, so I don't draw any unnecessary attention to myself when she finds out that people are making these types of comparisons."

The Prince lined the two women up in his mind and realized that the lady surely resembled his wife, Lady Naka, wondering if and how closely they were related to each other. They looked alike, but also quite different at the same time. While his wife was obviously the superior in terms of distinct elegance and sophisticated beauty, which could be even intimidating to others at times, this lady in Uji was utterly charming and adorable. Although there was a chance that her appearance might not prove as fine as it seemed from a distance, or that he might end up finding some unbearable flaws in her character, it was impossible for him to leave there that night with nothing to show for it, after all the zeal and passion he had put into creating this opportunity to see her again. Watching her so close at hand, he was much too eager to exercise any discretion, and he tried to think of how to make this lady his own. He couldn't take his eyes off of her and remained there perfectly still for quite a while. Then her servant Ukon gathered together the fabrics she had been sewing and hung them on a room partition saying,

"I'm too sleepy to carry on with this sewing. Last night, I sat up until dawn for no particular reason. I will finish these for you early tomorrow morning, my lady. Your mother's attendants will arrive here to pick you up around noon at the earliest."

She lay down on a nearby cushion and fell instantly asleep. The lady slid backward to the wall and lay down, too. Ukon then woke up briefly and went to a room on the north side to get some blankets. Returning to the room, she fell asleep near the hem of the lady's skirt.

As Ukon fell fast asleep immediately after lying down, the Prince could think of nothing to do other than knock lightly on the lattice door through which he had been peering. Hearing this, Ukon quietly asked who was there. The Prince answered with a slight cough which sounded dignified enough to be that of some nobleman. Ukon woke up, thinking that it might be the Commander.

"Open the door first, please," the voice outside said.

"What's going on? How can you visit here so unexpectedly at this late hour? It is already well past midnight."

"I was so surprised when Senior Secretary Nakanobu told me that my lady was going away for a while, that I dashed out of my house without properly preparing for the long trip here. Unfortunately, I also met with many misfortunes along the way. Let me in, please."

Since the Prince expertly mimicked the Commander's voice while speaking in hushed tones, Ukon believed it to be him and opened up the door without hesitation.

"Could you please turn down the light? We encountered bandits en route and I look quite frightful now."

In this way, the Prince was able to have the room darkened before he entered.

"Oh, dear!"

She hastily took the room lantern away upon hearing that. The Prince had more than enough wits to trick some simple, country servant.

"I don't want anyone to know that I'm here or catch sight of my appearance. So, please leave everyone asleep as they are now."

It was easy for him to pretend to be the Commander in the dark because their voices were naturally quite similar and he had known the man for such a long time. He entered the room, behaving in exactly the same manner as Commander Kaoru would. Ukon was so sorry for him and worried about how badly the bandits may have injured him, but she waited behind a partition, so that she couldn't see him directly or disturb them, as he had requested. He was wearing a very smooth, soft gown and the very rich scent of perfume which was usual for the Commander. As he came closer to the lady resting under a quilt, he took off his clothes and lay down quietly beside her. Then Ukon said to him from behind the partition,

"Please go ahead and relax in the bed as usual."

Not knowing where the bed was in the darkness, he did not reply. Shortly thereafter, Ukon brought some bedclothes for him to wear and woke those servants who had been sleeping around the lady to hurry them out of the room so that the Commander and the lady could be alone. Since it was customary for the servants there not to attend to the followers of Commander Kaoru, they too didn't realize that it was another person. One of the servants commented knowingly, saying,

"He came all the way from Kyoto just to see her even this late at night. How impressive is that? Our lady must now certainly understand his feelings for her and appreciate him as he deserves to be appreciated."

"Quiet now. Whispering sounds louder at night," Ukon said, and went to bed.

It was when he lay down next to her that the lady noticed that this man was not the one she had expected. She panicked at this unbelievable turn of events, but he wouldn't allow her to make any noise. Considering the fact that he had committed such a disreputable act at Nijo Palace the other day, when his wife and followers were around, he felt much more freedom in an isolated temple here in Uji. His behavior was hopelessly imprudent that night. If she had realized that it was not her man from the beginning, she could have rejected him outright. Although it was all too late, she was still unable to accept what had just happened to her and felt that it must have been some kind of nightmare. Meanwhile, the man started telling her how he had fallen in love with her at first sight and how much he had pined for her over these five months since. This was how she came to know that the man she had happened to sleep with was Prince Niou, the husband of her half-sister, which shocked her even more. She could think of no way to express her feelings but by softly sobbing, thinking of how Lady Naka would feel about this. Tears flowed down her cheeks like rivulets streaming from an endless spring. The Prince also started to cry himself, but for a very different reason. What made him feel so sad was the realization that finding another opportunity to see her again would be nearly impossible.

The night turned to morning in the blink of an eye. When one of his followers cleared his throat at the door to let him know that it was nearly time to leave, Ukon heard him and went to wake up who she thought was the Commander. Upon hearing her knock at the door, he realized he had no desire to leave so soon. Knowing that it was unlikely that he would be able to return in the near future, despite his strong feelings for her, he made up his mind to linger there longer. He thought to himself,

"Today I will stay with her all day, no matter how desperately people in Kyoto might be searching for me. If I leave her now, my heart won't be able to carry on beating, now that my love for her is the only thing giving me inspiration to live another day."

He called Ukon into the room. After explaining what had actually transpired the night before, he asked her a favor.

"I understand that you now no longer respect me, but there is no way I can convince myself to return home today. Please tell my men to hide out somewhere nearby and wait for me. Tokikata should return to Kyoto alone and tell those looking for me that I have secretly gone away to visit some remote temple in the mountains or fabricate some other such excuse."

Ukon was too distraught to reply at first. Since it was obvious that the incident had occurred last night due to her negligence, she felt so much remorse that she almost fainted away. Somehow, she managed to gather her wits and tried her best to deal with the situation as calmly as possible. Any grieving or crying wouldn't change what had already taken place. Moreover, they might make the situation worse by being impolite to the

Prince. She convinced herself that this was the inevitable outcome of Prince Niou falling for the lady in Nijo Palace. No one could have done anything about it, for it must have been destined long before this lifetime. She humbly replied,

"What about her trip to Hase Temple? Her mother is planning to arrive this morning to pick up our lady and take her there. I have no intention of placing blame on anyone or commenting on last night's fateful encounter, but it is very bad timing. I'm afraid it would be better for you to return home early for the time being, realizing of course that you are very welcome to return here at some other time if your interest in our lady still remains."

He found the situation unacceptable.

"Listen. I have been much too infatuated with her for the past few months now to get on with anything else in my life. I don't care about what they say or think about me anymore, because this lady here is all that I want now. If I were the kind of person who cared only about his status or reputation, then I wouldn't have taken such a huge risk coming here in the first place. You can give whatever excuse you like to her mother in order to put off the trip, provided no one finds out about us. It's for the good of everyone involved, and I don't feel the need to have any further discussion with you about this matter."

He seemed to be utterly entranced by the adorable nature of the lady. His mind was filled with so many passionate feelings for her that there was no place for the opinions of others.

Ukon walked out of the room and told the man waiting outside what the Prince had said.

"This is what he said to me, but you must persuade him to go home, otherwise this will destroy the reputation of both your lord and our lady. Although I'm not in a position to stop this unbelievably outrageous behavior of his, he will listen to his best men. You are the only ones who can change his mind now. How could you bring him here in the first place without thinking twice about the consequences? What if some fierce bandits had attacked him along the way? It is a more risky journey than you may believe."

The followers left, completely baffled by the unforeseen turn of events, without any idea as to what to do. Ukon asked for the man called Tokikata and relayed the Prince's message to him. He laughed.

"Actually, I had hoped to leave here shortly, even without his leave, because you frightened me too much with your fierce accusations," he said sarcastically. "But in all seriousness, the fact we brought him here in the middle of the night doesn't mean that we didn't hesitate to do so. Having seen how desperately in love he was with your lady, we dared to risk our lives to fulfill his wish. At any rate, I should go. It sounds like people are beginning to stir." He left the temple hurriedly.

Ukon didn't know how she could possibly conceal the situation. She collected the female servants who were beginning their morning tasks and said,

"Although the Commander arrived last night and has yet to leave, he seems to have encountered some serious trouble on the way here. Since he doesn't want this to develop into a big incident, please keep this visit to yourselves and stay away from him until he recovers. If someone brings his clothes or other things to the room, it should be done after dark so that you don't get a clear look at him."

The ladies made a fuss upon hearing that, as they always did about anything.

"That really scares me. Do you know Mt. Kohata, which is located on the way from Kyoto? I've heard it's such a terrifying place. The Commander would have walked through that area in humble attire, taking only a few men with him. It must have been an extremely harsh experience for him."

Ukon was feeling quite nervous inside but said in an even tone,

"Please calm down, all of you. Things will get even worse if people outside catch wind of this."

Praying to the Goddess of Mercy in Hase Temple for her assistance in somehow getting through it all, she was very worried that Commander Kaoru might send a messenger to the lady at this most untimely moment, which would surely be the end of them all. Meanwhile, the lady's mother was arriving shortly to pick up her daughter for the trip to Hase Temple. Since everyone there had purified themselves carefully to prepare for this occasion, it was disappointing for most of the servants to learn that the lady wouldn't be traveling today.

As the sun was rising higher in the sky, Ukon went to wait on the Prince and opened the latticed doors to let in some fresh air. All the blinds around the main house were shut so that no one could see inside, and signs were hung on the walls outside notifying passersby that there were people taken by bad spirits in the house. That was the only excuse that Ukon could think of to explain the situation if her mother were to come in person to collect her daughter.

Ukifune held up a basin to make it easier for the Prince to wash his face, as she usually did for her man. Prince Niou didn't care for this, however, because it made him feel superior to her. As his lover, he treated her equally, regardless of their difference in status.

"After you, my dear," he said, offering her first use of the basin.

In contrast to Commander Kaoru, a very thoughtful man who was always in control of his feelings, the Prince was incomparably romantic and passionate. He even begged her to stay with him longer, as he claimed he would perish from missing her too deeply. Beginning to wonder if this was how a man truly in love was supposed to act, she was confused by her sudden change of heart. When she thought of what would happen if this relationship should become public, the feelings of Lady Naka were the first to come to her mind. She wouldn't tell him who she was, no matter how many times he asked her.

He said, "I don't understand why you do this to me. I don't care how noble or humble you are. I just want to know you as you are. I swear that the more I find out about you, the more I'll love you."

Although he persisted, she continually refused to answer his questions about her identity. She did, however, answer all of his other queries in such a lovely, friendly manner that the Prince became more and more entranced.

People from her parents' house arrived there late in the morning. Two carriages and seven or eight horsemen, who looked as wild and rough as usual, passed through the entryway with many other men accompanying them. Their harsh rural dialect shattered the relative calm and peace of the temple. The female servants felt awkward when greeting them, so Ukon told the ladies to go back inside and continue with their daily tasks. However, she wasn't sure about how to respond either, mulling over several possibilities in her mind,

"What should I do now? Since the Commander is such a great nobleman, it may be common knowledge among the people of Kyoto whether he is in the capital or not. In that case, even if I tell them that he is staying here, they'll find out sooner or later that this is not the case."

She took it upon herself to write a letter to the lady's mother.

"Our lady's time of the month visited her last night, and she also suffered from a strange nightmare. Although she truly wished to accompany you, it would be better for her to stay here, at least for today, and take time to fully cleanse herself before going to the sacred Hase Temple. This is such unfortunate timing that we suspect some unknown power is allied against us."

After enjoying a lunch prepared by the servants attending Ukifune, the entourage turned back for home. Ukon also sent a message to Ben-no-Ama, the nun who lived in a separate house on the same property, relaying the news that the lady wouldn't be able to visit her place that day because she was in her time of purification.

The afternoons in Uji had always bored the lady, even in this beautiful season of spring, and viewing the mountain scenery with its cover of mist was the only thing which helped her endure another day, although it didn't provide enough joy to overcome her deep loneliness. That day when Prince Niou was next to her, however, she felt time flying swiftly by for the first time in a long while. The Prince, for his part, cherished every minute he spent with the lady so intensely that it was killing him inside to see the sun sinking slowly in the sky. On such a fine, peaceful day, there was nothing to distract him from her. He spent hours looking at Ukifune, but he could never get his fill. She seemed to have her own unique feminine presence, which appeared moderate but strong, while also maturely tender yet as charming as a child. As a matter of fact, it was apparent to the Prince that this lady was not superior to Lady Naka, although they were related by blood. Moreover, she was no comparison to the Prince's first wife, Princess Roku, whose beauty was so flawless that it took people's breath away. Even so, he was too smitten by her in that moment to acknowledge any of this, taking her for the one and only woman capable of enchanting him with her perfect loveliness. For her part, she had thought that the Commander would be second to none in his graceful appearance and decency, but the Prince seemed to be at another level entirely in terms of his caring attitude and dignity.

He drew an inkpot to his side and began practicing calligraphy. Watching him expertly sweep the brush across the writing paper and produce such impressive images, it was no wonder that a young woman like her came to be so drawn to him.

"Even when things conspire against us and I cannot come to visit in spite of my desire, just gaze at this and find me there."

So saying, he passed her a drawing in which there was a beautiful couple lying down together.

"I wish that we, like them, could be together forever."

When he said so in a small voice, tears filled her eyes.

"長き世を頼めてもなほかなしきは

ただ明日知らぬいのちなりけり

(Everyone wishes for a long life, knowing the tragic reality that even tomorrow may never arrive.)"

He added this poem beside the picture and said,

"I cannot believe how I feel at this moment. I sense that I will spend

the rest of my time struggling to find a way to fulfill my desire for you, although the suffering I endure may hasten the end of my life. Why did I ever seek you out in spite of the cold attitude you displayed toward me the other day?"

The lady took the brush that he had been holding and responded to his poem with one of her own.

"心おばなげかざらまし命のみ
　　さだめなき世と思はましかば

(We wouldn't cry over a change of heart, if life were the only mutable thing in this world.)"

He fell even more deeply in love with this lady to know that she had begun to love him in return and had revealed in the poem that she would bear him a grudge if he turned his back on her. He laughed a little and asked,

"Are you worried because you had a similar experience with another?"

He wanted to know in detail how Kaoru had come to be acquainted with her and why he ended up leaving her alone in Uji. His questions about their relationship embarrassed her greatly.

"You know I cannot answer such questions. Please, stop teasing me like that."

The Prince found her sudden sulky behavior adorable. Although he knew that it would be a simple task to find out the truth, his hopeless curiosity drove him to make her speak the words herself.

Prince Niou's chamberlain, Tokikata, returned from Kyoto after dark and spoke with Ukon.

"A messenger sent by the Empress arrived at Nijo Palace. It seems that the Great Minister of the Right has flown into a rage this time. The Empress said that it was shockingly reckless behavior for a person of the highest social status to leave the house secretly in the middle of the night, and that not everyone was respectful towards members of the Royal House, especially bandits who become active after dark. She was worried that she would be placed in a very difficult position if the Emperor were to find out about this. Her tone was quite serious, so I told them publicly that Prince Niou had gone to visit a saint of high standing in the eastern outskirts of Kyoto. Women are such sinful people, aren't they? They not only get unrelated people involved in their outbursts, but they also put someone like me in a position to have to lie in front of so many others."

Ukon smiled lightly and said,

"A saint? That's such an honorable way to refer to our lady. I think your offense can be forgiven for that. To be honest, the Prince seems to have lost his senses these days. What made him grow up to be like this? If only he had let us know about his visit in advance, we would have been very happy to prepare properly for both him and his men with all due respect shown to the Prince. His visit was too reckless and impulsive."

Ukon explained to the Prince what Tokikata had told her was going on in Kyoto. Hearing this, he could easily imagine those exhausting people in the capital making such a great fuss. He thought to himself,

"I'm fed up with the surroundings of my office, which nearly choke me out of breath. I wish I could be like those officials of lower status, even if only for a short time. Well, what should I do? I cannot keep hiding myself here forever, so I must go back and face the scandal I have created. My concern, however, is for Kaoru. We have enjoyed a very special relationship, both as close relatives and also as best friends since we were born. In case he should come to know about this, I don't know how I could face him ever again, much less beg his pardon. Besides that, I must protect the lady as well because, as the old saying tells us, Kaoru may blame her for her unfaithfulness, brushing aside his own fault in having not paid enough attention to her by leaving her alone for such long periods of time. That's my greatest concern. I'd therefore like to take her to such a place as people would never even dream of searching."

Although his feelings for the lady seemed to have a will of their own, there was no way that he could stay there for another day. He had to leave as soon as the day broke, promising to leave his soul in her sleeves, as an expression of his utmost devotion.

Just before dawn, one of his men cleared his throat in front of the room to let him know that it was time to go. Since the lady accompanied him onto the porch, it was even harder for him to turn away and set off on his way home.

> "世に知らずまどうふべきかなさきに立つ
>   涙も道をかきくらしつつ
>
> (I will be lost like no one before, for my tears will precede me, wiping away my path home.)"

The farewell brought a deep feeling of sadness to Ukifune as well.

> "涙をもほどなき袖にせきかねて
>   いかに別れをとどむべき身ぞ
>
> (These mean sleeves are barely wide enough to conceal my tears, revealing both my unworthiness and inability to keep you near.)"

The wind blew fiercely and there was a heavy frost blanketing everything in sight shining brightly in the dawn sunlight. The Prince and the lady dressed before saying goodbye, as had been sung in the old poem, but the warmth they had felt together had dissipated and a bitter cold was all that remained. Getting on his horse, the Prince felt that his heart still lingered and wouldn't permit him to leave. As his followers implored him many times to make haste, he finally summoned up the will to turn his back and head home. He was so empty inside, as his soul stayed behind. The Senior Secretary and Tokikata took the leads of his horse, in spite of their relatively high rank, to help guide Prince Niou over the steep mountains. They remounted once they had ascended a sharp rise onto a flat path. The sound of the footsteps of the horses on the icy water along the riverside made him feel sad and unsettled. He had known the same feeling a long time before on the same route back to Kyoto, although the lady he had been missing at that time would be waiting for him in Nijo Palace. What a bittersweet coincidence, he thought.

Back in Nijo Palace, Prince Niou went to bed in his room, where he thought he would be the most comfortable. He wanted to avoid Lady Naka, due to her having hidden the truth about the lady in Uji. Being alone in his bed, however, did not bring sleep. The loneliness in his heart caused his mind to race and wouldn't let him be. In the end, he decided to go down to Lady Naka's room. She didn't seem to know what had happened while he had been away, looking as fine and elegant as usual. Although he had found the lady in Uji incomparably adorable, it always impressed him how splendid his wife appeared, with her beauty and gracefulness. Looking into her eyes, he remembered the lady he had left in Uji that morning. She resembled his wife so closely that his heart ached to think about her. He lay down on the bed with a serious expression on his face. Then he told Lady Naka to come to his side, and he said to her in a faint voice,

"I feel very ill today. I'm not sure if I can make it through this. No matter how much I love you, if anything happens to me, you'll get over me soon enough and go to Commander Kaoru. I know he is the one you have really loved. They say that it's true love that remains after all else is gone, don't they?"

Lady Naka was utterly appalled, and wondered where in the world he had come up with such a ridiculous idea. It seemed unbelievable to her that he should mention this all so seriously, although it had no basis in reality.

"Do you understand that it would cause a lot of trouble if anyone should hear what you just said? If such a rumor went around, the Commander would be extremely confused, and take me for a crazy woman, one who started this rumor with vicious intent. Since I don't have a family of my own to support me, even such silly, groundless gossip could easily ruin my name."

She turned her back on him.

Looking at the beautiful line formed by the nape of her neck, the Prince continued to speak to her in an even more serious tone.

"What if something were to happen to me? What do you think you would do? Am I a bad husband? I care about you and treasure you to such a degree that I am criticized for that, but you seem to be stacking me up against another man, and passing judgment on me from on high. Although I understand that everything in this world flows as is destined from our previous lives according to the Gods' design, it pains me so deeply that you would keep secrets from me."

Speaking of destiny reminded him that it must have been fated that he should encounter the lady, regardless of his actual desires. He cried while realizing the overwhelming, irresistible force of fate. Lady Naka noticed that something was quite different about her husband that day, and she started to feel sorry to see him so grieved, in a way that she had never seen before. When no words came to her, her heart ached to think what kind of story he had heard about her and the Commander which would lead him to believe such a horrible thing. She could imagine that he would regard her as susceptible to such behavior because she and the Prince had started out without having actually fallen in love. It was the Commander who had arranged their first meeting, although he hadn't been so close to her then. She regretted having jumped at Commander Kaoru's overtures of friendship too hastily, which later was the cause of her husband's mistrust and suspicion. Upon realizing this, she suddenly found it all rather meaningless and said nothing more. Prince Niou wouldn't talk to his wife about the lady in Uji for a while, although he had expressed his frustration toward her for having kept things from him regarding Ukifune's existence. Lady Naka, however, believed that he was truly suspicious about her possible infidelity, worrying that someone might have told him that his suspicions had merit. She needed more information about what had made him think this, whether he heard it from someone or if it was just a figment of his own imagination, before she confronted him in an effort to convince him that she was not, in fact, having an affair.

It was at that very moment that one of their followers entered the room and informed the Prince that a message had arrived from his mother.

Upon hearing this unexpected news, he returned immediately to his own room, although he was far from fully consoled. The letter from the Empress said,

"You don't know how much I worried about you yesterday. Although I've heard that you've been feeling sick these days, come and see me as soon as you feel better. I can't even remember the last time you visited."

Feeling sorry to have troubled his mother so greatly, he decided to stay in his room, since he really didn't feel well that day. A number of high officials visited him to inquire about his condition, but he attended them from behind a diaphanous room partition from which he did not emerge for the remainder of the day.

In the evening, when the sun was setting over the beautiful mountains, the Commander came to visit Prince Niou. The Prince allowed him inside and sat down before him, attired in quite casual clothing. Kaoru said,

"They told me that you had been very sick and that your mother is greatly concerned. How are you holding up?"

The Prince was acutely aware of the loud and rapid beating of his heart upon seeing the face of his long-time friend. He answered perfunctorily, while thinking,

"Although there's apparently nothing to make us doubt his integrity, he surely has a cruel side to him to have left such an adorable lady alone in that ominous mountain village. People may call him a saint, but he has a devil somewhere within who can comfortably sit back while another pines for him for months on end."

Kaoru's attitude and choice of words struck the Prince as quite haughty sometimes, as if he felt that he was a man of the greatest integrity. Since that truly irritated him, the Prince often pointed out Kaoru's defects and complained about them with a sense of humor. That day, however, knowing the biggest and most well-hidden scandal of this noble-looking man, he was unable to mention a word about it so as to keep his own secret safe. Without the Prince's cynical jokes or witty criticism, the Commander didn't feel the same.

"You don't look very good. It's most troublesome when one's condition doesn't get either worse or better for days. Please take good care of yourself so that you can recover from this cold."

He expressed his sincere wishes for the Prince's early recovery and left to return to work.

Everything reminded Prince Niou of the lady in Uji and he found it impossible to escape his thoughts for hours once his mind strayed down that path.

"Kaoru is too mature and sophisticated to prevent me from feeling intimidated. I wonder how I compare in her estimation."

In the mountain village of Uji, the trip to Hase Temple had been canceled and Ukifune couldn't escape her daily sense of boredom. Many letters from the Prince had arrived, in which his passion was fully evident in each sentence. To keep this secret, he had discreetly asked a follower of Tokikata, who had no idea of what was transpiring, to pass his messages along to her. Ukon told a made-up story to other people in the house that one of the Commander's followers happened to be her ex-lover and he hoped to rekindle their romance. Although the piles of lies weighed heavily on her shoulders, she had no other option but to stack them ever higher.

And then it was February. Prince Niou was still keen to see the lady in Uji again, but his busy schedule didn't permit him to do so. As he had thought of her every moment, his heart ached more and more painfully each day, so that he felt as if he were dying from her absence.

Meanwhile, Commander Kaoru visited Uji, although unofficially as usual, for the first time that year when all the excitement of the New Year's events had died down. He first worshiped in the temple he had built there and rewarded the monks who had read sutras for him. It was already evening when he showed up to see her. He looked absolutely gorgeous, even in his very simple yet still elegant clothing. She delighted at the graceful way he entered the room, while her heart was touched by the gentle way he treated her.

She was deeply conflicted, however, having no idea of how she could ever look the Commander in the eye again. It made her feel even more intimidated to think that God must have watched everything she had done. Flashing back, she recalled the intense fervor she had seen in the Prince's eyes, although the arms that would hold her tonight wouldn't be those of the same man. Her sense of dignity seemed to dissipate the more she thought about it.

"That night the Prince told me that the memories of all the women he had been with were fading into nothingness since I had come along. From what they say, it seems that he hasn't spent time with any women since our time together because of his sickness, and some monks have even stayed at his place to offer prayers day and night. How will he feel to know that I have slept with the Commander tonight?"

The image of Prince Niou's face came to her mind and caused her great suffering, although it was certainly not any fault of the Commander's. He was a true gentleman, who always looked and behaved absolutely stunningly. His words of apology for not having visited her for such a long time were chosen so carefully and thoughtfully that they were extremely convincing, even without any dramatic expression of how much he had missed her or how sad he had been while they were separated. On the contrary, the few decent words he uttered showed his bitter sorrow over the absurdity of a long-distance relationship in which he couldn't see his love whenever he wanted. As speaking more about something didn't always lead to greater understanding, the Commander impressed people to their core with his reserved personality, rooted in an impregnable dignity. Everyone gave him full credit for his renowned reliability as well as his generous nature. Lady Ukifune was so afraid that it would be the end of her, with no room for excuses if he should discover her infidelity. She was sure that it would be an unforgivable mistake, knowing better than to choose the Prince, who had been utterly infatuated with her though their connection was reckless and tenuous. If he had thought of her as bothersome and turned his back on her, she would have lived a miserable, lonely existence, and she knew how hard it would be to be abandoned once more. A stream of thoughts raced through her mind, putting a wavering expression on her face. The Commander noticed this, but there was no way he could understand the reason. He thought instead,

"She seems to have grown up so much since I saw her last, as she is clearly now mature enough to have doubts and worries on her mind. Her sensitivity must have been nurtured by having spent a long time alone in such an isolated place. I guess this environment makes people do nothing but imagine the feelings of others."

Feeling very sorry for having left her for so long, he tried his best to comfort her, saying,

"The place I'm preparing for you is nearing completion. I went to the site the other day and was immediately convinced that you'll love it there. A river flows close to the house and its current is so slow and peaceful, unlike the one here. The plants and trees in the garden will flower beautifully in spring and I can enjoy them with you at anytime, as my residence is close by. Although you may now be feeling so lonely and worrying constantly, once you move there, there will be nothing to make you feel so. I promise that I will arrange things by the coming spring and welcome you to your new house in the capital."

It reminded her of what Prince Niou had promised her in the letter she had received the day before. He also offered her a place to live in Kyoto so that they could spend more time together. She felt a lump form in her throat when imagining how disappointed the Prince would be to know that she was moving to the house that Commander Kaoru had built for her. Although she was clearly aware that it was wrong to be attracted to Prince Niou, his image appeared in her mind's eye and would not be wished away. Then tears spilled forth, for she couldn't stand feeling so ashamed and sorry for herself. Upon seeing this, the Commander spoke to her in a calm tone,

"Don't feel so sad. I miss your smile and gentleness, which used to make me feel so very happy. Did someone say something to you? If I were not serious about us, I wouldn't have come all the way here to see you. It would be too risky for something as fleeting as a mere flirtation."

He lay down close to the porch and looked up at the crescent moon. The man remembered his tragic love affair in the past, while the woman thought of the complicated situation which was threatening her future. Both of them sank deeply into their own grief.

The mountains were covered in mist and there were several magpies resting on the sandbank where the cold wind blew strongly by. Everything in the scene was made all the more stunning because the atmosphere of the place itself seemed to add depth and vibrancy to the surrounding colors. Many boats loaded with firewood came and went along the river, passing under the bridge which had once been the inspiration for a poem the Commander had written for his beloved. Since the scenery was unique to this place, the memories of Lady Okimi crowded in upon him on cresting waves of varying emotions. It seemed that he would be unable to escape the remains of what he had once felt, even if the person sitting opposite him looked nothing like Lady Okimi, much less her half-sister, Lady Naka, who also paled in comparison to the deceased lady. As Lady Ukifune appeared much more mature and accustomed to this style of high-class living than before, the Commander found her even more charming because of this burgeoning sophistication. As for Ukifune, however, it was impossible for her to stem the tide of tears issuing from the deep sorrow in her heart. Kaoru could do nothing but compose a poem to make her feel better.

> "宇治橋の長きちぎりは朽ちせじを
>   あやぶむかたに心騒ぐな

(You needn't worry, for our love is as eternal as the bridge which spans the Uji River.)

You'll come to understand how much I care about you some day."

She answered with a poem of her own.

> "絶え間のみ世にはあやふき宇治橋を

朽ちせぬものとなほたのめとや

(Although the bridge seems riddled with cracks, do you still tell
me to believe its collapse impossible?)"

It was even harder this time for the Commander to leave the lady
alone. He wished he could have stayed with her for a little longer, but he
knew that it was foolish to do so after all the effort he had made to keep
this relationship secret from the world. Since it would be much easier to
see her more often in the near future, he convinced himself to shake off
his desire to linger, and he left for home before dawn. It impressed him
how the young lady had grown into a mature woman while he had been
away. He couldn't stop thinking of her the entire trip home.

On the tenth of February, both Prince Niou and Commander Kaoru
were present at a poetry reading event in the Imperial Palace. Along with
the live accompaniment, so marvelous and apt for the early spring season,
the Prince's voice, intoning a poem about plum blossoms, resonated
vividly throughout the palace. He was such a flawless young man, except
for the shortcomings of his amorous nature which had drawn him headfirst
into a forbidden love.

Suddenly the mild weather was replaced by cascading snow. As the
wind was also beginning to pick up, the party was suspended even before
it reached the midway point. Some people then retired to a room prepared
for the Prince and enjoyed a meal and drinks. When the Commander
neared the door to ask someone a favor, he saw the snow twinkling outside,
which appeared to him like countless stars in the sky. He became rather
emotional upon seeing such a beautiful sight, and quoted an old poem,

"さ筵に衣片敷きこよひもや

我を待つらむ宇治の橋姫

(Lying down in her bed alone, my precious will long for me
tonight beyond the bridge across the Uji River.)"

There was no doubt that the Commander revealed his royal bearing
in his every movement, no matter how humble or reserved his nature.
Even a very simple poem of lovers sounded absolutely elegant when

recited by him. It seemed as if his graceful spirit had given life and sentiment to each of his words, in a prominent, but never excessive, manner. Prince Niou became upset upon hearing such a beautiful recitation while feigning sleep.

"It seems he is quite serious about the lady he hides in Uji. I have assumed that it would be just me who was suffering from the lonely nights away from her. Now that I can see he feels the same way, I don't know what to do with the longing inside of me. How would it be possible for her to choose to love me instead of a perfect, caring man such as he?"

Prince Niou was devastated.

By the next morning, the entire capital was hidden under a deep layer of snow. The Prince went through the snow-filled roads to the Emperor's palace to present the original poem that he had read at the party the night before. Not only his face but his entire appearance was resplendent. The Commander was a few years older than the Prince, and he behaved in a way that seemed more mature and considerate of others. Being the example of how a nobleman should carry himself, he was well-recognized by people as a perfect son-in-law for the Emperor. No one could ever match him in academic or political knowledge. The Prince's poem was recited by a professional singer in the presence of the Emperor and the crowd. After the performance, people came out to the hall and praised the poet highly and some raised their voices to repeat the lines. The Prince himself was completely indifferent to the accolades, however, wondering why these people could even make time for such a meaningless event. His fervent desires for the lady preoccupied him so greatly that he was absent amidst the crowd.

Having noticed how serious Kaoru was about her, Prince Niou was keenly aware that he needed to take immediate action in order to win the lady's heart. He resolved to take advantage of every conceivable opportunity to visit the lady who was constantly in this thoughts. He set off for Uji immediately. The deeper they went into the mountains, the thicker the snow on the ground, although the snow around Kyoto was already melting away. The road was in an even worse condition than usual and not a soul could be found anywhere on the narrow path. His attendants were nearly crying out in the dark for fear of being attacked by fierce local bandits, and they were also concerned whether this visit would cause their lord any social or political difficulties. The Senior Secretary of Central Affairs, who guided the party to Uji, concurrently held the post of Junior Assistant Minister of Public Ceremony. In spite of these quite important positions, his conduct was far from that of a high-ranking, responsible individual, but rather it seemed that he was enjoying the somewhat harrowing situation. As he walked, the skirts of his trousers were held up by his hands, and he looked like a little child playing in the snow.

The day arrived when the Prince had announced in a message that he would come to see the lady again. Ukon looked up at the sky and felt relieved to think that he would postpone the visit due to the heavy snow. Her prediction proved inaccurate, however, when she was informed late at night that a group of men from Kyoto had arrived. Not only was the lady surprised by his unquenchable desire to see her, but she was also deeply touched by the eagerness and earnestness he showed her. Ukon's impression of the Prince changed, owing to him have traveled all this way to be with her on such a terrible day. Feeling a great sense of foreboding, Ukon had no choice but to let him enter secretly, so that others wouldn't know what was really happening. She called over a young female servant who had been very close to Lady Ukifune to explain what was transpiring.

"Things are spiraling out of my control. Could you help me handle this situation?"

The young servant, called Jiju, agreed to be her confidant and hosted the party of Prince Niou with Ukon. His clothes, soaked from the rain, were very strongly fragrant and his noble scent filled the whole place. Although the attendants were worried that people might notice that he was present, it was unclear to those who had grown up in the countryside whether the perfume was that of the Commander or not.

The Prince had ordered Tokikata to arrange a place with a high level of privacy and security. If it were just for some hours from midnight to dawn that he could spend with her, it wouldn't have seemed to be worth taking such a risk. There were also too many people living in the Palace in Uji to continue to keep things secret. Tokikata had made a plan to take her to a house on the other side of the river and sent a messenger there in advance. The news arrived to him only a few hours before sunrise that everything was ready for their visit. After a while, Ukon was woken up by the sound of the men preparing to leave. She couldn't maintain her composure any longer, with her body trembling from the anxiety, not knowing of their intention to take Lady Ukifune away in the middle of the night. The Prince lifted his beloved in his arms and left without giving her servants a chance to ask where they were heading. Since Ukon had to stay behind to keep things quiet, she told Jiju to accompany them.

They crossed the Uji River on a small boat which the lady had watched coming and going day after day from the window of her room. As they started to drift down the river, she became as frightened as if she were departing for a far distant heavenly world. The Prince found her irresistible when her fear caused her to closely nestle herself to his chest. A pale moon hung high in the sky waiting patiently for the sunrise, while the surface of the water was as clear as a cloudless sky. Then the boatman pierced the mirror-like stillness of the river with his long pole and pointed across the water.

"You see the famous island of citrus trees over there? An ancient Emperor wrote a beautiful poem about it."

Prince Niou and Lady Ukifune looked in that direction and could vaguely make out its silhouette in the darkness. It appeared to be simply a big rock covered by evergreens.

"Look, while the tree itself has no special qualities, its deep green color is so vibrant that it seems that it has lasted for thousands of years," the Prince said.

He composed a poem to comfort her.

"年経ともかはらぬものか橘の
　　　小島のさきに契る心は

(How could my heart ever change its course, now that I have sworn a love as eternal as the legendary island of evergreens?)"

She responded,

"橘の小島の色はかはらじを
　　　この浮船ぞゆくへ知られぬ

(The pure green of the island will last forever. But I am like this drifting boat, I know not where the current will take me.)"

Being finally with his beloved in such visually sumptuous surroundings, Prince Niou became even more emotional about everything he saw or heard. Although her poem insinuated her doubts about their future, it did little to dull his enthusiasm.

As the boat crossed the river, they were brought alongside the wharf. The Prince didn't want anyone else to touch her, so he himself lifted her in his arms as he stepped onto the shore. His followers offered their support as he carried her into the house which they had prepared. Those who lived there were watching the whole scene from nearby, curious as to the lady's identity. They believed that she must have been an extremely noble woman from a truly great family to be treated in that way by the Prince. The modest house had been built by one of Tokikata's uncles on his own property. Since the construction hadn't yet quite been completed, the interior was a bit of a jumble, and the wind came in through gaps in the wall. There was a little snow left here and there on the hedges, while clouds still covered the night sky, bringing more snow to the land.

The day finally broke. The icicles hanging from the roof glittered so brightly in the morning sunlight that their reflection made Prince Niou appear even more radiant. Since the trip had been made in secret, he was dressed simply, so as not to draw attention to himself. She was attired only in a few layers of gown-like underclothes, for the Prince had asked her to remove her outer garments in order to see the curves of her wonderfully slim figure more clearly. Although it was unbearably embarrassing for the lady to appear before an aesthete such as the Prince without any makeup or having properly prepared herself, because of their sudden late-night departure, there was no way that she could conceal herself in private in the relatively small room. The layers of silky, snow-white gown emphasized her innocent charm, up to the very details of the ends of the sleeves and skirt. In spite of having had relationships with quite a lot of women, it was the first time for him to see one in such a defenseless state. Even those ladies who he had married or had long relationships with had always been perfectly done up whenever he visited them. It was her natural beauty, however, that made his love for her burn ever more brightly.

Jiju, the attendant of Lady Ukifune, was quite a proper young lady. When she came to the room to take care of things, she was somewhat shocked to find the lady dressed so inappropriately. While both of the ladies were feeling awkward to see or be seen that way, the Prince said, in order to hush up the servant,

"I don't know who you are, but you cannot let it be known that I'm here."

Jiju was too intimidated to reply and left the room.

Meanwhile, the manager and chief resident of that place mistakenly took Tokikata for the leader of the party and tried his utmost to meet his needs. Acting as commanding as he could, Tokikata made use of the misunderstanding to cover up the reality of the situation from the people living there. The manager said something to him in a low and polite tone. Finding it very amusing to pretend to be his lord, Tokikata couldn't speak up when answering him for fear that his actual lord, who was in the next room, might hear him and become angry. He managed to whisper the following words.

"A credible fortuneteller performed an augury for us the other day, and we had a horribly sinister result. I came here with my men to keep myself from the capital for a while to rid ourselves of those bad spirits. For everyone's sake, don't let anyone near."

The manager had no doubt that this was a man of great nobility.

Prince Niou was losing himself in the flow of sensual moments with his beloved. His proclamations of love were unending, free of any disturbance from the outside world. Suddenly, however, one thought passed his mind: that she might have done the same thing with Kaoru. In an instant, his deep devotion turned into jealousy, which showed clearly in the way he spoke to her. He also told her how much the Commander cherished his first wife and that she had been the most important person in the Commander's life. He didn't mention a thing about the poem cited by Kaoru at the poetry reading, which had clearly expressed his longing for this lady. Tokikata brought them some snacks and a bowl of water with which to wash their hands and passed them along to the lady's follower who was seated near the front of the room since she had been charged with taking care of things for the couple. The Prince noticed him and made a joke about the misunderstanding with the head manager of the house.

"Be careful, great man. Now that you seem like a very important person here, don't you think it would be quite inconvenient to be seen doing that for us?" Prince Niou laughed.

The lady's follower was young enough to become so excited at seeing the goings-on of a secret love affair that she couldn't help feeling like having the same experience with her own secret lover someday. Not surprisingly, she ended up becoming intimate with Tokikata and spending all day lying together with him.

In the beautiful evening, everything was covered with a thick pile of snow. Prince Niou looked over to the other side of the river where he had stayed the night before and saw nothing but trees in the distance through the heavy mist, which obstructed his view. The mountains were shining brightly with the reflection of the evening sunlight. He started to tell her many stories in order to impress her, such as how hard it had been to go through the snowy road over the mountains at night to come visit her. He drew an inkpot closer and wrote something down.

"峰の雪みぎはの氷踏み分けて

　　　　君にぞまどふ道はまどはず

(Steps forward on the mountain snow, paces ahead on the
waterside ice. Though I've lost myself en route to your love, I'll
always find a way to your side.)

Even if there hadn't been a horse left to ride, I'd have walked here."
The lady wrote in reply,

"降りみだれみぎはにこほる雪よりも

　　　　中空にてぞわれは消ぬべき

(Were I the snow falling in the gale, I'd rather disappear
somewhere in between the sky and the earth than remain frozen
still in time on the water's edge.)"

Having noticed its inauspiciousness, she blotted out the poem just
before she finished it. The Prince criticized her near-completed poem for
the part of being "in between" as an ironic metaphor for their love triangle.
Her regret over the immodest expression that she had used humiliated
her so that she tore up the writing paper. The Prince lost his sense of
superiority to see her in such a state of doubt. He had forgotten how
popular he was with other ladies or how women adored him, but instead,
he gave himself to her completely in every single word and attitude so as
to make her love him even more. It had become so clear in his mind that
the lady he gazed upon was the only person he wished to impress and win
as his own.

The trip to Uji was to last for two days, ostensibly for ridding the
Prince of the bad spirit that had possessed him, which allowed plenty of
time for the secret lovers. Their mutual sense of devotion grew even
beyond their own expectations. A deliveryman confidentially arranged for
by Ukon arrived in the morning with a box of the lady's clothes. Lady
Ukifune had her tousled hair combed, and then she changed into many
layers of beautifully colored gowns, with a chic pink-rose outer layer
overlapping one of dark purple. Jiju also changed from her shabby robe

into one of higher quality. Prince Niou took a piece of pinafore out of the box and asked the lady to wear it to help him wash his face and hands with a bowl of water. He thought that his sister, Princess Ichi, would take care of her nicely as one of her closest attendants. Although the Princess already had many servants of noble status in her employ, it seemed most unlikely that she had found anyone more attractive than this lady in Uji. They spent the entire day focusing their efforts on making as much love as was humanly possible. It didn't matter to them what others might think. The Prince not only told her over and over again that he wanted to run away with her, but also asked her to swear that she would ignore the Commander, and not allow him to visit her or, if he insisted on seeing her, to treat him with complete disregard. Lady Ukifune was at a loss as how to respond to all these impossible favors, while her tears showed the weight of her unavoidable emotional confusion. It broke his heart to see his obsessive attachment tormenting his beloved who still hadn't decided to abandon the other man. Yet, he couldn't control his emotions which caused him to continue with his demands throughout the night.

Before sunrise, he took her home cloaked in darkness. She was carried in his arms all the way, just as she had been when they first arrived there. He said,

"I know that you count on Commander Kaoru very much, but he wouldn't treat you as nicely as I, would he? Can you understand the depths of my feelings?"

The lady nodded her assent so adorably that he felt his heart fill with joy and relief. Ukon was waiting for them at the corner of the main house. Upon their return, she quietly opened a small side door to let the lady in. It plunged him into the depths of absolute despair to see her off.

As had become the norm, Prince Niou returned to Nijo Palace after his trip to Uji. He immediately became quite sick and was unable to eat anything at all. The more days he spent there, the paler his face became and the more weight he lost. It was so obvious that his condition was quite

serious that everyone, including the Emperor, became greatly worried
and watched him carefully, which hindered his ability to write letters to
the lady with any regularity. Meanwhile, Lady Ukifune's overly-strict nurse
had returned to Uji after helping with her own daughter's childbirth. Since
this old nurse wouldn't be happy about the lady's unfaithful relationship
with Prince Niou, it was no longer possible for her to read his messages
more than a few times a day, as she had done while the nurse was away.
Her mother, Lady Chujo, had hoped blindly that her daughter, who had
reconciled herself to such a miserable life despite what she deserved,
would be treated respectfully by the Commander as one of his official
wives. Nothing was more delightful for her, therefore, than the fact that he
was going to move Lady Ukifune to a house he had built close to his palace
in the capital city, for then there would be no one who could question the
Commander's commitment afterwards. Lady Chujo had already started to
look for extra attendants and new pagegirls to hire for her daughter to
dispatch them to Uji. Lady Ukifune herself was still unsure of her feelings,
admitting that the Commander would perfectly fulfill her every social
need, yet Prince Niou's face as he had been desperately telling her how
much he needed her remained locked in her brain. Everything that he
had dared to say or show to her, whether good or bad, was housed in her
heart. She even dreamed about him every night. She was so overwhelmed
with the indecisive nature of her own mind.

Into the rainy season of early spring, after days of terrible weather,
Prince Niou finally abandoned hope of traversing the mountains to see his
lover in Uji, although his feelings for her had grown so enormously. He
even wished rather ungratefully that his parents, the Emperor and the
Empress, could have laid less expectations on their children so that he
need not feel so constrained. His frustration led him to scribble down a
poem of his uncontrollable passion and longing for her.

"ながめやるそなたの雲も見えぬまで
空さへくるるころのわびしさ

(Just as my heart lost its last ray of hope without you, so the sky dimmed too dark for me to see you beyond the clouds.)"

His writing in the message appeared to be so impulsive yet tasteful that, especially for a young lady like Ukifune who hadn't experienced such an emotional approach before, he seemed very glamorous and cultured. Each message she received from the Prince made her miss him more and more. On the other hand, the Commander, who had promised earlier than Prince Niou to take care of her forever, seemed to be more considerate and majestic a person than one could ever imagine, though it might be only because he was the first man she had been so intimate with.

"How could I survive in this world if the Commander should find out about this and run out on me now? As my mother looks so forward to the day when the Commander will finally bring me over to Kyoto, she will be totally disappointed with my abandoning him for such an outrageous suitor, and she will desert me thereafter. Although the Prince says that he is very much in love with me now, I understand that no one can expect his favor to last for very long, as it is said to be his typical pattern in relationships. I'm sure that it's no lie to say that he loves me, but I must wonder what will happen after his capricious devotion comes to an end one day. Besides, even if I were fortunate enough to live for the rest of my life as his beloved mistress somewhere in Kyoto, I would be constantly in discomfort, thinking how much our relationship would be hurting Lady Naka. Since nothing can be kept confidential in this world, which was proven when the Prince found me somehow from the very small clues that he picked up in the evening when we first met, no matter where and with whom I end up in the future, it's impossible to disappear from the world completely."

Thinking and thinking, Lady Ukifune still couldn't make up her mind, understanding very well that it would be extremely foolish to cast aside the Commander's favor. It was then that a messenger from the Commander arrived.

Having letters from two very different but excellent men in hand, she believed it inappropriate to compare their messages in any way, which seemed to be what an amorous woman typically did, in order to enjoy a sense of superiority. She took up the one from Prince Niou first and lay down in her bed to follow his beautiful script with her eyes. Each line was filled with his passion, which, taken as a whole, represented a flood of emotions. Ukon and Jiju looked at each other and nodded, thinking that the lady must be in love with the Prince. Jiju said,

"No wonder that she's had a change of heart. I also thought the Commander was second to none as a nobleman and I honestly admired him very much. Then this Prince came along, however, and he was an absolute beauty. Especially when he takes his ceremonious air off and looks at you intimately, his charm enthralls beyond measure. If I were Lady Ukifune, I would never be able to remain calm even for a moment while being romanced by him in that way. I would happily serve the Empress, if possible, so that I could have a chance to see him every day."

Ukon was surprised at her words and instantly criticized them.

"Where lies your loyalty to change your mind so easily? Tell me, who could possibly be superior to the Commander as a person? Setting appearances aside, his personality and overall bearing are exceptional. There is no doubt that Prince Niou has a reckless nature, as has been proved by his previous indiscretions. If our lady chooses the Prince, no one would ever feel secure about her future, don't you agree?"

Talking with Jiju in private, Ukon found a degree of comfort in having someone to worry about the lady's predicament with, though it was hard for them to see eye to eye. It brought her some much needed relief to try to work things out with someone who cared about the situation as much as she.

The letter from the Commander was opened next, which read,

"I'm sincerely sorry that I have been unable to visit you as often as I'd like, but you are always on my mind. It would make me happy if you could find time to write to me as well. Although it's been so hard for me to get in touch with you because of my onerous schedule, you must never think that it indicates a change of heart."

50

He also added a poem at the end of his letter.

"水まさるをちの里人いかならむ

　　　晴れぬながめにかきくらすころ

(Being hemmed in for days by the rains, my only care is about my lady in the distant village of a river basin, threatened undoubtedly by rising waters.)

I miss you even more on rainy days."

It was written on a piece of fine white paper, folded neatly and wrapped quite formally, as if it were an expression of his character. Although the writing itself wasn't particularly tasteful or artistic, his still-water personality could be seen running deep between the lines, which contrasted with Prince Niou's message with his direct and passionate expressions of adoration, folded up small and casually. Both of them were very attractive in their own way.

"You should write back to Prince Niou now, while no one is around," Jiju said.

"I don't feel like it today."

Lady Ukifune hesitated to do so and eventually expressed herself in a poem.

"里の名をわが身に知れば山城の

　　　宇治のわたりぞいとど住みうき

(The name of this village is associated not only with my family's history but also with my destiny which confines me to Uji's[1] environs.)"

Looking at the drawing that Prince Niou had left for her the other day, the lady couldn't help crying over her emotional inconstancy. No matter how many reasons she thought of to break up with the Prince, convincing herself that their love affair wouldn't last forever, it would still hurt to be a stranger to him after moving to Kyoto and being recognized by people as the Commander's woman. She finally wrote back to the

---

1. Lady Ukifune is making a play on words in this poem. Uji, the name of the village, is very similar in pronunciation to *ushi*, meaning 'suffering.'

Prince.

"かきくらし晴れせぬ峰の雨雲に

浮きて世をふる身をもなさばや

(Living disoriented in life without a flicker of clarity, I shall be the
clouds over the mountains bringing darkness to the sky.)

I won't be able to see you again once I vanish in a puff of smoke and
am swallowed up by the dark clouds."

Immediately upon reading the letter, Prince Niou howled in despair.
Yet, he was still sure somehow that the lady missed him as much as he did
her, imagining her suffering in deep dismay. His mind was wholly occupied
by his yearning, crowding out all other thoughts.

The famous "man of integrity," Commander Kaoru, also received a
poetic reply from the lady. After having read it thoroughly, one word after
another, he came to feel great sorrow, considering how painful it must
have been for her to live in such an isolated village alone. Understanding
her situation, he missed her even more. The poem she sent to him read,

"つれづれと身を知る雨のをやまねば

袖さへいとどみかさまさりて

(Although the endless rain falls upon me, reminding me how
much misery I was born to endure, my tears flood out to soak
my sleeves before even the river can follow suit.)"

He read her beautifully-worded poem over and over without setting it
down.

The Commander finally decided to confess his relationship with Lady
Ukifune to his wife, Princess Ninomiya. While they had a private moment,
he broached the subject.

"I'm so afraid that this might upset your feelings, but I want you to
know that, in the end, I'm simply a man. What I mean to say is, there is
another woman with whom I have had relations for several months. Since
she has been spending time alone in a remote village outside the capital, I
felt it better to bring her over someplace nearby. As you know already, I

have always had a life philosophy different from that of others. It's because I wanted something extraordinary out of life, and had even planned to become a monk at some point, though that was all until you came along. Now that I'm so very fortunate a man to be married to you, it has become virtually impossible to abandon everything for the life of a hermit. However, I honestly feel that I need to make up for the sins I have committed in my life by starting to take matters seriously with this lady."

"I don't see any reason for you to be so daunted to say such a thing," his wife replied composedly.

It was her dignity and noble breeding that enabled her to respond in that way.

The Commander heaved a sigh and answered,

"Some people may report this to the Emperor in a somewhat vicious manner. It can strain the limits of the imagination to realize how excited people can become about rumors, simply for the purpose of amusing themselves. I feel, however, that this lady from Uji is too worthy to be the object of such public scrutiny."

The Commander had begun secretly preparing to welcome Lady Ukifune to his newly-constructed house. It was to be expected that some of the more curious members of the public would spread licentious gossip about his building a new house in Kyoto for his secret mistress. In order to avoid being drawn into such a tiresome and nonsensical situation, he chose a team from among some of his closest followers to be in charge of interior decorations. In the end, however, this turned out to be an exercise in futility because he selected the Senior Assistant Minister of the Treasury to join this group due to their amicable professional relationship. Unfortunately, this man was the father-in-law of the Senior Secretary of Central Affairs, the one entrusted by Prince Niou to arrange for meeting the lady in Uji on his first visit there. Thus, everything the Commander said eventually made its way directly to the Prince. One day a follower of the Prince appeared and reported,

"We've heard that the interior designers and painters of the house were selected from among the Commander's inner circle of associates. Therefore, the commissioning of the art work has been restricted to a small group of people who are doing a very careful and elaborate job."

Prince Niou became greatly worried upon hearing that news. He suddenly recalled that his nurse, who had lived alone in her house in Kyoto in order to take care of the Prince since his youth, had very recently married a Governor of some far-off district and was scheduled to leave to join him soon. The Prince immediately sent a message to her new husband to ask him a favor, saying that he'd greatly appreciate it if he and his wife could help the Prince hide the lady. There was no way the Governor could refuse, having been asked by a person such as the Prince. The Governor told the Prince that it would be an honor, although he privately wondered what sort of woman would inspire the Prince to make such an odd request. The Prince felt a little relieved to have secured this hideout, which the Governor and his wife would quit in late March for his place of service. The Prince was determined to take her away on the same day that they planned to vacate the house. He sent off a quick message to his nurse.

"So, this is what I'm thinking to do. Please keep this only between the two of us."

Still, it was impossible for the Prince himself to visit the lady in Uji. Ukifune also wrote him back, saying that it would be difficult for her as well to welcome him because she was under the ever-watchful eye of her own nurse.

The Commander chose the tenth of April for welcoming Lady Ukifune to Kyoto, although she wasn't excited to hear the news. Feeling as insecure as a floating weed regarding her future, she wished to stay with her mother, Lady Chujo, for a while, until she found some way to reconcile herself to her fate and marry the Commander. At that time, however, her step-sister was about to give birth to a child of the Lieutenant who had once been engaged to Ukifune. The palace of the Governor was so unsettled, with a cadre of monks reading sutras and praying all day long for the safe and easy delivery of the child, that Lady Chujo couldn't call her favorite daughter over to her place nor accompany her on the trip to Hase Temple. She was, however, able to take some time off and visited Uji instead.

On her arrival in Uji, Ukifune's nurse gladly reported to the mother,

"Commander Kaoru has generously arranged for many things, such as new clothing for each of us to wear on the day we are scheduled to move to the capital. We try to look and behave as gracefully as we can, but I'm sure that I'll embarrass myself in Kyoto every now and then because my country upbringing comes out in whatever I do or say."

Lady Ukifune saw her mother happily talking with her nurse about the big move. She felt her heart ache so badly, peeking from behind the screen. She lay down on her bed, thinking,

"If things should go wrong and my relationship with the Prince became a public source of heartless gossip, what would people think of us? Since Prince Niou is indifferent to what others think, he will find me no matter how I feel or where I go, even deep in the mountains or up in the clouds. That's how I believe we will ruin ourselves together at the end of this lover's tale. Another letter from him arrived today, saying that he wanted to leave everything behind and run away with me. What should I say?"

Being sunk in her thoughts and wavering emotions, she felt too depressed to get out of bed. Her mother came to her room and looked upon her daughter's face anxiously.

"Why in the world does she look more pale and haggard than ever before?"

The nurse explained,

"She has been unusually sick these days and has spent most of her time in bed without eating anything at all."

Lady Chujo found the condition of her daughter very odd, worrying that she may have become possessed by some evil spirit.

"I need to know exactly what is happening to her. I fear it has something to do with us being unable to visit Hase Temple to purify our souls this year."

Lady Ukifune felt so sorry that she had been hiding all these matters from her mother, and she was unable to look Lady Chujo in the eye due to an overwhelming sense of guilt.

After dark, the moonlight was shining brightly, which reminded Ukifune of the night sky she and the Prince had gazed up into while on the boat, shortly before daybreak. She couldn't hold back her tears, blaming herself for having fallen into such an immoral affair. Her mother and the nurse invited Ben-no-Ama, the nun who lived in a cottage nearby, to join in their conversation about the old days. The nun grieved over Lady Okimi's passing, telling them how loving and considerate she had been and how destiny had instantly turned the tables and extinguished such a brightly burning soul.

"If she were still alive today, she would be enjoying the prime of her life as her sister, Lady Naka, does. They would still be close and would often enjoy talking about how they were getting on. I had really hoped to see both of them being happily married to great men after all the struggles they endured in childhood."

Lady Chujo felt slightly bothered by this story, thinking that her daughter was no less excellent than either of these sisters, and everyone would come to appreciate this if her relationship with the Commander worked out as planned. She proudly said,

"Although there have always been a lot of things to worry about over this daughter of mine, I feel more at ease now that she is moving to Kyoto after having fallen into the favor of such a great nobleman. From now on, I may not have as many chances to visit here, but it would be my pleasure to talk about those old stories whenever I am able to see you again."

Ben-no-Ama replied,

"I have kept a certain distance from your beautiful daughter because I've been fully aware that I'm not in a position to say anything to her, considering my humble status as a nun. Though I know I will miss her deeply after she departs, having been greatly concerned about such a young lady living all alone, I couldn't be happier for her at the same time. The Commander has always been an exceptionally thoughtful person in my eyes, which was why I agreed to arrange his initial meeting with Lady Ukifune. I just knew that they would be a perfect match as a couple. It seems my inspiration wasn't completely off the mark, was it?"

"Well, no one knows if it will work out in the long run, but for now I must be very grateful that you introduced my daughter to such a wonderful person. Based on the fact that he promised to be with her forever, you don't know how much we appreciate you for what you've done. Lady Naka used to feel sorry for my daughter and so had allowed her to live at her palace, but due to an unexpected occurrance we were forced to leave there suddenly. It was nearly the end of the world for us at that time, when you literally swooped in to save us from complete disaster," said Lady Chujo as she bowed down.

The nun seemed to understand what she had meant and laughed reservedly.

"I've heard that it's difficult for a beautiful lady to serve Lady Naka because of her husband's being such a womanizer that he often makes trouble. An attendant of Lady Naka once told me that they were almost perfectly paired as a husband and a wife, though when it came to the Prince's affairs with the ladies working there, Lady Naka always blamed the women, not her husband, as being the instigators, regardless of their lower status, which has proven quite troublesome over the years."

Lying down in bed, Lady Ukifune heard them talking and thought that if even an unrelated servant was accused by Lady Naka of having an affair with the Prince, how much more blame would be heaped upon her own sister.

Lady Chujo was surprised by the story which had just been told.

"Jealousy changes people, indeed. The Commander is also married to a daughter of the Emperor, but it doesn't really bother me whether she accepts his relationship with my daughter or not because we don't know her personally. Nonetheless, if my daughter were one of the mistresses of

Prince Niou, or in some sort of unfaithful relationship with him, in spite of what Lady Naka had kindly done for her, I would never return to see my daughter no matter how painful or hurtful it would be."

The lady was totally stupefied, listening to their conversation, and thought to herself,

"I'd rather just disappear now. As long as I linger in this world, our secret will always be in danger of being revealed. Things would become very ugly for all involved if the truth were to come out."

Then her mother heard the current of the Uji River roaring ferociously past and spoke to her daughter in an assuring manner,

"Not many rivers sound as terrifying as this one here. As you have been waiting for so long in such a desolate place as this, no one will argue that you now deserve to be cherished by the Commander."

As people were talking about how fast and dreadful the current of the Uji River had been throughout history, one of the servants in the room started to tell a story of a recent accident.

"The grandchild of a local boatman erred when poling his grandfather's boat across the water and fell headlong into the river only to drown. Once its fast current takes people under, very few have even the slightest chance of survival."

The ladies from the area seemed to concur. Lady Ukifune's thoughts went beyond simply feeling sorry for the tragic accident.

"What if I go missing just like the child? People may grieve for a while, but if the relationship between the Prince and I were somehow discovered, I would have to live with public contempt for the rest of my life, causing a lifetime of humiliation for everyone around me."

Reflecting over what to do, she gradually came to realize that there was nothing preventing her from making the fatal decision to end her own life. Her mood suddenly cleared, thinking of things this way, although it couldn't be helped that a part of her hoped to avoid choosing this last resort, when actually faced with the sadness of doing so. While listening to her mother grumbling about her worries over her daughter, with her eyes closed as if asleep, Lady Ukifune could think of no other way to relieve herself of this emotional confusion.

Lady Chujo looked into her daughter's sleeping face, which appeared too pale to be healthy, and cautioned the nurse to be more sensitive to the young lady's condition.

"Please arrange to have appropriate rites undertaken for her quick recovery. As for the ceremony, it must be ...."

Lady Ukifune remained motionless in her bed, listening to her mother asking her nurse to make certain that various things went smoothly during the ceremony to rid her of the evil spirit which plagued her. Ukifune thought that what she really needed was, as had been described in an ancient love story, to cleanse herself of her passion in a sacred river so that she would be incapable of falling in love once again. Her mother was making such a fuss in organizing the event, having no idea at all what her daughter was thinking. Lady Chujo continued,

"It looks like we are short of female attendants. Do you know of any ladies who would want to work for us? But leave new recruits here. It's very difficult to get along with a noblewoman such as Princess Ninomiya. Though in many cases the noblewoman herself takes on a generous attitude to the second wife of her husband, her people tend to have conflicts with the servants of the new lady, which causes so much trouble over time. Do not be too obvious, and do keep what I just told you in mind."

After confirming everything and leaving nothing to chance, Lady Chujo prepared to return home.

"My other daughter also needs my help in delivering her first baby," she said.

Lady Ukifune felt hopelessly lonely and weighed down with a heavy heart. It seemed that this may be the last time for her to see her mother before something terrible befell her.

"I still feel very sick, mother, especially when you are not around. I am always nervous and wish that you could stay with me. Could I come with you and stay by your side for a spell, please?"

Being begged so unexpectedly by her beloved daughter, Lady Chujo burst into tears.

"I feel the same way, my dear, but it's just not a good time at our house. Besides, your people will be so frustrated by the lack of space, being unable to do anything to get you ready for the move. I promise, no matter where you travel to after marriage, I will come any distance to see you, even before you call. It's such a shame, however, that a humble woman such as myself can offer you no real support. I'm truly sorry for that."

Her tears ran dry as soon as she finished speaking.

Commander Kaoru sent another letter that same day. As Lady Ukifune had written in her last message that she didn't feel well, he was deeply concerned about her condition.

"Although I wish I could visit there myself, I cannot because of the many duties I must attend to here. It excites me beyond measure just thinking about welcoming you to Kyoto in the coming days that I don't even know how I will spend these interminable moments until then, now that missing you has become nearly unbearable."

A message from Prince Niou also arrived in Uji. As was usually the case, he expressed his devotion for her using all of the passionate expressions at his disposal, although the letter closed thus, revealing his anxiety,

"What makes you hesitate so much? I feel as if I'm going crazy just thinking you may have given your heart to another. Nothing else can hold my attention. It's as if I'm obsessed with thoughts of only you."

He must have been feeling uneasy, for she hadn't responded to his proposal to live in some hidden place together, a proposal he had included in his letter from the day before.

On a rainy day, a messenger from the Commander happened upon another messenger exiting the gate at the lady's house in Uji. As he had met him before on some occasions at the house of the Senior Secretary, he began speaking to him.

"Hello. How have you been? What sort of duty brings you out this way?"

The other messenger answered,

"I'm on my own business this time. I come here on occasion to see my woman."

"You must be joking. Who would hand deliver a letter to his own lady? I think that you might be hiding something from me. Tell me, what is it?"

The other messenger answered hastily,

"Well I mean, it's actually my master, Lord Tokikata. He is secretly in touch with a lady here."

Although his story seemed odd and inconsistent, the Commander's messenger didn't ask any further questions and saw the man off, avoiding being rude by prying too deeply into the affairs of others.

Nonetheless, the Commander's messenger was a clever man as well as possessing a great deal of common sense. He ordered his pageboy to follow the suspicious messenger and confirm that he returned to Tokikata's. The boy came back later and reported,

"He entered the palace of Prince Niou, although the letter was handed to the Senior Secretary."

Actually, the Prince's messenger had undertaken the risky task, unsuitable for one of his humble position, without much understanding of the situation. It was still very shameful for him, however, to have spilled the secret so easily to the modest follower the Commander had happened to send to Uji. As soon as he heard the report from the young male servant, the messenger went to the Commander's palace and passed the letter from Lady Ukifune to one of the aides there. Commander Kaoru, dressed in casual attire, was just about to leave for Rokujo Palace, with only a few followers in tow because it was only an informal visit to his older sister, the Empress. Handing over the letter to his superior, the messenger said in an intentionally loud voice,

"This time, it took me longer than usual, because I needed to look into a suspicious man I ran into at the lady's place."

The Commander, leaving the house, heard the messenger's words and approached him.

"Then, tell me what you've found out," he said.

The messenger, however, didn't mention a thing at that time. The Commander understood through eye contact that it was neither the time nor the place to discuss the matter, and withdrew without uttering another remark.

As it had been reported that the condition of the Empress was worse than ever, the Princes and Princesses flocked to her palace that day to see for themselves how their mother was holding up. The presence of many high government officials added to the liveliness of the gathering. Fortunately, the Empress didn't seem as ill as had been rumored. When the Senior Secretary of Central Affairs showed up later with the letter from Uji, Prince Niou was talking with some of the female attendants in their waiting room. On being informed of the Senior Secretary's arrival, the Prince called him over to one of the outside gates to receive the reply from the lady. Meanwhile, the Commander had just been excused from the room of the Empress. As he was leaving, he found the Prince in a corner of the garden with a letter in his hands. From how keenly he was reading it, the Commander thought the Prince had to be utterly infatuated with its sender, but he was too cautious to walk directly past the Prince. All he could recognize at that distance was the rich scarlet color of the paper, on which the vague outlines of small letters were written. The Prince was too engrossed in its contents to pay attention to anything or anyone around him. At that moment, the Great Minister of the Right, Yugiri, who was an uncle and father-in-law of the Prince, also excused himself briefly from the Empress's room. Since it would be inconvenient for the Prince to be seen so caught up in reading a letter from another woman, the Commander gave a slight cough in warning. At almost the same time that the Prince looked up and stashed the letter away, his most powerful uncle appeared in front of him. While Prince Niou immediately tidied up his clothes in surprise, the great authority figure of the times went down to his knees and bowed courteously to him.

"I'm afraid I must leave. Although the Empress's condition has been stable for the past few years, we have to be careful from now on. I'll ask my men to invite the most highly-ranked monk from the renowned Enryaku Temple in Mt. Hiei."

Upon saying so, he quickly arose and left to organize things for the monk's invitation.

It was already deep into the night when people left for home. As Prince Niou was departing, Great Minister Yugiri accompanied this promising son-in-law of his, as an expression of his humbleness and loyalty. After walking the Prince to his room, the great uncle left for home surrounded by a brace of his sons, who were high-ranking government officials in their own right. Commander Kaoru emerged from the room after everyone else. While his followers went ahead of him to the gate, being busy preparing the lights for his departure, the Commander called the messenger over, wondering what information he possessed.

"What did you try to tell me earlier?" he asked.

"Sir, this morning a follower of Lord Tokikata, the Governor of Izumo, was at the lady's house in Uji. He handed a message written on a light purple-colored paper attached to a cherry tree twig to an attendant at the door on the west side of the house. When I asked him about this, his stories were so changeable and inconsistent that I was hesitant to believe him. So I ordered my men to follow him to find out why he had acted so oddly when I questioned him. It turned out that he went straight back to the palace of Prince Niou, and the letter went to a Mr. Michisada, a Junior Assistant Minister of Public Ceremony and Senior Secretary of Central Affairs."

The Commander found it all very strange and asked,

"How did the attendant in Uji pass along the letter to the messenger?"

"I wasn't present when she handed it over to him. I guess they passed him the reply at some other door away from where I was standing, for it was inconvenient to do so in front of me. One humble servant told me, however, that the beautiful paper the lady used for the letter was a vivid scarlet."

Taking everything into consideration, the Commander was almost certain that it had to be the very letter Prince Niou had been reading that afternoon. Although he was impressed by the messenger's quick thinking in having the stranger tailed, and wanted to ask him more about it, he hesitated to do so, being aware of others milling about.

On his way home, the Commander couldn't conceal his displeasure at what he had just discovered.

"When it comes to love-related issues, it's surprising how careful you must be around the Prince. How in the world and when could he have found out about the lady and, what's worse, made advances towards her? It was foolish of me to think that the village was so far away that there would be no chance of this sort of trouble occurring. Though I wouldn't blame him if he had swept away some random woman whose lover was a stranger to him, this time it was my woman and he knew it. Not only have we been as close as brothers since childhood, but I am also the one who introduced him to his beautiful wife. How unforgivable of him to mock me in this way!"

His mind was becoming occupied with spiteful feelings.

"Although I have yearned for his wife, Lady Naka, for years, I've never crossed that line thanks to my sense of morality. It's not some capricious passion, but a long and sad history between us that makes me long so deeply for her. Despite all of that, I've never done anything over which to feel guilty about, which has enabled me to view myself as a good human being. Now that I know how ungraciously he betrayed me, however, all the efforts I've made seem so stupidly meaningless. I wonder how he could keep in touch with a lady living as far away as Uji, while having been sick these days and preoccupied with receiving many visitors while confined to bed. With such a long distance between them, how far has their relationship progressed? I heard that he once went missing for a couple of days and people had desperately searched for him high and low. The cause of both his disappearance and sickness had been unknown, but it seems so obvious now. Looking back to when he fell in love with Lady Naka, at first sight no less, he was continually depressed because he couldn't travel to Uji that often. Everyone worried about him very much at that time as well."

In addition to recalling the Prince's behavior when smitten, the Commander began to understand why Lady Ukifune looked so troubled the other day. The more it finally seemed to make sense, however, the more unbearably his heart ached.

"It's others' feelings that we can never understand. She appeared to be very modest and reserved at first sight, but there was also something amorous about her. In that sense, they make a good match."

He tried to compose his emotions by changing despair into indifference. It then began to feel completely natural for him to give way to the Prince and drop out of the love triangle, although the other half of him still cared about her.

"Since the very beginning I hadn't considered making her my wife officially, which is to say, I could have kept our relationship a secret. Even if I break cleanly from her, it'll only make me miss her more for having spent so much time apart when we were together."

A torrent of different emotions swept him into a state of anguish, so that he could no longer maintain his usual equanimity.

"If I should desert her now, the Prince will take her somewhere else and cherish her passionately for a while. That, however, will expose her to a lifetime of misery, where she must face the very cruel reality that both the Prince never thinks about others when making his decisions and that his interest in her will have faded. I've seen a few former beloved mistresses of the Prince end up becoming servants of his sister, Princess Ippon. If I hear them say later on that Lady Ukifune has fallen to such a humiliating station, I will never be able to stop regretting my decision."

After deep consideration, he found it impossible for him to completely sever ties with her. He wrote another letter to ask how she was doing in Uji and called the same messenger over to entrust its confidential delivery. The Commander asked,

"Does the Senior Secretary of Central Affairs called Michisada visit his wife often? I mean, do you think they are still on good terms?"

"Yes, they seem to be, sir," the messenger answered.

"The man you met the other day in Uji may have regularly been dispatched there. Michisada must have become interested in this lady when he found such a beautiful young thing left lonely and unhappy for such a long time."

The Commander sighed deeply and continued,

"Since this is a very shameful situation for me to be involved in, deliver this letter as confidentially as you can, please."

The whole story was intended to make his messenger believe that the man called Michisada was the one who was secretly in touch with Lady Ukifune. It worked out quite well for the humble man, who finally came to understand why the Senior Secretary was always probing into how the Commander was or what the situation in Uji had been like, although he was too afraid to mention anything directly. The Commander was also very hesitant to ask more questions, for he didn't want to provide him with too much insight into the matter.

At the house in Uji, the more often the messengers from both Commander Kaoru and Prince Niou began to show up with their letters, the more important it became to keep them from bumping into each other. In his latest message, the Commander simply wrote,

　　　　"波こゆるころとも知らず末の松
　　　　　　待つらむとのみ思ひけるかな

　　(In my utter ignorance that your heart was turning offshore, how
　　　　blind I was to have believed in your eternal longing for me.)
Don't make me everyone's fool, please."

Lady Ukifune felt the pangs of guilt in her heart, although she was unsure exactly what the Commander meant to say, so unexpected was his message. It wouldn't be a wise choice for her to either reply as if having understood the whole meaning of the poem or to write excuses, which would be too contrived to erase his doubt. Therefore, she put the letter back into the original envelope and sent it back to the Commander with a note saying,

"I guess you've sent this message to the wrong person. Incidentally, I apologize for having been too ill to write you for a while."

The Commander smiled bitterly upon reading her reply.

"I must admit that I was impressed by how shrewdly she escaped my snare. She just proved her mettle in an unexpected way."

To his dismay, however, he became even more enchanted to see this other side of her.

Although the Commander hadn't mentioned it directly, it was quite obvious by then that he was aware of the love affair, which made Lady Ukifune fret greatly. She despaired to think that she would be ruined for what she had done. It was then that Ukon came to speak with her.

"Why did you send the letter back to the Commander? It's a most sinister thing to have done."

"There must have been some mistake. I don't think it was intended for me," Lady Ukifune answered.

The truth was, however, Ukon had sensed something unusual about her reply to the Commander and had already opened the letter before passing it on to the messenger. It wasn't anything a prudent attendant would ever do. Without confessing that she had read it, she said,

"You must be very upset. It seems to be a dire situation, now that he must have found out what's going on."

Lady Ukifune blushed upon hearing those words and was momentarily speechless, realizing that Ukon knew what had been written in the Commander's letter. Nonetheless, she didn't even imagine that her long-time attendant would have opened the letter, but that the only possible way she could have learned this information was that one of the

Commander's companions had somehow discovered it due to his odd recent behavior and leaked the news to some of her ladies in Uji. Being too shocked to ask how Ukon had come across this piece of gossip, Lady Ukifune felt extremely embarrassed, just thinking about how she would have appeared in the eyes of the others who now knew the truth. Although it was far from what she had hoped for, she tried to reconcile herself to the hard luck she was destined to endure as she lay quietly down in her bed. At that moment, Jiju, the attendant who had accompanied Lady Ukifune and Prince Niou to the other side of Uji River, joined in the conversation. Ukon started to tell her story.

"An older sister of mine used to have relationships with two different men when she lived in the Hitachi region. I guess this sort of situation can happen to anyone, no matter how important they may be. Both of them were very much in love with my sister and they showed almost the same great degree of passion. The one who came along later, however, completely stole her heart away, which enraged the first man and drove him to kill his rival in the end. After the incident, that fellow stopped seeing my sister as well. As a consequence of the love affair, not only did one of the most promising young men in the region lose his life, but the other was also accused of committing a heinous crime and was banished from the region, in spite of having been highly regarded as a capable follower of the local Governor. As for my sister, she was considered to be responsible for the whole matter and forced to move out of the Governor's house, in which she had served for a long time. She ended up living in the far eastern regions, separated from her people. Her nurse still cries over her. My sister made a lot of people unhappy in that sense, which I think is a very sinful thing to do in one's life. I know that talking about her now can be a bad omen, but all I'm asking for here is your awareness that love affairs can truly ruin people's lives, whether humble or noble, and it's very wrong to be indecisive about this sort of issue. Although usually it doesn't involve the loss of one's life as it did for the young man who pursued my sister, everyone, regardless of social class, will have to lose something in some painful way as a result of their unfaithful deeds. Especially when it comes to noblemen, they'd rather choose death sometimes over humiliation and disgrace. So, please choose one of them now before it's too late. If you think that Prince Niou loves you more devotedly than Commander Kaoru, as he continually claims, just make up your mind to love only him and waver no more. Thinking too much only weakens you and won't bring you any relief. You have seen how much your mother has worried about you, as well as how busy your nurse has kept herself in preparing for your move to Kyoto. The Prince is so desperate to come here and take you to his place before the Commander whisks you away from him. You cannot just leave all of these people to continue with what they are doing for you now. It's too cruel."

The other attendant responded,

"It's terribly inappropriate of you to tell us such an inauspicious and unsettling story. As you know, it all comes down to where your destiny takes you, regardless of what you do in this life. If Lady Ukifune loves one person more than the other, it should be a sign. For my part, I understand why she is not particularly excited about moving to Kyoto for the Commander, who seems now to be hurrying up the preparations to bring her over as soon as possible. It was unbelievable how passionate the Prince was for her the other day. I believe that she should choose the man she feels more strongly for, although to do that, some time needs to pass so that the situation can settle down."

Although Jiju claimed that it was the lady's choice to make, her loyalty was evident.

Ukon didn't concur with Jiju, however.

"Well, I don't know if that's such a good idea. Either way, bringing her a life of peace is all I have asked for when praying to the Gods of the temples in Hase or Ishiyama. According to what I hear, those in charge of the Commander's properties are a quite violent people who live in this area in large numbers. Their reach also grows as they bring even distant relatives into the fold. One of the sons-in-law of their patriarch is now their de facto leader, and he has been promoted to Lieutenant of the Right Division of the Inner Palace Guards. Whatever order the Commander gives goes directly to him. Although a highly-titled nobleman wouldn't expect his men to take any type of extreme action in executing his commands, when it comes to uncultured country people, like those working here as night watchmen, they sometimes go too far to satisfy the dictates of their lord and foul things up in the end. Oh, and speaking of going too far, that night when Prince Niou took Lady Ukifune out very late at night, I was so terrified of what might have happened on the way. Since he was disguised as a commoner with only a few guards to accompany him, if he had been discovered by any of the Commander's rough and overzealous underlings, the situation could easily have turned deadly."

Lady Ukifune became more distressed to hear them talking that way, as they didn't understand the true cause of her suffering. She thought,

"It's truly embarrassing that they take it for granted that I've already chosen Prince Niou, when, in reality, I don't regard either of them as better than the other. They are both wonderful men, and it feels like a dream to be loved by them both, with no idea which to choose. I am very grateful to the Prince for loving me so passionately, although I wonder what it was that attracted him so strongly. The Commander, on the other hand, has graciously taken care of me and has been so steadfastly reliable for the past few years. I never want to end my relationship with him, which is why I'm troubled so. What if things go as wrong as they did for Ukon's sister while I'm pondering thus?"

She was consumed by one thought.

"I'd rather just slip away from this world. I must be destined to live this life the least happily of the most ordinary of people. Even the humblest would never have as much trouble in living as I have had."

She lay face down in bed in despair. Ukon tried to encourage her by saying,

"Don't be so pessimistic, my lady. All I meant by telling that story was to let you know that this kind of trouble can happen to anyone and that you can choose either suitor free of any pressure. To be honest, I am very concerned about you lately, because you used to confide in me all of your troubles or worries, but since this love affair with the Prince started, you have been quite hesitant to share your feelings with us, and instead have piled up all of your stress inside."

Those who knew the reality of the situation were all too distraught about the future of Lady Ukifune to do anything, while her nurse, being out of the picture, was contentedly working away, preparing the clothing for their day of departure. Upon seeing Lady Ukifune lying alone on the bed looking distraught, the nurse called over a few young female servants who had just started to work there and said to Ukifune,

"Why don't you get yourself up and spend some time relaxing with these young servants? If you continue to waste your time in bed like that, some evil spirits will lead you away from the goodness in your heart."

In spite of these encouraging words, the nurse was deeply concerned to see Ukifune's hopeless expression.

Several days had passed without any type of reply from the Commander. It was then that the head of the local family in power, who Ukon had described as violent and rough, showed up. As he was an old man with a wild appearance, a big, strong frame and a deep, hoarse voice, everyone could tell that he was someone to be feared. He asked for an audience with the chief female servant, and therefore Ukon came out to attend him. He said,

"Our lord called me over to his palace in Kyoto this morning and I've just now returned. Along with many other details regarding our duties, he questioned me about the night-watch around this compound. As you probably know, the Commander has never assigned any extra people to guard this place at night, even though his lady stays here. He thought it to be unnecessary because my men had to work here both day and night and there wouldn't be any opportunity for others to sneak in. However, he's received some information recently which leads him to believe that there are some unknown men often visiting their ladies here. He severely reprimanded us for letting such an inconvenience occur on his property, saying that those who had been working on the night-watch should have known something about it, because if not, he said that they could not have considered themselves fit to be called guards. So I told him that, to my shame, I wasn't informed of anything, since I had been absent from duty for months due to a serious illness. I also said, 'Although I don't know anything concrete about what is going at the palace, I can assure you that my men have carried out their job on my behalf as carefully and enthusiastically as possible, and if such a horrendous thing had taken place, there would have been no way it would have gone unnoticed.' Then the Commander warned me that not only should I be more careful but also that I would be punished severely if anything untoward should be discovered for certain. Although not fully understanding some of what he was talking about, I have sworn absolute obedience to his command."

Ukon felt cold shivers up and down her spine. Even the inauspicious hoot of a night owl couldn't be more terrifying than the story she'd just heard. She didn't know what to say, so she excused herself without giving him a proper reply.

Upon returning to Lady Ukifune's room, Ukon sighed deeply.

"Here it comes. This is exactly what I told you the other day. The Commander must have noticed something, which is why he hasn't been writing recently."

Then, despite the intensity of the atmosphere, the nurse gladly said, having heard a part of the conversation between the patriarch of the family and Ukon,

"How kind the Commander is to take notice of such a thing! I've been so worried because, despite the great danger of being robbed in the surrounding area, the men of the night-watch were becoming indolent and careless these days, unlike how they carried themselves at the beginning. All they do is send their humble followers in their place, and these men are too useless even to patrol at night."

What a happy person she is, Ukon thought.

Lady Ukifune faced the fact that she was on the verge of losing everything. What made her even more confused was the constant stream of letters from Prince Niou, all of which asked her whether or not she would accept his proposal, and telling her how much he suffered while anxiously awaiting her reply. She came to feel exhausted and thought,

"Whichever I choose, there will be unavoidable consequences for everyone concerned. I guess the only way to remedy this situation is to disappear. Compared to those heroines in ancient tales, who threw themselves into a river after wavering between two equally excellent men, even without actually having been intimate with either, much more do I deserve to die. Besides, I am certain that life will never stop treating me harshly. My mother will cry over me for a while, but I'm sure she'll recover before long because she has many other children with which to keep herself occupied. I'd rather die than create a humiliating scandal and live on as a public laughingstock."

It was surprising for Lady Ukifune to come up with such an extreme idea, one in stark contrast to her delicately gentle and innocent appearance. One reason for this might have been her childhood experience in the countryside, far from the world of the aristocracy where the practically moderate way of getting along in life held sway.

She told them to tear up all the letters from Prince Niou, so that things could be kept only between the three of them after her death. She disposed of them not at once but in different ways, little by little. Some pieces were burnt in the flame of a room lantern and others were thrown into the river. Those servants who didn't know about their love affair thought that Lady Ukifune was discarding things that would no longer be needed after the move to Kyoto, such as her calligraphy, which had been written during her long, uneasy life in Uji. Jiju found Lady Ukifune throwing away these scraps of memories and said,

"Why do you have to do that? Since you two are very much in love and the letters fully expressed his feelings for you, it would be best to keep them perhaps at the bottom of some box or somewhere unlikely to be found, so you can read them again and appreciate them from time to time in later years. The Prince not only used the most gorgeous stationery, but also selected the most excellent words to describe his passion. It is such a heartless thing to tear them all up in such an utterly disrespectful manner."

Lady Ukifune, however, didn't heed her words and answered,

"I must do this, because it will cause a lot of trouble later if someone should find them. I don't have much time left in this life, anyway. It won't make him happy, but instead he will be bothered by my insensitivity for having left these letters behind, which would humiliate me the most."

Confronting a growing sense of fear and despair, she hadn't realized that she'd made up her mind to die. It was then that an old saying suddenly popped into her head: 'The biggest sin was to die before your parents.' Although she couldn't remember where she'd heard it from.

March was already coming to a close. The place where Prince Niou was planning to move secretly with Lady Ukifune was to be vacant on the 28th of that month. A letter from him arrived in Uji, saying,

"I will come to you that night. Be wary of your servants, so as not to let them suspect anything is amiss. You needn't worry about anyone from my side betraying us. You have my word."

Lady Ukifune was pleased and saddened at the same time, thinking,

"Even if the Prince finds a way to come here somehow, he won't be able to talk with me or even to see me, now that the night-watch has been reinforced. I don't see any chance for us to spend time together once more. He will have to go back home feeling greatly disappointed after all the rigorous effort he put into this plan of his."

Once she imagined him going back to Kyoto with a broken heart, his shade continued to haunt her, causing her heart so much pain that she tried to cover up her face with the letters clutched in her hands. Although having held the waves of emotions at bay for some seconds, she finally broke down into tears. It didn't take much time before her sobbing turned into a howl. Ukon gently tried to calm her down, saying,

"My Lady, don't feel so sad. People will wonder why you are acting like this and some may eventually figure out what is really going on. I've heard there are already some people who doubt that you have been sick for such a long time, claiming it is unnatural or suspicious. Although there's no need to take it all so seriously, why don't you write him back so as to reassure him for the time being, whether you mean it or not? Remember that I'll always be by your side to help you with anything and to make things right. Besides, when you think about it, Prince Niou is one very bold man, one who would be brave enough to fly to you if it were his last resort. It is child's play, therefore, for such a man to carry a slip of a thing like you away with him on the wind as you are blown far away from here."

Ukon put it in such an exaggerated way just to cheer up Lady Ukifune, who spoke up after taking some time to compose herself.

"I honestly hate it when people speak as if they know that I've made up my mind to be with the Prince. If I were in a position where I could feel completely comfortable in choosing him, I would be glad to do so. Unfortunately, this is not the case. As far as what he wrote in his messages, it seems as if I were party to his plans, which is also not the case. It is possible to predict what will happen to me, what he is going to do about me, and that makes me feel miserable, as if I have no control over my own life."

The messages from Prince Niou sat in a pile at the edge of her desk, unanswered.

Meanwhile, Prince Niou was feeling more and more irritated, as days had passed without having received a reply from his beloved. He constantly tried to reconcile himself to the fact that she would have made the safest choice to be with Kaoru. Although that was totally understandable considering how eloquently the Commander was at convincing others with his artful words, the state of his mind was far from one of resignation. As the Prince was sure that Lady Ukifune had once loved him in return, it was unbearable for him to think, as was most possibly the case with her, that her change of heart had been caused by the silly preaching of her older female attendants during his absence from Uji. Deeper and deeper he sank into frustration at every thought, and he eventually lost himself to despair. It was as if his vision had been thickly veiled by a dark sandstorm stirred up by his hopeless desire for Lady Ukifune. It was then that Prince Niou resolved himself to take all the risks necessary and strike out for Uji.

The Prince, accompanied, as always, by his closest followers, arrived near the house in Uji. Tokikata went ahead to check the opening in the reed fence surrounding the house, where they had always entered from in previous visits. This time, however, some watchmen seemed to have quickly noticed a suspicious presence outside the fence. One of them asked loudly,

"Who goes there?"

The voice didn't sound lazy or sleepy in the least, but very cautious, unlike any quality expressed in the watchmen before. Tokikata beat a hasty retreat and sent in one of his men who had actually visited very often to see his own woman. To the party's surprise, the guards stopped this frequent and recognizable visitor to question why he was there. The forcefulness of the new security policy annoyed the man a little, but he answered calmly,

"I've come from Kyoto to deliver a letter. It's urgent."

He asked politely for their permission to complete his "assignment," naming one particular attendant working under Ukon whom he said he needed to meet. Ukon got a message from Prince Niou through this servant, expressing how complicated the situation had already become.

"I'm terribly afraid that tonight cannot be the night," she responded.

Prince Niou was very disappointed to read the message, yet was unable to give up. It was extremely disturbing that everyone seemed to be allied against him, trying to keep him and Lady Ukifune apart. He ordered Tokikata to enter the compound alone.

"You go and meet the attendant called Jiju and convince her to help us somehow."

Tokikata showed his cleverness in making excuses to gain entry into the grounds and was able to meet with Jiju. After listening to his explanation, she told him what she knew.

"Though I'm unclear about the details, it is said that the Commander called over the head of the village and told him directly to reinforce the night-watch. It's so very troublesome for us, now that they are taking control of everything. When you look at Lady Ukifune, she seems to be feeling so down these days, which I guess is because she is extremely intimidated about all the excessive attention the Commander has paid to her lately. We feel very sorry, by the way, that she isn't able to see the Prince tonight. If anyone should find out about their relationship, things would turn out badly for them both. I sincerely promise that instead we will somehow sort things out for the night when your lord is planning to take our lady away."

She also told him that they had to be careful with Ukifune's nurse, who was ever alert, even about the smallest noises at night. Tokikata begged her to come with him before the Prince to explain the situation directly.

"You must understand that it was not easy for the Prince to come here, considering the recent circumstances surrounding him. Since he was dying to meet Lady Ukifune tonight, it will be absolutely impossible for me to tell him what I've just heard from you by myself. Would you please come with me and repeat to him exactly what you just told me? I'm begging you, please."

Although she insisted over and over that a humble servant such as herself was incapable of doing what he requested of her, Tokikata continued to press her for hours. While their argument continued, it moved deeper and deeper into the night.

The Prince was waiting on his horse a short distance away from the house, though he was disconcerted by the wild dogs which often appeared before his party barking fiercely. Another great concern of his was that local bandits might happen upon them, since he had only a few of his followers around and they were all dressed like ordinary countrymen. He could tell that everyone was feeling very apprehensive. Meanwhile, Tokikata had finally convinced Jiju and was hurriedly walking with her to where the party was awaiting his return. As he desperately encouraged her to go faster, the beautiful attendant tied back her hair, which was much longer than she was tall, tucked it under her arms and held it in front of her body to move more easily. Tokikata tried to get her to ride on horseback, but she resolutely refused. He reluctantly continued walking beside her, therefore, helping her to walk by holding up the skirt of her gown. He had also borrowed a pair of poorly-made shoes from one of his men, so that Jiju could wear his well-tailored boots suitable for mountain hiking.

On their arrival, Jiju approached the Prince and roughly explained the difficult situation surrounding Lady Ukifune. Since he wanted to listen to her more carefully and certainly not on horseback, some of his men were immediately ordered to find somewhere for their conversation to take place. They discovered a house hidden in the mountains and unfolded a large mat over weeds in the garden. Upon dismounting and sitting down on the mat to speak properly with Ukifune's attendant, Prince Niou was brought to tears, thinking,

"What a pathetic man I am, now that I find my love precariously balanced at the edge of a cliff. With this huge emptiness in my heart, how could anyone possibly expect me to live like others do from now on?"

His tears seemed to flow endlessly over the blinding sorrow he felt. Jiju was a woman with such a tender heart that she totally sympathized with the Prince to see him grieving so. She thought that even the most malignant creature made of all the spiteful feelings in the world would shed all of its grudges before the Prince's divineness. After somewhat regaining his composure, the Prince asked Jiju,

"Can't I have even a minute with her tonight? How did it all happen since the last time I saw her? I know that her sudden change of heart has

78

something to do with other ladies in the house. They must have supported the Commander as the more suitable choice, no?"

She recounted the goings-on of the past few weeks and then said,

"Please decide on the date when you will come back here to take her away and make your preparations in complete secrecy. Having seen many of the tears from both of you spilled over this affair, I fully understand the depth of your feelings for each other. I solemnly promise to even risk my life to do what I can for you both."

To preserve his dignity as a man, it was necessary for him to accept her suggestions with grace, rather than continue to complain so effeminately, since he cared what his people might have thought after witnessing him crying over a woman.

Midnight had already passed. Every time the wild dogs were scared away from the Prince's party, their barks resonated so loudly in the mountains that those night-watchmen stationed around Ukifune's house became ever more vigilant. They made noise by forcibly plucking the strings of their bows, followed by their gruff voices shouting warnings like "Be on the lookout for fire," to warn off whoever was around their property. Hearing them, Prince Niou felt as if he were being pushed down the road back home. He was greatly dispirited to realize he had to soon leave.

"いづくにか身をば棄てむと白雲の
　　かからぬ山もなくなくぞ行く

(Where will I be able rest in peace, if not on the mountaintop below the white clouds? I'll walk this trail away from you, though my tears refuse to cease.)

Thank you for coming. You can go back now."

Thus he spoke, allowing Jiju to return to the house. When she looked at him, it touched her so greatly to see the grace of his aura, with the scent of his fragrance superbly intensified by heavy night fog, that there were no words in which to frame her feelings. Tears of sympathy were all she took home with her.

Lady Ukifune heard from Ukon that she had rebuffed the Prince's proposal to take her away that night. She was staggered to hear that the Prince had come there for her, and she had to lie down to let the feeling subside. It was then that Jiju came back to report what she had seen and heard while with the party of Prince Niou. After listening to Jiju's words in silence, Lady Ukifune's eyes filled with tears eventually, although it made her feel embarrassed to think that the ladies around her would consider it a clear sign of her strong devotion to the Prince.

The next morning, she hesitated for a long time before getting out of bed, expecting that her eyes would be swollen and dulled from last night's weeping. When she finally roused herself, she donned a shawl typically worn for the recitation of the sutras and concentrated herself on imploring God's forgiveness for her having chosen to pass from this world before her parents. She came back to her room and took out the painting that Prince Niou had drawn for her. Staring at it very closely, she could still clearly remember the aesthetic curves of his fingers as well as his adorable face and every other part that fascinated her, as if he were still sitting there right in front of her eyes. It was her greatest regret that she was unable to bid him a final farewell the night before. She also felt very sorry when she thought about the Commander, who had graciously promised his enduring affection and had built a new house near his palace, hoping to install her in a more tranquil setting. Having understood that some cruel people might speak ill of her or spread shameless rumors after her death, which would cause the Commander a bit of trouble, Lady Ukifune thought it to be better for her to choose to die, rather than live on with such a dishonorably scandalous image and let those rumors tarnish her man's majesty. She put her feelings down in a poem.

"なげきわび身をば棄つとも亡き影に
　　うき名流さむことをこそ思へ

(Throwing myself into the current may end my life in sorrow, though the shadow of notoriety lingers over my mourning.)"

Lady Ukifune also missed her mother greatly and even remembered the ugly faces of her half-sisters with fond memories, which came as a surprise to her. As thoughts of Lady Naka, who had treated her very kindly, came to mind, Lady Ukifune was surprised at how many people she wished to see once more. While she sat in this state, the female servants attending her had kept themselves busy with the considerable tasks they needed to complete before the move to Kyoto. In the daytime, even when they were talking about seemingly important things, Lady Ukifune didn't pay them any attention. While during the nights, when everyone was back resting in their rooms, she started to plan ways to sneak out of the house without anyone noticing. She got so caught up in her scheming that she was unable to sleep properly or even maintain her sanity. As the first light broke each morning, she always gazed at the river nearby, telling herself that the end of her life's journey was coming closer and closer each day.

In his letters, Prince Niou wrote about many important things related to his plan for their flight. Nonetheless, Lady Ukifune couldn't reply to them for fear that their secret should be found out by the guards before the letter could be passed on to the Prince. The only message from her came in the form of a poem, which read,

> "からをだにうき世の中にとどめずは
> いづこをはかと君もうらみむ
>
> (Suppose I left no remains of this life, at what would your lament be vented, if not at my grave?)"

She also wanted to tell the Commander how grateful she was in the last moments of her life. Since the Prince and the Commander were very close to each other, however, it was certain that one day they would realize that her last messages had arrived to them at almost the same time, which would make them believe she had been fickle and untrustworthy. Her heart ached so badly just thinking about this that she changed her mind to not tell anyone what had really driven her to take her own life.

Then, a letter arrived from her mother in Kyoto.

"Since you appeared so ominously in my dream last night, I can't help but feeling anxious today. I had already ordered some monks from the nearby temples here to chant a prayer for your sake, but when I then took a nap, having not slept well after having been awoken by last night's dream, I dreamed this time of what is said to be yet another inauspicious sign. I was so shocked that I felt it necessary to dash off this letter to you now. Please be careful in all the actions you take. Especially when living in such an isolated place, you must be aware of how other women involved in relationships with Commander Kaoru can bring you harm. I'm becoming obsessed with this great sense of misgiving because this occurred when you have been seriously ill for weeks. Although I truly wish that I could be there for you, your sister's condition refuses to stabilize as the birth of her first child draws near. The concern here grows, as it seems that it's not simply a sickness but a malady caused by evil spirits. My husband told me over and over to keep my eyes on her at all times. Although I can't make it to your side at the moment, make sure you ask some people in the temple near your place to say a prayer for you, too."

The messenger on Lady Chujo's errand was also carrying her letter to the local monks along with a gift to offer them as a reward for the invocation. Mournfully, Lady Ukifune thought of her mother, whose loving feelings toward her could be seen between the long lines, although she had no idea that her daughter had already made up her mind to shortly end her life. The messenger left at once for a nearby temple to finish his business there, and Lady Ukifune wrote a reply for her mother in the meanwhile. There were so many things she wanted to say, but only a single line made it into the letter.

"のちにまたあひ見むことを思はなむ
この世の夢に心まどはで

(I'll meet you in a later world, so please don't let such dreams disturb you, no matter how real they may seem.)"

The bell was rung at the beginning of the sutra-reading ceremony held at a nearby temple. Lying down on the floor, Lady Ukifune hung on to the resonant sound travelling on the wind. Shortly after the toll had ceased, the messenger came back with a report on how the rites had been carried out. Lady Ukifune expressed her thoughts in a poem.

"鐘の音の絶ゆるひびきに音をそへ

わが世つきぬと君に伝へよ

(The fading toll of the temple bell resonates with my sobs of grief, please tell my mother that I am done with this world.)"

She wrote it on a page of sutras from the temple, but as the messenger said that he wasn't going back to Kyoto that night, she re-wrote it on a beautiful piece of stationery which she folded neatly and tied to a twig, so that her mother would be sure to notice it.

The nurse was also feeling very uneasy and called over a servant to say,

"I've a really bad feeling. Lady Chujo said in the letter that she had a strange dream about Lady Ukifune. Caution the night-watchmen to be especially vigilant tonight."

Hearing the nurse's words, Lady Ukifune expected it to be incredibly difficult to run away from the house even in the dark. The nurse looked at Lady Ukifune and talked to her gently, trying to encourage her somehow.

"You can't keep refusing to eat, my dear. Just a little bit of boiled rice soup would help."

Lady Ukifune appreciated that the old lady's advice, though tiresome at times, arose out of genuine consideration for her.

"Although it seems that she thinks she is holding up very well by herself, now that others seem to regard her as a nagging old lady with whom they don't feel comfortable, I wonder how she will survive without me."

Just imagining how tragic the life of the nurse would be after her death, she felt so sorry that she wanted to tell the nurse the reasons why she had to resort to such an extreme course of action. Every time she tried to think of how to express her thoughts, however, the waves of emotions crashed against her heart, so that in her struggle to hold her tears back, the words could find no space into which to flow. Then Ukon came into the room and lay down next to Lady Ukifune to try and relieve the young lady who had so long been trapped in indecision.

"Don't be so distressed all the time, Lady. It has been said that those who become too absorbed in worrying allow their souls out of their body to wander around. It might be your soul freed into the air that caused your mother to have those nightmares. Just choose either the Prince or the Commander, and let it all be as it was meant to be."

Ukon took a deep sigh. Lady Ukifune listened to her words, covering up her face with the sleeve of her starched gown.

8. The Mayfly

The Mayfly

CHARACTERS

Commander Kaoru

Prince Niou

Lady Chujo, Ukifune's mother

Lady Naka, Prince Niou's wife

The Empress

Princess Ippon, the Empress' daughter

Lady Ninomiya, the Empress' daughter
and wife of Kaoru

"Lady Prince," daughter of the late Prince Shikibu
and now the Empress' lady-in-waiting

Tokikata, Prince Niou's retainer

Lady Kosaisho, Princess Ippon's lady-in-waiting

Lady Chusho, Princess Ippon's lady-in-waiting

Lady Ben, the Empress' lady-in-waiting

Ukon, Ukifune's lady-in-waiting

Jiju, Ukifune's lady-in-waiting

Ukifune's nurse

Ben-no-Ama, a nun from Uji

Hitachi-no-Kami, the Governor of Hitachi
and Ukifune's stepfather

Yugiri, the Minister of the Right

Ajari, a monk

People were shocked to discover that Ukifune had disappeared from her house in Uji and began a desperate search. Unfortunately, they unearthed no clues as to her whereabouts despite their considerable efforts. The situation was reminiscent of the kidnapping of a princess in a classic fairy tale.

Out of concern for her daughter's welfare, Ukifune's mother sent another messenger from Kyoto before even the roosters had stirred, as the one dispatched previously had spent the night in Uji and was yet to return. The nurse and the other ladies did not know what to make of this confusing, chaotic situation. For most of those present, conversations revolved around what could have happened to Ukifune. While everyone panicked, only two, Ukon and Jiju, who both knew of her extraordinary grief and unbearable suffering, could come to guess that she might have thrown herself into the Uji River. Crying for her, they unsealed her mother's letter.

"It may be just because I cannot sleep well tonight, worrying so much about you, but I cannot see you clearly even in my own dreams. Once I fall into sleep, something terrifying comes to mind and causes this anxiety, making me feel ill. Knowing that you are moving to Kyoto in the coming days, I'd like to have you stay here in my house until then. I feel that today may not be the best choice since it is going to rain, but..."

Ukon then opened the letter that Ukifune had written the previous night in reply to her mother. Reading it through, more tears came to her eyes. In the letter, Ukifune revealed her desperate loneliness. Ukon's grief grew further after reading it, as the fact that Ukifune had not confessed any of her feelings, or intimated even the slightest intention of committing suicide, seemed so terribly sad to Ukon, since the two of them had grown up together and were still close friends, able to share everything in their hearts. She could not bear this horrible state of affairs, and stamped the ground like a child. Although she had understood that Lady Ukifune had grieved deeply, it still seemed hard to believe that she should have conceived of this tragic notion, considering her pure and gentle nature.

Ukon was left with a weight of infinite sadness, and found herself unwilling to accept that her closest friend was already dead. The nurse was so distraught that the only thing she could say was, "What can we do...? What should we do...?"

Niou sensed that something was wrong after reading Ukifune's letter. Although he was sure that she held some affection for him, he also thought that she may have hidden herself away because of her insecurity over his feelings, which, given his history with women, would have normally been on the verge of shifting away at any moment. He sent a messenger to Uji in an effort to discover her intentions.

When the messenger reached Uji, the house was filled with ladies' sobbing, and no one came to receive the letter he brought. He asked the maid what had happened. She answered,

"Last night Lady Ukifune passed away suddenly. Everyone is in shock and feels completely at a loss. I don't think there is any chance that they can attend to your message at the moment."

Knowing nothing about the complexity of the situation, the messenger returned without inquiring further into the matter.

Upon his return, the messenger told Niou what he had witnessed at the house. Niou could not believe his ears and felt that he must be caught in the midst of some cruel dream. Ukifune had made no mention of having suffered from a serious disease of any kind. Although she occasionally mentioned that she did not feel well, in her last letter she had seemed fine and had expressed her feelings for Niou more deeply than ever before. Niou could not grasp what had really happened. He decided to dispatch Tokikata to Uji, in order to confirm that the messenger's story was correct. Tokikata hesitated, saying,

"I'm afraid that Commander Kaoru might know something about this turn of events already. They say he has ordered his security forces in Uji to be more vigilant in order to ensure that all are safe. He has already tried to block my servants from going in and out of the house, and his men have become much more circumspect. I think it will be a serious problem if I suddenly appear there for no particular reason and Commander Kaoru finds out about it. Especially now, since Ukifune has succumbed to some sudden disease, many people will be at the house."

"Yet, I cannot let this go without knowing the truth. Could you please fabricate a plausible reason to visit the house so as to meet someone with whom you can communicate secretly? I need to know what in the world made them tell my man that the lady is dead. I know that common people are prone to exaggeration."

Tokikata felt so sorry for Niou, watching him worry about the lady so intensely, that he left for Uji that afternoon. Since he was a skilled rider, he arrived in Uji in a short time. Although it had stopped raining, the road he had taken was in a terrible state. He wore poor clothes, which had become covered with mud along the way, and therefore he looked like a working-class man. This helped him get through the gates into the already crowded property. He was very surprised to hear some people say that they were going to hold a funeral that night. He asked for Ukon, but she refused to see him. She did, however, relay a message through one of the servants.

"At the moment, I do not know what is happening, and I do not have even enough energy left to pick myself up. Visit me again later tonight. It is a great shame that I cannot see you at this point in time."

"I understand how hard this is for her, but there is no way that I can return without a more detailed report. Please let me speak with someone else," Tokikata begged, and another lady appeared.

"Who could have imagined that an event like this would transpire? She died in a way no one, even herself, would have ever imagined. No words can describe how we feel right now. Please tell your lord that everyone here is grieved and shocked, feeling like they are trapped in a living nightmare. After a spell, when we have had a chance to recover from this horrible tragedy, I will tell you how much she suffered, and how sorry she was on that night when your lord came to see her. Please come back once the period of mourning has passed."

As she finished speaking she began sobbing bitterly.

Tokikata heard many others further within the compound crying out. The voice of the nurse cried,

"Where are you now, my lady? Please come back to us. What a great pity that we cannot even find your body! After so many years spent by your side, I could never get my fill of seeing your beautiful figure each day. I have lived just for the opportunity to pray for your happiness. But now you are gone, without letting me know where. I would not allow even a demon to take you away. They say *Taishakuten*[1] can bring back a person whom others fervently wish to see once more. Whoever took away my precious lady, please bring her back to me. Even just her body, please..."

Hearing this, Tokikata felt that something was amiss and asked,

"Would you please tell me what actually transpired? Did someone steal her away? My lord sent me here because he eagerly yearns to learn nothing but the truth. For now it may seem acceptable to leave things somewhat unclear, but I do not want to be embarrassed and blamed when my lord finds out what really happened. Don't you think it honorable that my lord asked me to come here and listen to you in person, simply because he still clings to the slightest hope that the lady still lives? Although I know that there have been many men who have fallen in love with women throughout history and in all parts of the globe, I believe that the dedication and devotion that my lord has shown for Ukifune is second to none."

The ladies appreciated his honesty and thought that they should talk about it now, as it was inevitable that an unusual incident of this nature would become a popular subject of rumor.

"If we could believe someone may have hidden her away, we wouldn't grieve like we are now. Our lady had been depressed for quite a while, as the Commander had already expressed his concern. Both Lady Ukifune's mother and nurse expected her to marry the Commander, who had been engaged to her for some time, and were more than happy to prepare for

1. The god of life and death.

that outcome, while she was secretly falling for Prince Niou. This emotionally trying situation brought her too much suffering and ultimately caused her to end her life. No one, however, could have anticipated that this sad incident would actually occur. That is why the nurse is crying so plaintively, with such pitiful lamentations."

Tokikata thought she was still not speaking directly, hedging her words very carefully.

"That will suffice for now. We will come visit here again, when things calm down. Besides, it is not very polite to stand around talking so much. Soon, my lord will also visit here himself."

"I'm afraid that won't be necessary. Of course the fact that your lord cared about our lady is an honor, but revealing the nature of their relationship would irreparably harm her reputation. Therefore, we think it would be better for us to keep it a secret, considering that the lady herself concealed it in life."

Trying to disguise the truth that Ukifune had died an unusual death, the lady led Tokikata out of the grounds, for fear that being seen talking with him would provide an unwelcome hint to even a casual observer.

Lady Chujo, Ukifune's mother, arrived in the rain. She was clearly grieved, saying,

"In this mutable world, we sometimes have to resign ourselves to fate, seeing that someone we loved has died. It is sad, but that's how we live in this circle of life, but this time, without her body before my eyes, I will never be able to stop thinking about her."

Lady Chujo thought that some monster might have eaten her or a fox might have taken her away, as often happens in old, twisted fairy tales. The idea that Ukifune ended her risky, love-driven suffering by throwing herself into the river never even crossed her mind. She also suspected that the nurse of Commander Kaoru's principal wife, Princess Ninomiya, played some role, as Ukifune had always been intimidated by the Princess. It seemed a simple task for her to find out that the Commander was hiding Ukifune here and to send someone to kidnap her. Lady Chujo asked a servant if anyone unfamiliar or suspicious had begun to work there lately. The servant replied,

"Uji is so quiet and isolated that new people are generally disinclined to remain here for long. We are told they will rejoin us as soon as they return from Kyoto. That is why there are no such people here at the moment."

Even some ladies who had been employed there for a long time went back to their parents' homes, so that fewer people were there working. Jiju and the others remembered that Ukifune had been in anguish and, while weeping, said that she would rather be dead. When they were reading the letters and poems that Ukifune had hidden, they came across one of her poems, 'Shadow of Notoriety,' under an inkstone, in which she expressed her deep grief. This despairing piece of writing created the image in their mind of the roaring Uji River swallowing her, which frightened them greatly.

In any case, it did not seem good for Lady Chujo to suspect that her daughter who was dead might actually have been kidnapped. Ukon and Jiju talked it over and decided to tell Lady Chujo the truth. Since the incident and the following secret relationship were beyond Ukifune's control, explaining the cause of her death would not hurt her dignity, and it was the best way to lift her mother out of her mental chaos. They also thought that the unusual way in which they had taken care of their lady's death would become suspect eventually, and the world would learn the secret sooner or later. They had to be ready to respond to the impending scandal, and the first thing to do was, of course, to tell her mother the truth.

Ukon explained everything to Lady Chujo, who could not help becoming upset, listening to this highly unexpected piece of news. Even Ukon felt like she would almost faint away from the telling of the story. Picturing her daughter going into the river, Lady Chujo emotionally traced Ukifune's steps all the way to her death. The mother insisted on searching for her daughter downstream in an effort to at least recover the body.

Ukon and Jiju, however, disagreed, because the search would achieve nothing, presuming that the body must have washed out to sea by now, and such a search would lead people to develop further suspicions about Ukifune's death. Lady Chujo did not know what to say or do, being subject to the powerful waves of sorrow which threatened to overwhelm her at any moment. The two supported her as she walked to the carriage, and they brought her some of her daughter's things which had been left behind, such as a cushion, her daily items and nightclothes, and placed all of them into a trunk. They also confessed the secret of this funeral to those who were to spend thirty days in mourning together in the house, including a monk whose mother had been Ukifune's nurse, this monk's uncle Ajari and his followers, and an older monk who had been close to the family. The nurse fell to the ground weeping, being too grieved to stand while they held the funeral, pretending all the while that there was a body in the coffin.

Kaoru's men who had earlier spoken harshly to those in the house came down and said,

"You must first discuss the funeral arrangements with the Commander and instead hold a much larger ceremony at a time preferable to everyone."

The ladies replied,

"We have good reason to do this tonight, as well as to keep it quiet."

The men were made to keep their distance from the funeral, in the field on the opposite side of the river. The coffin was cremated in the presence of only those who already knew the truth. The fire did not last long. People in the countryside have a greater appreciation for traditional manners and are more superstitious than those in the city. Some said that the funeral was far too small and poor for a lady from such a noble family, and others said that it was indicative of the ungrateful nature of people in Kyoto to treat the death of a concubine in such a manner. Those rumors ran through the area, and started to impugn Ukifune's reputation.

They were sure that on hearing that she had died but no body had been left behind, Commander Kaoru would suspect that Ukifune had actually disappeared. Prince Niou would also know the truth sooner or later, since he was a close relative of the Commander. Although the Commander might think at first that Prince Niou had sheltered her, he would begin to suspect others of hiding her too. Ukifune had enjoyed good fortune in life, being loved by noblemen, and therefore it was unfair that her reputation be disgraced by this type of shameful doubt. Some of the female servants quickly muzzled those who had discovered the truth in the confusion during the morning of Ukifune's disappearance, while Ukon and Jiju worked hard to make those still ignorant about the actual circumstances believe that the lady's death was nothing out of the ordinary. Although at some point in the future they would be able to tell both Prince Niou and Commander Kaoru how Ukifune came to commit suicide, they had to conceal the true reason for now, since it seemed too cruel for her suitors to discover what had compelled her to take her own life. To learn of this would cause even Kaoru's deep sorrow for Ukifune to dry up.

At that time, Commander Kaoru was staying in Ishiyama Temple with his ill mother where he was being busy praying and putting things in order. Although he was deeply worried about Ukifune, Ishiyama was too far away for him to know what was transpiring in Uji, and, in fact, people felt it was dishonorable for the Commander to have sent no one to the funeral. It was only when a messenger from the manor in Kyoto arrived in Ishiyama that he found out that his lady was dead. He was devastated to hear the news, and sent his closest man, Okura-Tayu, to Uji early the next morning to deliver a message.

"I have just received some unbelievably sad news. Knowing that I should travel to Uji as soon as possible, I cannot do so at the moment because we are bound to stay here for a certain length of time to pray for my mother's recovery. I've heard that the funeral took place last night, but why was I not consulted about this? Isn't it usual to delay such an event? Besides, it is disrespectful for you to have held only a small ceremony. Although there is nothing I can do about it, now that it's done, I am mortified that her reputation might be ruined by such a simple funeral, which should have been one more fitting for the end of a noble lady's life."

This message raised anew such a deep sadness in people's minds that they were at a loss as to how to respond. They weren't able to express themselves clearly in the reply, sending only their tears of sadness as an excuse.

Kaoru blamed himself for the unexpected death of Ukifune, because it was he who had sent her to Uji, where it is said that demons live which cause all manner of misfortunes.

"Why did I let her stay in Uji for such a long time, without noticing that such a place was doomed to tragedy? My carelessness also allowed for that unpleasant secret relationship to occur."

Thinking of these matters in such a way, he couldn't help regretting his foolishness in everything he had done, which caused him even greater sorrow. He thought it unwise to suffer from any sense of responsibility for the lady's death, especially while his mother was praying eagerly for her own recovery. He went back to Kyoto but did not go to see his wife. Instead, he wrote to her,

"It is not a matter of great importance, but someone I know passed away quite recently. I'd like to keep myself away from you until things settle down, for fear of passing on any ill tidings."

Alone in his room, he went through a period of deep sorrow. Reminiscing over Ukifune's attractiveness and beautiful face made him grieve for her. He felt sorry that he didn't realize her preciousness in life and had left her alone for so long without visiting with any real frequency. The sting of remorse rushed up from the bottom of his heart and grabbed firmly hold of him.

"I'm destined to keep suffering from the agony that love brings. Is this all God's will for me, someone who wishes to follow a spiritual path but cannot leave this worldly life? He treats me in this cruel way so that I will become spiritually aware and can enjoy His mercy in the future."

Believing this to be the case, he spent most of his time offering up prayers.

Prince Niou was a mere shell of a man for several days following the loss of Ukifune. People worried because it was as if he were possessed by an evil spirit. It was when he let all the tears inside finally escape that his feelings started to subside, that the sorrow he was carrying changed itself into a longing for the woman who lived in his memories. He thought no one would know why he was in such deep distress because he kept the truth to himself, claiming instead that he had a serious illness. People around him, however, could see his grief coming out spontaneously, in unexpected bursts. Some wondered what sort of misfortune had befallen him, and why he suffered so greatly that even his life seemed to be in danger. Eventually, this talk reached Commander Kaoru's ears. At that point, he came to be dead sure that the two had had an intimate relationship behind his back. He thought,

"It was not just writing to each other or something along those lines. It would be natural for him to fall in love with Ukifune at first sight. She deserved it. If she were alive, I would be a cuckolded fool by now."

Thinking this way helped him feel much less pity for his deceased lover.

Kaoru went down to Nijo mansion. He hadn't sent anyone to inquire after Prince Niou despite the heightened public concern over his condition, and he was worried that people would notice that there was something between the two of them. Kaoru dressed in light black, symbolic of the death of a remote relative, because he had lost his uncle, Prince Shikibu, a few months prior. Of course, this period of mourning was also dedicated to his deceased lover. The years had thinned him down and he looked even more splendid. Silence was their only companion that evening, after the other visitors had taken their leave.

Niou surely looked ill, but he could meet with those whom he knew very well, as the illness was borne of his emotions. Kaoru was let in to see him. Prince Niou felt so embarrassed and uncomfortable upon seeing

Kaoru that he burst into tears due to his fragile emotional state. He tried in vain to conceal it.

"Although the illness is not that serious, everyone says it is going to get worse and will become the subject of rumor. I am somewhat apprehensive since my father and my mother worry about me so much. At any rate, all the things that have happened lately make me realize how meaningless life is."

He tried to wipe away his tears with his sleeves, but they continued to spill forth, and controlling them was an impossibility. He was aware that crying this much in front of others could damage his dignity. At the same time, he also thought Kaoru would never know that these tears were for Ukifune, and instead would think that Prince Niou was just experiencing a bout of lingering attachment to this life. How could he know what Kaoru was feeling then? The Commander thought,

"As I imagined before coming here, he has been devastated by Ukifune's death. How long had they been together? They must have laughed at me and taken me for a fool."

His sadness abated somewhat when he viewed things in this manner. Prince Niou noticed Kaoru's outward calm and thought,

"How can he look so indifferent when his lover has passed away? When feeling painfully sad, a normal man will be very sensitive, and tears will fall ceaselessly, responding to every little thing happening around him. Even the songs of birds in flight are the cause of sorrow, reminding you of what has been. If he realized what makes me so grieved, he would be able to sympathize with me. Only a person like him, who has gained an insight into the sense of mortality in life, can be so calm in a cruel situation such as this."

He thought highly of Commander Kaoru, and felt that he would never be his equal. Knowing that he also loved Ukifune, Prince Niou felt a slight affection for him too. Imagining that one day Ukifune sat opposite the Prince intimately, Kaoru's mind was flooded by memories of the lady.

After they chatted for a while, Kaoru came to feel that it was time to broach the subject of Ukifune.

"Since our childhood, I've felt guilty about keeping secrets inside. Time has slid on by and now even someone like me has become a man of station. Of course one has no time to spare, keeping oneself constantly busy in dealing with various matters of state. This is why I have not been able to visit you for an evening chat, like we used to enjoy in the past.

Let me tell you a story of mine. I heard that in the mountain village you also know well there was a lady, a relative of my ex-lover who had died young. I wanted her to be a form of solace for me, to share reminiscences of my ex-lover on occasion. At that time, however, people would have criticized me if they had found out about our relationship, so I kept the lady hidden away in the isolated village. I didn't visit her very often, and it seems that I was not the only object of her affection. Although infidelity cannot be overlooked in a wedded wife, it is not something forbidden a lover, so I appreciated her as a pretty diversion with whom I could seek comfort. Surprisingly, however, she passed away suddenly. This reminds me how much pain life can give us, and now I feel very sad. I suspect you may have already heard about this particular turn of events."

He started crying then. Although Kaoru had admonished himself for showing his sorrow, he couldn't stop the tears once they began flowing. Prince Niou sensed that those tears came from another source and felt sorry for Kaoru, but he pretended that he didn't notice anything out of the ordinary.

"Please accept my condolences. I heard about it only yesterday. Although I wanted to help you get through your pain, I held back because I also heard that the relationship was a secret one."

He spoke only briefly about the matter, as he could not bear talking about it any longer.

"She was the kind of woman in whom anyone would be interested at first sight. In fact, you may have seen her already, as she was related to your wife," Kaoru insinuated without elaborating further.

"Well I guess it is not good to talk too much about this tiresome world when you are ill. I don't want to interrupt your time of rest. Please take good care of yourself," said Kaoru as he bid the Prince farewell.

Kaoru thought,

"The Prince was more grieved than I thought he would be. Ukifune's life seemed to be a misery, but it was actually one filled with great potential."

The Emperor and the Empress had raised the Prince so well, he seemed more beautiful than all others, and was one of the most intelligent people in his world at that time. Despite having several great wives, he had devoted himself fully to Ukifune. Although many oracles in the house were intoning all manners of prayers and invocations for the Prince's recovery, unbeknownst to them, it was all caused by the little lady's death.

"I myself have now acquired the title of Commander and have a daughter of the Emperor as a wife, but still I cared about the lady as much as he. Especially now that Ukifune is dead, my feelings for her have grown enormously sorrowful. I must look quite undignified. It is imperative that I banish her from my mind."

He tried to hide his feelings, so as not to be seen as grieving, but he was still so upset that he went back to his room, after acknowledging that human beings are made of neither wood nor stone.

Kaoru imagined that Prince Niou wouldn't be happy with the simple funeral held for the lady. It was a disagreeable turn of events, even though he could understand that it might be because her mother was of humble origin and her brothers and sisters were still alive. They were afraid that they could tarnish their reputation for doing something unworthy of Ukifune, he thought. Knowing very little about what had happened, he had much to wonder about. He wanted to visit Uji by himself, but it seemed too much to stay there until the period of mourning was over. At the same time, it was definitely not right to visit and return to Kyoto so soon afterward.

The next month, Kaoru decided to travel to Uji. That evening was so painfully beautiful and the scent of citrus reminded him of Ukifune, which made him miss her all the more. At that moment, two nightingales flew by. He uttered a fragment of an old poem, "The nightingale sings its lonesome song...." As it was the day when Prince Niou was scheduled to travel to Nijo mansion, Kaoru snapped off a citrus twig and attached it to a poem, which he sent to the Prince.

"忍び音や気味もなくらんかひもなき
しでのたをさに心通はば

(You too would cry silent tears if your spirit were bound to that of the one who died and left you behind.)"

When he received the poem from Kaoru, Prince Niou was sitting at the edge of the garden with his wife, who comforted him simply by her close resemblance to Ukifune. The Prince sensed a veiled implication behind Kaoru's words and replied,

"橘の匂うあたりはほとどぎす
心してこそ鳴くべかりけれ

(The citrus flowers in your garden stir up memories of your lost love. In such a place, even nightingales will sing as if in mourning.)

It seems as if you have something you want to tell me."

Lady Naka eventually learned quite a bit about the tragedy. She was puzzled as to why she still lived, after having lost both of her sisters due to matters of the heart.

"Is it because I'm the most thoughtless one of us all? After all of this sorrow, how much longer must I endure this life?"

The Prince told his wife about his relationship with Ukifune, yet he softened the details ever so slightly as he felt suffocated by his sense of guilt, and he knew it would all come out sooner or later.

"I felt very sad and jealous because you hid it all from me," said Lady Naka amidst her smiles and tears.

Looking at her, Prince Niou could clearly see that she was indeed Ukifune's sister, which briefly filled his mind with an overwhelming sense of peace.

In Rokujo palace, there existed the tendency to blow even the smallest things out of proportion, so when it was learned that the Prince was sick, everyone went nearly insane from worry. An endless line of visitors came to visit him while he was there, and moreover his wife's brothers and father, the Minister, annoyed him by constantly hovering nearby. Fortunately, he could relax here in Nijo mansion, and felt comfortable and meditative in the quiet environment.

He was unable to accept Ukifune's passing, as it still seemed more of a dream than reality. It was a mystery to him why things had suddenly turned out the way they had. He ordered his men to go to Uji and bring Ukon back to Kyoto.

Lady Chujo, Ukifune's mother, returned to Kyoto, since the sorrow caused by the sound of the Uji River was unrelenting, and she came to think that the siren call of the water sought to pull her under as well. The house was still filled mostly with silence, save the low droning of the monks chanting a prayer to the Buddha. Prince Niou's men easily passed through the gates, as no one remained to guard the house. Tokikata remembered that the guards had rebuffed Prince Niou's attempts at entry when he came to see the Lady just before she had departed this world. Now, standing in the same place, with no security forces accosting them, Tokikata wondered regretfully what would have happened if they hadn't stopped the Prince that fateful night. In Kyoto, there were many who were unable to understand why Prince Niou had allowed himself to drown so deeply in his own sadness, and they thought it inappropriate to grieve so obviously for a lady of such humble upbringing. Once they arrived at Uji, however, remembering the Prince overcoming all obstacles to visit his love, pictures of the beautiful Ukifune and the Prince riding together in the boat rushed clearly back into their minds, prompting them to break down in tears. It seemed completely natural for Ukon to appear before Tokikata still crying profusely. He informed her that they had been sent to bring her back to Kyoto.

"I'm afraid I must refuse the invitation since I don't want to give anyone the opportunity to question the death of our Lady. Besides, even if I accept the honor of speaking with Prince Niou, I don't think I am yet ready to explain all of the details. After mourning for forty-nine days, before which time it seems inappropriate to leave the house, I will come to the Prince, regardless of whether he has invited me or not, and tell him all that he wants to hear, the entirety of which still seems too sad to be true. Although I don't feel like I shall still be of this world at that time, if I am, I promise to go."

Ukon wouldn't say another word or even stand up.

Tokikata replied between sobs,

"I didn't clearly understand what their relationship was like, nor how the two were in private, but I did know the depth of his love for her. That is why I was in no rush to really get to know you, thinking that I would have ample opportunity to become more familiar with you later on as my master and your mistress would be formally linked. After this tragedy occurred, I realized how much trouble we caused you, and I felt great respect for you for having been so dedicated to her in life."

Tokikata begged,

"As our Prince himself sent this carriage for you, I cannot take it back empty. Could the other lady come with us in your place?"

Ukon called for Jiju and told her to go to Kyoto on her behalf. Jiju replied,

"When even you are not ready to speak with him yet, how can you expect me to do so? Besides, isn't it inauspicious for someone in mourning to visit another house?

Tokikata urged,

"Now, the Prince is saddened that there are many things he has to sacrifice in order to maintain a public face, but when it comes to Ukifune, he seems unable to keep up such appearances. At any rate, having loved her so deeply, he may unwisely go into mourning himself. You have only a few days left in your mourning period, correct? Please come with us, just one of you."

Jiju finally agreed to go with them, for she appreciated how Prince Niou grieved, and she thought this would be the last time for her to see him. Since her Lady had passed away, there had been no official head of the household, and therefore she didn't have appropriate mourning clothes to wear in the presence of a noble person. She put a grey formal outfit in her trunk instead. On getting in the carriage, she was suddenly struck by the image of Ukifune. If she were here alive, Prince Niou would have sent the same carriage to collect her, and Jiju realized how very happy she would have been to come to Kyoto in her service. It made her even sadder to think about this, and she sobbed all the way to Nijo mansion.

Prince Niou emotions ran high just to hear that Jiju had arrived at the palace, but he mentioned none of this to his wife. He moved to another wing of the palace to welcome her, and ordered them to park the carriages near the passageway leading to that wing.

He asked her a string of questions about Ukifune. Jiju told him that she had suffered deeply for a long time, and that she had wept inconsolably the night before she had passed away.

"She didn't talk much and she was very shy. There were no last words of any kind. No one had ever imagined that she would do such a terrible thing as throw herself into the river."

The Prince felt himself drawn ever deeper into sorrow. How much easier would it be to accept if her death had come from some disease or another more inevitable fatal event? From the bottom of his heart, he regretted not having tried to understand that she had been holding in so much silent pain that she ended up killing herself. He thought that if he had known, he could have tried to relieve her suffering and save her life. Realizing that it was all too late, his sense of frustration grew even stronger.

Jiju said,

"I profoundly regret that none of us understood the depth of our Lady's desperation when she burnt those letters."

Their exchange kept them awake throughout the night, but still they continued to speak. Jiju told him about the poem Ukifune had written to her mother in reply.

After talking about Ukifune for such a long time, Prince Niou felt a certain degree of closeness to Jiju. He said sympathetically,

"You can serve here, if you like. The lady of the house is no stranger to Ukifune."

"I appreciate your kindness, but I am currently in mourning, and I don't think this is a good time to start working somewhere new. After this mourning period has passed, I will then take time to consider my options."

Jiju delicately declined his considerate offer, so he told her to come visit again at a later time. Unexpectedly, he felt sad to see her off to Uji, and he gave her a set of combs and a box of clothes which had been made for Ukifune. Although there were many more gifts he had had made for the lady, he gave her that which he deemed appropriate for someone of her station. Jiju at first hesitated, anticipating that everyone in Uji would wonder what she had been doing while she was away if she were to return with these gifts in hand, but there was no way she could politely refuse them.

Back in Uji, Ukon and Jiju secretly opened the gifts from the Prince and took a close look at each of them. In the box, they found brocade clothes, which were so gorgeously embroidered that they couldn't help but weep. At the same time, they didn't know where to hide them while they were in mourning.

Commander Kaoru also decided to go to Uji to assess the situation. On the way, many old memories flashed through his mind. He retraced the steps of his misfortunes.

"What sort of destiny drew me to Prince Hachi in the first place? I failed in love with two ladies from his family, and in the end, even a humble lady, whom her father didn't acknowledge, made my life harder than I could have imagined. Since this family came into my life, I have experienced immense suffering. All of my misfortunes may result from my weak character, having abandoned faith for frivolous love. All of this despite the fact that I had lived with Prince Hachi, a venerable man deserving of respect, while waiting for His guidance for my next incarnation. I may be justly served for perverting the course of true faith."

The Commander tried to talk with Ukon, but his overwhelming sadness prevented him from speaking easily. He finally asked,

"Although it would have been more prudent of me to visit after the period of mourning had concluded, which is only a few days from now, I had to come here today because I couldn't contain myself any longer. I must know, what disease was responsible for the lady's sudden death?"

Ben-no-Ama, a close friend of the Commander's, had already realized that the lady's body was missing. It seemed only a matter of time before he discovered the same thing. The least desirable outcome for Ukon was that her lies would result in complicating things and damaging Ukifune's reputation. Although she had prepared some excuses which she was going to use in a case like this, all of them slipped her mind when confronted with the Commander's sincere attitude. Finally, being too afraid to continue lying, she felt compelled to tell him the truth.

Her unexpected reply left him speechless.

"This is unacceptable," he said as he thought,

"She was the kind of person who was too shy and gentle to express things people usually say or think. How could a person like her concoct such a terrifying plan? Are they telling me this in an effort to hide something else?"

His confusion was overwhelming. It was evident by Prince Niou's depression that he was not the one who took her away. Looking around, he could sense no strangeness in the atmosphere of the house, which would naturally emerge if this whole thing were a ruse.

"Is there anyone who disappeared with her? Tell me all of the details. Even if she found me unfaithful, I don't think she would leave me for another man. I don't believe that she has done this for no particular reason."

This cross-examination was exactly what Ukon had been afraid of.

"As I think you know, she had never been welcomed by her father. She always held so much distress inside. Her depression grew since she moved to this quiet, isolated village. Her life took on color only when you visited her. It was not often, but she lived with her unhappy past which continually caused her great pain, waiting for the day to come when you would arrive, although she wouldn't mention this to be the case. Lately, as her sincerest wish was coming true, we were very happy to prepare for that day. Lady Chujo was also very happy for her and tried to take care of things in Kyoto. Then your letter arrived. She couldn't understand what made you doubt her love. The security detail you sent said that you admonished them for allowing some of the ladies to behave immorally. We didn't know who you were talking about. The guards were quite vulgar in delivering their warnings, and Ukifune hadn't heard from you for a while. She was worried that her mother, who had known how hard life had treated her and wanted to give her daughter the peace and happiness in life that others experience, would have been very disappointed if you left her then since people would have made a fool of her. She insinuated this constantly and was much aggrieved. These are the only possible motivations I can think of for her suicide. Even if a monster had come and taken her away, there would have been traces of her body left behind."

Kaoru found it intolerable to see Ukon talking about Ukifune while crying so mournfully. Knowing about the secret relationship with Prince Niou had done much to relieve his sorrow, but then Ukon's tears reminded him afresh of those feelings. There was no way he could hold it inside.

"My life is no longer mine alone. Now that I'm a man of title, I have forced myself to remain calm even when I feel as if I'm dying inside, wanting to see her and comfort her. I was going to invite her to live near my house and I was also going to talk with my wife to make her understand our relationship. It was all for our future happiness. If she doubted my sincerity, it might be because she was unfaithful herself. I didn't mean to come here to ask this, but now, between just the two of us, please tell me the truth. I'd like to ask you about Prince Niou. How long had they been together? I am well aware of his charms, and I'm sure that Ukifune must have been greatly attracted to him. To be honest, I think it is possible that she died because she missed him too much, even though it was impossible for them to meet that often. Be straight with me. I'm ready to hear anything as long as it is true."

Ukon realized for the first time that this man knew everything. She felt sorry for him as well as for Ukifune.

"You've heard a nonsense rumor, Commander. I was with her everywhere all the time."

After seconds of silence, she continued,

"Then I guess you've heard of this story as well. When she visited Lady Naka and stayed at Nijo palace, Prince Niou happened to gain entrance to her room. We all ran him out, knowing that it was not appropriate behavior for a man of his station to exhibit. Actually, the reason why she decided to take up temporary residence in a small hut was that she was terrified by the incident. Since then she never let him know where she lived. Suddenly, however, the first letter arrived this February, followed by more soon after. The letters kept coming, but she didn't pay them any attention. Then we advised her that treating the words of such a great man so ungraciously could have dire consequences. I think she replied to the Prince once or twice after that. That was all that occurred."

He understood that there was no way that he could expect more than that from her and felt bad about having asked, thinking,

"Ukifune would have loved the Prince, but I guess she also cared about me. Thinking too much killed her in the end. If I hadn't taken her to a lonely place like this in the first place, no matter how hard her life had treated her, she would have never taken things this far. The river invited a very sad ending, indeed."

Commander Kaoru was staring fixedly in hatred at the Uji River. Although he had visited Uji many times to see the ladies he had loved, he had never felt it particularly tiresome to come and go, taking long journeys on steep mountain paths. Now he didn't even want to even hear the word 'Uji.'

He remembered that when he said that he wanted to have a doll of the deceased Lady Okimi, Lady Naka joked that Ukifune was like a living version of such a doll. Since dolls are set afloat on the river to purify evil, it had been a sort of ominous augury. He blamed himself for his carelessness which seemed to have caused her death, and he thought of Ukifune's mother, whose status was so low that her daughter's funeral needed to be small and simple. Although he was dissatisfied with that, after hearing it all in detail, he still felt sorry for her.

"I cannot imagine how sad this is for her mother. Ukifune's beauty and grace were extraordinary gifts bestowed upon the daughter of a lady of such low status. Her mother won't know what was going on between her daughter and Prince Niou, and she detests me for some horrible thing that she incorrectly assumes I must have done."

Although there would not have been any evil spirit in the house since she died outside these walls, he didn't step into the house in the presence of others, and had been talking with Ukon while sitting outside on a small chair used to hold the carriage in position while parked. It made him uncomfortable to keep talking while seated thus, so he repositioned himself on a carpet of moss under a densely-leafed tree and took a rest.

As coming here caused him so much emotional pain, this visit would be his last. He gazed around while writing a poem, which read,

"われもまた憂きふるさとを荒れ果てば

たれ宿木の陰をしのばん

(If I leave this village of sorrowful memories behind to fall into ruin, who will remain beneath this tree to recall my old days.)"

By then Ajari had become a Risshi, the third greatest monk in the temple. The Commander called him in and ordered him to organize a memorial service for Ukifune. He also made them increase the number of monks involved. His intention to make up for the sinful death of the lady was reflected in the size of the ceremony set up on the seventh of July, for the purpose of praying for the lady's peaceful rest. As he was leaving Uji, his heart ached profoundly, realizing that he would have stayed there that night if she had been alive. He also sent a man to call on Ben-no-Ama, but she refused to come out to talk with him, saying,

"I'm a touch depressed since I feel as if I'm the one who carries around all the misfortunes of this world, which are responsible for my going even more senile these days. As of late, I do nothing but lie in my bed."

He didn't try to make her see him against her will. On his way back home, he regretted that he hadn't brought Ukifune over to Kyoto as soon as possible. His anxiety remained as long as the sound of water could be heard. The fact that he hadn't made any attempt to find her body also pulled him further down into a state of remorse. He disconsolately imagined the lady lying at the bottom of an unknown sea encircled by shells.

Lady Chujo couldn't stay in her own house for fear of taking on any of its bad luck, which was to be especially avoided because her other daughter in Kyoto was soon to give birth. She moved from one place to another, which gave her no chance to rest. She was quite nervous about whether this delivery would go well, but, in the end, her daughter gave birth without incident. However, Lady Chujo hesitated to visit the mother and child because of the misfortune she was carrying. She couldn't think about any other child and she felt quite lost. It was then that a messenger secretly arrived with a letter from Commander Kaoru. Even though her mind was too blurred to see things clearly, she was surely happy to receive the message, yet saddened at the same time.

"We all experienced the unexpected misfortune of Ukifune's death. I wanted to be the first to send you a letter expressing my condolences, but I couldn't do so because every time I tried, I became too upset, and the tears darkened my sight to the point that I was unable to write. I cannot imagine the sadness you must be enduring. A considerable time has passed during which I hesitated to write this, thinking that you wouldn't be able to read it anyway. The true nature of mortality shows itself clearly and scares us so deeply. If I am strong enough to hang onto this life in spite of my sadness, I hope to help you in any way I can, as a man who loved your daughter in life."

His gentle and considerate words affected her deeply. The messenger also passed along the Commander's unwritten message.

"Since I had regarded my relationship with Ukifune as a lifetime commitment, I didn't rush things, and it might have given you the impression that I was not a truly dedicated suitor. From now on, however, I will make your family my priority and never forget my obligations. You can fully rely on my assistance. I have heard that you also have young sons. If they have aspirations to become officers, I will certainly support them."

Lady Chujo invited the messenger to her room, as the misfortune she was carrying was not deemed to be severe. She wrote a reply while crying profusely.

"It would be no wonder if this much pain should kill me, but I am ashamed to be still alive. I received your words of kindness, which were more than I could even have dreamed of, and I feel so very grateful. Growing up, Ukifune had been unsure about her future. Even though I cared about her deeply, I also knew that the very reason she was suffering was because of me and my low status. Then, when you came along, for many years we trusted in your words as our only hope. However we ended up disappointing you with this incident involving my daughter. There must be a fatal connection between this place and our family. Thanks to your considerate message, I'm now motivated to live longer. Of course, I look forward to your support when my sons come of age. Forgive me for not coming up with the words to fully express my gratitude, as I still feel as if I'm going blind from the tears which refuse to leave my eyes in peace."

She took a fine belt and sword, which Lady Chujo had prepared to give Ukifune in the future, and placed them in a bag as gifts for the Commander, which she loaded into the carriage when the messenger was climbing in, since it seemed inappropriate to offer mere ordinary gifts in this situation. She left him a message.

"This is the will of my deceased daughter Ukifune."

When the Commander saw what the messenger had been given in Uji, he said that she needn't to have done such a thing.

The messenger told the Commander,

"Lady Chujo came out to talk with me herself, even though she was in a depressed state, crying all the time. She said she was very grateful that you had offered your assistance in furthering her young sons' careers, but considering her low-class status, she will send only the smart one to work under you, so that no one will wonder why you are offering her family your patronage."

Commander Kaoru thought,

"Some may find the relationship between myself and this family a little unusual, but I don't think there will ultimately be any problem, when you realize that it is not unheard of for even an emperor to take a lower-class rural woman as one of his wives. As long as the lady is presentable and the emperor loves her, no one will speak badly of him. In the case of lieges, there are many with wives who come from families of low status or who have been married before. Even if people find out about Lady Chujo's ancestry, I will not be put out. It will cause me no trouble since I did nothing wrong. A mother who lost her precious daughter in such an unfortunate way deserves considerate help from others in order to reestablish her family's honor. That is how a good man is supposed to behave."

Hitachi-no-Kami visited Lady Chujo in the villa where she was hiding. He was angry and spoke without taking a seat.

"How can you stay in a place like this during such a tumultuous time for our family?"

Even though he hadn't heard anything about Ukifune for many years, he hadn't really cared at all, thinking that there would be nothing special to hear. Lady Chujo had been planning to tell him about the honor Ukifune was going to bring to the family after the Commander moved her to Kyoto. As she had passed away, there was no point in keeping it secret. The mother told her husband the truth with tears in her eyes. She showed him the letter from the Commander. Hitachi-no-Kami, a typical country man who admired nobles and was impressed by everything they did or said, felt intimidated at first, but read it over and over.

"She has indeed thrown her extraordinary fortune away by committing suicide. Although I have worked for him as one of his many subjects, I have never had the chance to serve him directly. He is a truly noble, great man. It is very encouraging and comforting that he has offered his support to our sons."

He spoke in a delighted voice. The mother couldn't help thinking about how things might have been if Ukifune were still alive, and she collapsed into tears. Watching her crying, Hitachi-no-Kami finally felt saddened, and tears came into his eyes. However, he realized that if Ukifune still lived, the Commander wouldn't have cared about her family so deeply. He understood that the Commander felt duty-bound to help the mother escape her sorrow, regardless of others' reactions, all from a sense of guilt, which stemmed from the fact that their daughter might have died because of him.

Kaoru organized a memorial service forty-nine days after Ukifune's passing in a temple in Uji, although he still wondered exactly what had happened to her at the last moment of her life, and couldn't get the mystery out of his mind. At any rate, he thought it would not be such a bad thing to

hold the ceremony, regardless of whether she had actually died. He
lavishly rewarded the sixty monks involved. Ukifune's mother attended
the service and did what she could for her deceased daughter. Prince
Niou had sent Ukon a silver pot filled with gold. Because of his intention
not to stand out, it fell upon Ukon to bring the gift to the ceremony herself,
causing people to wonder how she was able to procure such a fabulous
offering despite her low class. The Commander invited many men from
his inner circle. People were quite surprised to see such a grand ceremony
held by Commander Kaoru for a lady nearly unknown in society. It piqued
their curiosity and caused them to wonder what she had been like in life.
Hitachi-no-Kami made his appearance and behaved as if her were the
host of the service. Everyone viewed him with suspicion. He had previously
tried his best to celebrate the birth of the Lieutenant's newborn baby in an
extremely ostentatious manner. He acted so unbecomingly for his status
and had even removed everything from the house in order to replace it all
with high-end foreign goods. His effort, however, was a complete aesthetic
failure due to his lack of discriminating taste. Compared to his attempt,
this ceremony was far more superb, and he realized that if Ukifune had
been alive, she could have escaped her destiny of being in the same class
as he. The wife of Prince Niou commissioned the reading of a sutra by the
Seven Monks. Belatedly, the Emperor came to know that Commander
Kaoru had had a secret wife. He assumed that the Commander had loved
her deeply but would have hesitated to make the relationship public for
Lady Ninomiya's benefit. The Emperor felt sorry that the Commander
had to hide his lover in Uji out of consideration for his principal wife, which
ultimately might have been what was responsible for this young lady's
death.

The two young noblemen had suffered from an emotional pain which
seemed to torment them endlessly. This was especially true for Prince
Niou who had lost his lover while his passion was soaring, so that the
depth of his sorrow was extraordinary. However, he was surrounded by
many different ladies through which he could make himself feel better, as

he was, by nature, fickle in love. Commander Kaoru, who was in the process of caring for those who were close to Ukifune, could not break free of his despair over missing her.

The Empress Akashi was still in Rokujo mansion in mourning for her uncle, the former Prince Shikibu, whose name her son, Niou, had adopted after his passing. With having inherited such a noble title, he could no longer visit his mother so often. He instead often came to his sister, Princess Ippon, seeking in some way to alleviate his sadness. What he found unsatisfactory was that he couldn't see any of the beautiful ladies up close, particularly a stunning lady called Kosaisho, who was on intimate terms with Kaoru. She was respected as a lady of great merit, who played many instruments beautifully and whose way of writing and speaking was considered extremely sophisticated. Prince Niou had also desired this lady for years and had tried his best to get to her, in keeping with his favored routine. She, however, had kept rejecting his flirtatious advances because she was not interested in being just one of his many conquests. This attitude of Lady Kosaisho attracted Kaoru, being so different from that of the other ladies. She sent a letter to Kaoru, because she had heard that he had been lost in thought those days and she couldn't stay silent. It was written on tasteful stationery.

"哀れ知る心は人におくれねど
　　　数ならぬ身に消えつつぞふる
(Although no one feels more sorry for your loss, knowing how little I mean to you, I remain silently by as if fading away.)

I wish I could have died in her place, so that you wouldn't be this sad."

Kaoru felt relieved to read the message because it helped him pass the melancholic evening quietly alone. He expressed his appreciation in his poetic reply.

"つれなしとここら世を見るうき身だに
　　　人の知るまで嘆きやはする
(I have seen a world of misfortunes and learned much of life's

mutable nature, but, in truth, I am not as grieved as others believe.)"

He went to Lady Kosaisho's house to tell her that he was very grateful for her words of comfort, especially on such a wistful evening. Owing to his great status, the Commander had a solemn atmosphere. As he had never visited a middle-class lady's house before, he found it poor and ramshackle. Lady Kosaisho found it strangely amusing to see the distinguished Commander sitting by the small door of a very humble room, but she had a nice conversation with him, feeling no shame over her plain dwelling. He thought,

"She may be even more brilliant than my deceased lady. Why does she work as a servant?"

He did not know why, yet he wished that something more appropriate might be arranged. But he revealed none of this in his behavior.

In summer, when the lotus flowers were blooming their most beautifully, Empress Akashi hosted a series of sutra reading sessions called 'Mihatsukou (Lectures on the Eight Volumes),' each of which was dedicated to those who had recently passed away, such as the Lady of Rokujo-in or Lady Murasaki. It turned out to be a very dignified and venerable five-day-long gathering. The Volume Five session was so worth watching that many people desperately sought the honor of being in attendance, using any of their trivial personal connections with the ladies of the house to their advantage.

On the morning of the final day, after the last of the sessions had finished, people began cleaning up all the decorations that had been put up for the event. They worked so hard returning things to their original places that the house was in total disarray. Princess Ippon had been temporarily housed in the west wing, until the situation settled down in the north block. Many ladies were back in their own rooms, tired from listening to the sessions for days. There were not many remaining around the Princess. In the evening, Kaoru changed his clothes and went to a house called Tsuri-dono (The Fishing Pavilion) because he had some business with one of the monks leaving that day, but he found they had already left. As there seemed to be nothing else to do, he took a rest by the pond.

Since only a few people were walking around that area, some ladies were resting in a room created by divider screens. Kaoru heard someone moving around. He thought it could be Lady Kosaisho, and peered into the nearby room through a crack in the sliding doors. The room was tidily arranged, with a fine interior, which was unusual for a room of average ladies. The screens were staggered, and he could see inside through the gaps between. Some ladies were laughing while trying to crush ice on the lid of an elegant old box. The three ladies and a young girl were in casual clothes, and they didn't appear to be in a noble lady's presence. Then, his eyes were caught by a beautiful lady in a white gown, who was watching their actions with a piece of ice in her hand. The beauty of her smiling face defied description. It was such a hot day that she had pulled her hair to one side. Her figure was beyond imagination. Although he had seen many outstanding women before, this lady was unique in her dignity and bearing. Before her brightness, the faces of the other ladies in the room looked as if they were besmirched in soot. When he calmed himself down and looked at them once more, he found that the manner in which a lady in a yellow gown fanned herself was rather refined and feminine, as she said to the other ladies,

"It's so difficult to crush the ice. Why don't we just leave it and feel all the cooler simply watching it?"

Her laughter was charming. From the voice he could tell that it was Lady Kosaisho.

Laughing at her suggestion, they succeeded in crushing the ice and held some pieces in their hands. Some of them started fooling around by putting the ice on their heads or by chilling their chests with it. Lady Kosaisho wrapped her piece with a slip of paper and handed it to the Princess, but she wiped her hands on the paper and said,

"I don't want it, thank you. Its drops are a little troubling to me."

Hearing the faint sound of her voice, Kaoru was gladdened. He recalled the time he had seen the very young Princess, who had impressed him with her loveliness. Although he hadn't had a chance to see this lady since then, he was happy that the Divine had given him another opportunity to gaze upon her. At the same time, however, from his past experiences it seemed more than possible that a glance at such a splendid lady would be the end of him emotionally, as by the Gods' design. Although he became anxious inside, he still couldn't take his eyes off of her.

It was then that one of the ladies remembered that she had left the door to their room open when she had earlier been called to some urgent business. She became worried, because she would be scolded if someone were to find out. She ran back to the room. Finding a man in front of the door peering inside, she was so curious about his identity that she hurriedly walked straight to the room without hiding herself. Kaoru stepped back into the shadows, so as not to let the lady know that he was there, for fear of being viewed as indelicate. For her part, the lady thought she was in trouble.

"This is a problem. I left all the screens slightly open, so that others could look into the room. Is he one of the young men who live here? It would be impossible for a stranger to gain entrance. If this incident becomes public, they will wonder who it was to have left the door open in the first place. Since he was dressed in silk, the people in the room would not have noticed the sound of his approach."

Kaoru feared he had found yet another troublesome love.

"I was once nearly a monk, but when I met my ladies in Uji, worldly desires conquered my mind yet again. In a similar way, my feelings for Princess Ippon will undoubtedly cause me great suffering. If I had become a priest when I was twenty, I would have gotten used to an isolated lifestyle deep in the forest and would never have had to endure this type of emotional anguish. Why did I wish to look at the Princess longer? What does it mean anyway? This will certainly cause me nothing but future agony."

The next morning, waking up beside the beautiful figure of his wife, Lady Ninomiya, herself a half-sister of Princess Ippon by different mothers, Kaoru tried to convince himself that the lady he had seen the day before was not as beautiful as she, but he was not entirely successful. Princess Ippon seemed very special, unbelievably refined and gorgeous. He even thought that her grace exceeded that of a mere human, and he could find no words to sufficiently describe her. In an effort to rein in his passionate appreciation, he questioned whether he had simply built up his estimation of her in his mind, or if the situation itself had made her appear so beautiful. He told a female servant,

"It's getting very hot. I wish to change my esteemed lady's clothes to something lighter. Sometimes, dressing differently proves a much better choice. You shall go to the equerry and ask her to fashion a lighter set of clothes and bring them to Lady Ninomiya."

They thought that the Commander wanted to appreciate his wife in different apparel. In the afternoon, when he got back from the room where he always meditated alone, the dress he ordered had been prepared and hung on a screen.

"Why don't you put on this clothing? It might not normally be appropriate to wear clothing through which your skin can be seen when there are others around. But now it is all right, wouldn't you agree?"

He dressed her himself. The richness of her hair and the way that the clothes hung on her body gave her quite a splendid appearance. However, when he compared her to Princess Ippon, she was no equal to the latter's beauty. He even asked for pieces of ice to be brought and put one of them in the hand of Lady Ninomiya. He knew that it was foolish, but when he thought about those who stare at a painting instead of their lovers, he viewed his own actions as acceptable since his wife was similar in appearance to the lady he had fallen for. Even so, he couldn't stop sighing lamentably, thinking that it would have been so nice if he could have joined the Princess' party the day before and gazed upon her to his heart's desire.

"Do you write to Princess Ippon?"

"When I lived in the Emperor's house, he told me to write to her, so I did, although we haven't been in touch for so long."

"I imagine that she doesn't write to you any more because you married below your station. It is sad, isn't it? I can tell sometimes that you feel reproach towards her."

"I have felt no reproach towards her. It would be unnecessary."

"Then, I can tell her that you refrain from writing to her because she looks down on you due to your lowered status."

Kaoru spent the day with Lady Ninomiya, and the next day he appeared in the house of the Empress. It was no surprise that Prince Niou happened to be there too. His dark-colored clothes mixed with red and yellow tones were very sophisticated and tasteful. His skin was fair and as beautiful as his sister's. Looking thinner than before, he appeared even more stunning. To Kaoru, he looked like his sister, Princess Ippon, which once again reminded him of his passion. He knew he shouldn't revisit those feelings and tried to calm himself. It was an emotional conflict he had never known before.

Prince Niou had had many paintings brought with him. He asked a lady to carry some of them to Princess Ippon's room. He himself left to see his sister.

Kaoru approached the Empress and highly praised the sutra-reading sessions which she had held. Taking a look at the paintings left in the room, he talked about Lady Rokujo and all the events of that time. He finally said,

"Actually I feel sorry to have seen my wife, who was high-born, become somewhat depressed after she moved out of this house. She feels isolated, because now that Princess Ippon has stopped writing to her, she believes that the bond between them has disappeared owing to her marriage to a man of lower status. It would be wonderful if she could have a chance to see fine items such as these paintings once in a while. What does your Highness think of this? Of course I will help in any way I can."

The Empress seemed surprised at his words.

"How could Princess Ippon stop corresponding for such a trivial reason? I imagine it was easy for the two princesses to send letters to each other while they lived in the same palace, but since Lady Ninomiya moved far away after becoming your wife, distance came between them and their correspondence dropped off after a while. I will talk to Princess Ippon and ask her to write to her sister, but I wonder why Lady Ninomiya didn't send a letter herself."

"I suspect she felt too intimidated to do so. Having a close relationship with you and your family, I am happy to make the acquaintance of even those who hadn't known my wife before our marriage. I think it must have been hard for her to stop corresponding with someone in the family who had known her for so long, especially after marrying someone like me."

The Empress didn't know that all these words were motivated by a man in love.

Kaoru left the presence of the great lady, and headed to the west wing of the palace to see his friend, Lady Kosaisho. Along the way he gazed longingly at the hallway from which he had seen the Princess, in order to briefly satisfy his passion. Other ladies behind the screens created a fuss about his coming to the house. He saw some young men, including his nephew, a son of the Left Minister, talking with some ladies. He sat down by the door and said,

"Although I have come to this palace very often, I haven't visited this wing for some time. Well, in the company of young people like yourself, I feel quite old, but I have decided not to let my age fill my life with boredom. If I seem funny and clumsy to you, it is just because I'm not used to this new approach towards life."

He glanced at his nephew's group and someone said,

"You'll be back fresh in youth once you start trying."

Even the lady who humorously said so was quite graceful. They didn't discuss anything in particular. The conversation was random and general, but also oddly comforting.

Princess Ippon came to the house where the Empress was staying. The Empress was asked if the Commander had come to see her in the palace. Her lady-in-waiting answered,

"He said he was going to discuss something with Lady Kosaisho."

The Empress herself continued,

"A serious man like the Commander doesn't want to open his heart to inconsiderate women. It will be naught but embarrassing for a lady of a shallow nature to speak with him, as he will see through her obfuscations and find out how unworthy she truly is. Lady Kosaisho is a perfect match as his intimate."

Although Kaoru was her brother, he still seemed troubled in love. She was hoping that the ladies would see to it that things went calmly. The lady-in-waiting explained the situation with a sense of humor,

"Lady Kosaisho is definitely the favorite of the Commander, and he often comes to visit her. They may speak intimately, and sometimes he leaves very late at night. However, the truth is that between them there is no romantic relationship such as people imagine. Apparently Lady Kosaisho has such a strong antipathy toward the amorousness of Prince Niou that she seldom writes him back, which is not the action a proper lady should take towards such a nobleman."

The Empress laughed with the lady and said,

"She must be quite perceptive to see the true nature of the Prince. I don't know how these trouble-making habits of his can be broken. I feel ashamed of his behavior, and I don't think that I'm alone in this."

The lady told the Empress a story she had heard.

"I heard a strange story that I think would interest your Highness. The Commander's deceased lover was a young sister of Prince Niou's wife in Nijo palace. They say the lady of the former Governor Hitachi is her aunt or mother, but no one seems to know the exact details. At any rate, Prince Niou had also secretly visited Kaoru's lover. Eventually Kaoru found out and decided to take her from Uji to Kyoto at once. While they were preparing for her relocation, the security of the house was fortified. When Prince Niou tried to visit the lady again, he couldn't get inside, and had to wait outside on horseback. In the end, he had no choice but to leave. The lady might have come to love him so passionately that she disappeared suddenly. They assumed that the lady had thrown herself into the river. Some elderly ladies, such as her nurse, were crying out for her. Of course, this is only what I've heard."

Not surprisingly, the Empress was quite shocked.

"Who told you that? What a sorrowful story! Although this type of gossip always spreads like wildfire, this is not your typical rumor. Kaoru mentioned none of this to me; he was just grieving over the sorrow of life, although he mentioned that it is lamentable that everyone in the family in Uji died young."

"Did he really? Common people always talk about uncertain things as if they are definite facts. A child who worked in the house in Uji recently came to a house of the parents of Lady Kosaisho, and said there's no doubt about this story's authenticity. Everyone in the house worked quite hard to hide the fact that she had died in that manner, and tried not to let anyone get the idea that she had performed such an outrageous deed. I think that is why the Commander hesitated to tell you about it in detail."

"Tell Lady Kosaisho that that child must never talk about this to anyone. Gossip like this can destroy the reputation of Prince Niou, and all nobility will despise him."

The Empress said this out of deep concern for the Prince.

After a while, Lady Ninomiya received a letter from Princess Ippon. Kaoru was very pleased to see her splendid handwriting. He was certain then that this woman was as excellent in character as he had suspected, thinking that he should have done something earlier to see her writing. The Empress had sent many beautiful paintings. Kaoru gathered up even better ones and sent them to her in return. The one which depicted a scene from a story where Serikawa, the main character, falls in love with Princess Ichi and leaves his house because of his deep longing, seemed to

succinctly express Kaoru's feelings for Princess Ippon. At the same time
he was saddened, knowing that his love was not going to have a happy
ending as in the story.

"荻の葉に露吹き結ぶ秋風も
　　　夕べぞわきて身にはしみにける

(Even the autumn breeze merging dewdrops on a leaf saddens
me, especially on an evening when I lose myself in thoughts of
beauty.)"

Although Kaoru wanted fervently to attach this poem to the reply to
the Princess, it was easy to predict that the world would react in an
extremely negative way if they caught even the slightest hint about his
feelings for her. In this way he suffered from forbidden love. In the end, he
came to think that his sorrowful past was to be blamed.

"If only Lady Okimi had lived and had been my wife, I would have
never fallen for another woman in my whole life. I would not have taken
even a daughter of the present Emperor. Anyway, if it was known that I
cared about my wife so much, who would want his daughter to marry me
in the first place? Lady Okimi's passing was the beginning of this chaotic
situation, indeed."

Blaming the lady from his past, he missed her and despised her at the
same time. It was his greatest regret that their time had passed him by
and would never return. After he managed to accept the fact that there
was nothing he could do about the things which had already transpired,
his regret spread to the matters with Ukifune, who had ended her life in
such a horrible way. Recognizing her youthful indiscretion at being
enchanted by Niou, he had also heard that she had been unsure about her
future after his attitude toward her had changed. He thought she was not
the mature type of lady with whom to have a serious relationship, such as
a marriage, but rather a charming young girl to take as a mistress and
spend time comfortably together. He finally reconciled himself to bring an
end to his seemingly endless pining away by laying the blame on his own
absurdity for leaving a young lover in a place like Uji. He also resolved not

to have any reproachful feelings toward either the Prince or the lady.

Since even a calm, moderate man like Kaoru suffered so greatly from love affairs that they affected his health, it was impossible for a man like Prince Niou to mend his broken heart after Ukifune left him in the way that she did. He had no one to talk with about his feelings for his lost love. Only Lady Naka listened to him, feeling sorry for the death of her young sister, but she shouldn't have felt very sad, having spent so little time with Ukifune in life. Besides, it was not in good taste for him to show his wife his feelings for another lady so directly. So he summoned Jiju.

After the death of their mistress, the people in Uji had left the house and lived on their own. Only the nurse, Ukon, and Jiju stayed in the house of mourning together, since they had been the closest to the deceased. Although Jiju had borne the fierce sound of the river, believing it was just for a short while until the day when they would take Ukifune to a mansion in Kyoto, now that the lady was gone, she could no longer endure the dark, terrifying atmosphere in Uji, which prompted her to move to a small house in Kyoto. Prince Niou located her and suggested that she work in his Nijo mansion. Jiju, however, refused his generous offer, as it seemed very possible that other ladies would speak ill of the forbidden love affair between the Prince and Ukifune, and speak critically of her as well. She told him that she wanted to work in the house of the Empress instead. The Prince replied,

"That's fine, and I will support you from the wings."

Jiju started working in the Empress' house, for she hoped that the work would help her get over the sadness she felt over her lady's death. People there considered her a humble servant of pleasing appearance and no one spoke ill of her. Since Commander Kaoru visited often, her sorrow reappeared when memories of the past flooded in every time she caught sight of him. Although she had heard that only noblewomen were there and she had come to know almost everyone in the house by then, she could find no one to rival Ukifune's beauty.

The former Prince Shikibu (Prince Kageroh), who had passed away in spring that year, had a daughter. However, her stepmother, Lady Kita, didn't care for the girl at all and had been thinking about promising the girl in marriage to her own brother, a mediocre keeper of horses. The Empress heard of this and was much aggrieved.

"That poor girl! It is absolutely unacceptable to ruin the Prince's precious, beloved child's life in that way."

The girl herself was very apprehensive about this gloomy marriage. Her brother, a noble equerry, recommended that she work for the Empress.

"Why don't you work for her majesty, the Empress? She has true compassion for you and your unfortunate situation."

The Empress had recently welcomed the girl to her house as a lady worthy of being Princess Ippon's conversation partner. Although she served there and received preferential treatment, the situation was a bit of a shock for a former princess. They called her Lady Prince and she was required to wear a *mo*.[2] Prince Niou thought she looked like his deceased lover, since the former Prince Shikibu and Prince Hachi, the father of Ukifune, were brothers. He missed Ukifune so much that his amorous nature got the better of him and encouraged him to view Lady Prince as an outlet for his passion.

Kaoru lamented how hard life had treated this young former princess. It was not so long ago that her father thought about letting her become one of the concubines of Tohgu[3], or of expressing his hope that Kaoru would take her as his wife. Facing a girl who once enjoyed a life of great prosperity that had changed in the blink of an eye, Kaoru thought that those who committed suicide by throwing themselves into a large body of water might have shown foresight in avoiding a situation such as this. He felt truly sorry for her.

Empress Akashi often stayed at Rokujo mansion because it was more spacious than her own mansion and had a cozy atmosphere. Even those

2. A formal kimono for ladies but not worn by princesses.
3. A mansion for the heir to the throne.

who didn't normally accompany the Empress didn't fail to visit. There were many ladies about, not only in the main house but also in all the detached houses and hallways. Yugiri looked after the mansion as expertly as his father, Prince Genji, had done. The family flourished even more after Prince Genji had passed away, and the magnificence of the Rokujo mansion of today seemed to surpass even that of previous times. If Prince Niou had been his normal self, he would have caused all kinds of trouble with a variety of ladies during the several months that the Empress was there. Actually, he was very quiet, and people around him came to suspect that he might have changed. After a while, however, he fell in love with Lady Prince and fell back into his old routine.

When the cool autumn breezes signified the passing of summer, the Empress began preparing to return home. By then, almost all the young ladies were staying not at their own houses but at Rokujou mansion, for they were keen to see the maple leaves change into beautiful colors at the peak of the season. Appreciating the flow of water and admiring the glow of moonlight, they held musical events almost every day. Prince Niou liked to be in Rokujo mansion for its cheerful atmosphere. He was always at the center of the action. The Prince looked wonderfully vibrant, like a flower which had just bloomed, even after days and nights of revelry. Since Kaoru didn't visit there so often, he made the young ladies of the Empress nervous. On one occasion, these two young noblemen came to the Empress's room at the same time. Jiju peeked inside the room from her place of hiding and she thought Ukifune should have lived to be loved by either of these noblemen. Ukifune had thrown her great luck away. Jiju was angry at herself since she had told no one about the house in Uji or the fact that Ukifune was the secret lover of the Commander. While Commander Kaoru was leaving the room, Prince Niou was trying to tell his mother a story surrounding the details of what had happened in his house. Jiju hid herself away because she didn't want the Commander to find her and think that she didn't adore Ukifune, since she had left Uji before the first anniversary of her landlady's death.

When the Commander was walking the hallway in the east wing, he found some ladies talking in whispers by an open door, so he approached them and said,

"Why don't you want to fraternize with me? I think I am a great man to be with and you can feel more comfortable with me than with other ladies. Besides, being a male friend, I can tell you what only men can know, which may help you gain some insights into our psyche. I'm confident to say that you will understand sometime how worthy I am of your attention."

The awkwardness prevented anyone from saying a word. Then an older woman named Lady Ben answered,

"Well, I think a lady can fraternize comfortably with someone only when she knows that the person is not a desirable object of her love. It is a female dilemma indeed, isn't it? Now I'm not talking to you like this without deliberate intention, but I spoke up because if a lady like me who is always loud, which is what everyone thinks of me, doesn't say anything back to you, who would?"

"I'm sorry to know that you don't take me as a desirable man to have as a friend."

He made a joke and threw a look into the room. They had taken off their *kuraginu*[4], and set them aside. It seemed that they had been relaxing and enjoying creating random bits of calligraphy. He saw some flowers and grasses plucked short lying on the cover of an ink stone. The ladies had probably picked them themselves. One lady hid behind the screen, one looked the other way, and a third sat behind the open door so that his view of her was obscured. He only saw the shapes of their heads, which impressed him very much. He took up a brush and wrote,

"女郎花乱るる野べにまじるとも

　　露のあだ名をわれにかけめや

(Even when I enjoy the company of ladies who appear like yellow

---

4. A formal kind of kimono for middle-class ladies.

patrinias scattered about a field, no one would suspect me of indiscretion.)

It's a shame that you don't wish to be unreservedly familiar with me."

He passed what he wrote to a lady who was sitting close to him but gazing in the other direction. The lady didn't move at all but calmly and immediately answered,

"花といへば名こそあだなれをみなへし

　　なべての露に乱れやはする

(Speaking of the flower, its name sounds like a lady whose feelings are very often fickle. Are those yellow patrinias gathered by the dewdrops which rest upon their petals)?"

It was not a long reply, but its elegance impressed the Commander. She was there because when she had hoped to pass through this door to the Empress's room, Kaoru had happened to arrive and detain her.

Lady Ben told Kaoru,

"Your mind must be truly aging for you to mean what you just said. Your words are provokingly good though."

And she also said,

"旅寝してなほ試みよをみなへし

　　盛りの色に移り移らず

(You need to make sure that you are not likely to be attracted by the blooming flowers in their prime while residing here for only one night.)

Then we will more fully understand your nature and know if you are truly a serious man."

The Commander replied,

"宿貸さばひと夜は寝なんおほかたの

　　花に移らぬ心なりとも

(If you let me stay at your place, I will sleep there for one night, although my heart is unmoved by most flowers in the world.)"

Lady Ben became somewhat upset at what he had said and replied,

"Now you have insulted me. When I say 'flower,' I wasn't speaking of myself. I was speaking only of ladies in general."

Since the Commander had been reluctant these days to make jokes or utter witty phrases around people, the ladies still wished to hear more from him.

"It seems I was thoughtless. I will leave you now, as I imagine there is some reason for you to be so unfamiliar towards me."

Seeing him leaving, some of the ladies were worried that he might think everyone there was as immodest as Lady Ben.

Commander Kaoru was looking out at the shrubbery, leaning on a parapet at the end of east wing. Nearby were some flowers which seemed like they were blooming for the first time in the beautiful sunset. Everything touched his heart. He mumbled in a low voice, "Looking at the clear autumn sky, memories of her fill my heart with sorrow." He could hear the rustling gowns of the lady he had just spoken with. She passed through the sliding doors to the opposite side of the central room, out of Kaoru's sight. Shortly after, Prince Niou happened by and asked another lady,

"Who was the lady who just walked away?"

Kaoru heard someone answer from behind the screen,

"It was Lady Chusho, an equerry of Princess Ippon."

This can't be good for her, Kaoru thought. If a man can learn information about a lady so easily, anyone who becomes interested in her will rush to find out her identity. Kaoru felt sorry for the lady who had just had her name and title revealed. At the same time, he found himself jealous that ladies got along so well with Prince Niou that they hid nothing from him.

"This is probably because the Prince can easily befriend anyone, and his technique in seducing and attracting ladies is beyond compare, while I am a little clumsy with women and it is difficult for me to make close connections with others. The Prince should experience the taste of mortification like I have in the past. In order to bring this about, I need to become intimate with a lady to whom the Prince has been recently devoted. Although she will undoubtedly choose me over him if she is a smart woman, no one can know beforehand whether or not she is of such exceptional character."

When Kaoru took a dim view of the future of his plan, things with Lady Naka slipped into his mind.

"Lady Naka faces her husband's faithlessness, which allows him to have open relationships with others freely, and yet she appreciates my love very much. I also think it is exceptionally wise of her to maintain our friendship, knowing that we cannot become too intimate, as people would roundly criticize the relationship between the two of us. I'm very glad that she keeps doing the right thing. I wonder if I can find even a single woman as brilliant as her in this mansion filled with ladies. It may be because I don't pay close enough attention to them, but the possibility seems quite remote. Since I constantly wake in the middle of the night and am not feeling well these days, it may not be so bad to learn to play the game of love, to alleviate my stress."

Knowing it would not be such a bad thing after all, he was still not in such a mood.

It was a strange coincidence that Commander Kaoru should have once again walked by the Fishing Pavilion on the west side of the palace, where he had seen the Princess for the first time, at the same time that a group of ladies were there together, relaxing and enjoying the beauty of the moon without the company of the Princess who had left her own house for her mother's that evening. Kaoru heard someone playing the *koto* with gentle and melancholic notes. They were surprised to see Kaoru in such an unexpected location.

"Why do you play the *koto* as if you are trying to make someone fervently wish to catch sight of your visage?"

He quoted a phrase from a scene where a man meets a girl playing the *koto* in 'Yusenkutsu,' a classic Chinese novel. One of the ladies sat up and answered him without pulling down the blind, which had been raised a little higher than usual, knowing that there was a description of the girl's appearance in the book which claimed that she and her brother looked very much alike.

"I'm afraid I haven't a brother who resembles me."

The speaker was, in fact, Lady Chusho. He replied with a joke citing a phrase from the same scene.

"Actually I am a maternal uncle of the girl you are looking for."

He then asked her,

"It seems that Princess Ippon has gone to the house of the Empress. What does she do while she is there?"

"Wherever she is, she is up to nothing special. She just takes life as it goes, like we are doing right now."

He gave a sigh to find how easily the Princess takes it in, in spite of his suffering for her. He started playing the *koto* offered by the ladies without tuning it, so as not to let anyone who heard his sigh know his true feelings. The sound of the instrument was the perfect accompaniment to the autumn scenery, and even though he played it casually, it was quite pleasing to the ear. However, when he stopped in the middle of the song, those who had been listening intently felt annoyed, gasping for the rest.

"My mother's status was as high as Princess Ippon's. Although the Princess is a daughter of the Empress and my mother was that of another lady, they are both loved very much by their fathers, the Emperors of their respective generations. It's remarkable how fortunate the Princess is. Empress Akashi must have brought something special to her children."

Having one of the Empress's daughters as his wife, he thought that destiny must have put him in a good spot as well. On top of that, if he could also have Princess Ippon as his wife, his life would be glorious beyond compare, even though it was clear even to him that what he was contemplating was sheer fantasy.

Lady Prince had a room in the west wing of this palace, where Princess Ippon lived. She heard many people gathered together and looked outside to find them enjoying the moon in the garden. Kaoru remembered that she was another beloved daughter of the former Emperor. As her father used to think that Kaoru would make a wonderful husband for the former Princess, he decided to come and talk to her. A few girls in casual attire were relaxing on the porch, but as soon as the nobleman showed up, they looked embarrassed and hid themselves away inside, which he found unsurprising. He went to a room at the south end of the house and cleared his throat. Then an elderly lady came out. Kaoru said,

"I would not say things like 'I am your secret admirer.' Everyone uses this expression and I realize it's tired and trite. Besides I'm too old to pretend to be an amateur in love. I'm looking for the right words to describe my feelings for Lady Prince."

The woman wouldn't even inform Lady Prince that he was here, and said, affecting to be wise,

"We feel sorry to see her in a position of a lady yet serving another, remembering how much love the former Prince Shikibu showed her, and how much happiness he wished for her future. She appreciates your support and kind words, which have helped her greatly."

Kaoru refused to accept her words, for she treated him with half neglect and showed him no consideration. He was annoyed by her attitude and said,

"Considering the fact that we are relatives and that relationship will never change, it is more than fair for her to count on me, especially in times like this, although I cannot do what I am capable of when I am unable to see her in person and need a go-between just to have a simple conversation."

The old lady was convinced of his sincerity, so she pushed Lady Prince out in front of the Commander.

"For a lady like me, who has no one to depend on in the world, having someone who offers his unconditional support means a tremendous amount. I appreciate it from the bottom of my heart."

Her voice, which he heard for the first time without anyone to pass the message between them, went through his ears vivaciously, charmingly and tenderly. He would have liked her very much if she had been just an ordinary lady. However, when he thought about her current situation, in which she had reconciled herself to speak directly to someone like him, he couldn't help being disappointed and anxious about her future, remembering how magnificent she used to be when her father had been still in life. Although he was sure that she looked beautiful too, feeling keen to see her face, it was so easy for him to imagine that she was to be a new object of Prince Niou's passion that Kaoru hesitated becoming any more intimate with her. He felt so fed up with the world, where it caused him so much trouble to meet a decent, attractive lady who was right for him.

"Although Lady Prince had been cherished by her noble father and showered with so much love, I think there will be many others who are her equal. What I cannot understand is how the ladies in Uji, who grew up by the saintly Prince Hachi's side in the mountain village, were completely flawless. Even the youngest daughter, who seemed like a shallow, thoughtless lady, was aesthetically as elegant as Lady Prince."

Everything seemed to remind him of the family in Uji. On one evening, he was remembering all the unrealized promises and pledges he had made with his ladies in the pages of his past. In his lonely reflection, mayflies danced about him idly.

> "ありと見て手にはとられず見ればまた
> 行く方も知らず消えしかげろふ
>
> (Visible, although not tangible, a mayfly flew by and left me alone without sharing its destination.)

Just like the old poem which begins 'Wondering if they are really here or not...'" he muttered to himself, feeling empty inside.

9. Writing Practice

Writing Practice

CHARACTERS

Ukifune

Commander Kaoru

Sozu, a high-ranking monk

The sister nun, Sozu's younger sister

The mother nun, Sozu's mother

Ajari, disciple of Sozu

The caretaker of the villa in Uji

The Empress

Sho-sho, a nun

Captain Chu-sho, son-in-law of the sister nun

The Governor of Kii, grandson of the mother nun

Lady Kosaisho, Princess Ippon's lady-in-waiting

Ukifune's younger half brother

In those days, there lived a great monk called 'Sozu of Yokawa' on Mount Hiei. The venerable man resided with his mother of eighty odd years and a sister of around fifty. The two nuns had wished for many years to visit Hase Temple and their prayers had finally been answered. Sozu asked Ajari, his right-hand man, to accompany them in order to dedicate images of Buddha and some hand-written sutras. After having accomplished so much during their visit to the temple, they turned back for home. When they were passing over Nara Hill, the mother suddenly fell ill. Since they were unsure whether she could survive the trip to Kyoto, they decided to err on the side of caution and let her rest for the night at the house of one of their acquaintances in Uji. Deep in the night, as her condition worsened, a messenger was sent to Sozu. Although he had taken an oath preventing him from descending the mountain that year, he couldn't let his aged mother die mid-journey without being by her side. As soon as he received the news, he immediately came down to Uji, filled with a sense of unease.

Although people may have thought that his mother had already lived a full life, Sozu called together some of his more highly esteemed fellow monks and began to pray with them for her recovery. The landlord heard the hustle and bustle in the guestrooms. At that time, the people of the house were in the midst of purifying themselves, preparing for their own visit to Mitake Temple. They were very worried, because if the old lady died there, the house and all its inhabitants would enter into an official state of mourning. Sozu came to know that they had been talking about this potentially troublesome situation. He found their concerns quite justified, and he sympathized with them. On top of that, considering the size of the house and the poor maintenance of the rooms, it seemed better for Sozu and his party to move out. His mother had recovered somewhat by then, enough to withstand the long journey to Kyoto, but the direction to their house was not auspicious in terms of Yin and Yang philosophy, so he needed to take them somewhere else. Sozu recalled that there was a house nearby on a former estate of the deceased Emperor Suzaku. He sent a messenger to the keeper of the house, a man who was familiar to

138

him, asking for a few days accommodation. The old keeper returned with the messenger and told him that everyone in the house had left for Hase Temple on the previous day. He said,

"If you come, you can use the main house, as it is currently unoccupied. Those who go to Hase or Nara always stay there."

Sozu was glad to hear that.

"That will be just fine. I know the house is an official government holding, but I think it will be a comfortable place to stay with no one else around."

He sent some of his men to look into the condition of the building. The keeper had become accustomed to accepting such travelers, so he went back to the house and returned as soon as he had prepared for their arrival.

Sozu set off for the house earlier than the two nuns. The place had fallen into ruin, and he was struck by a sense of impending doom. Looking around, he told his men to read protective sutras in loud voices. Ajari, the monk who had accompanied the nuns to Hase Temple, and another monk of the same class felt oddly compelled to search behind the main house, and they took along a more humble monk who lead the way with a torch. They found a gigantic tree, which was almost like a thick forest unto itself. Their gaze was drawn to the foot of the tree, as if their eyes had been caught by some horrifying force, they found a white form spread out over the tree's base.

"What is that?"

They stopped and illuminated it with the torch. It looked like someone sitting in a crouched position.

"Is it a fox trying to trick us? You will never succeed! I will uncover your disguise this instant," said one of the monks as he tried to move in closer. The other monk stopped him saying,

"Don't approach it. I don't think any good can come of that."

He crossed his fingers to make a sign to ward off sorcery, and pointed the resulting symbol at the thing, all the while unable to tear his eyes from it. Although the situation was terrifying enough to cause them to tremble and their hair to stand on end, on impulse, the humble monk moved closer and studied the creature carefully. It appeared to be a lady with long shiny hair, sobbing over the sturdy roots of the tree.

"This is rather unusual. I think we should ask Sozu what to do."

"Yes, this is quite a mystery."

One of them went back to Sozu and told him what had just happened.

"I've heard that foxes can turn themselves into other forms, but I've never seen such a thing with my own eyes."

Sozu came down from the main house to the backyard.

Most of the people in the house were working quite hard to prepare for welcoming the two nuns who were soon to arrive. They brought everything inside and organized it all as quickly as possible. Meanwhile, the back part of the palace was quiet and only four or five people were there, watching the strange creature in the backyard. It hardly moved. It was such a mysterious and intriguing sight that they continued to watch it for a few hours. Sozu thought,

"I can't wait here for the sun to rise in order to tell if it's a person or some other creature."

He recited a spell repeatedly in his mind, making the sign with crossed fingers, after which he reached a conclusion.

"This is a person. It is neither terrifying nor mysterious. Move in closer and speak to it. It is not dead. Or it was once dead but has come back to life."

Ajari doubted his words.

"I'm afraid that cannot be true. Who could throw a dead body away here in the palace? Even if it is a real human being, the only possibility is that a fox or a spirit of the tree had kidnapped it and brought it here. At any rate, this is not a good sign. There must certainly be some evil spirit present."

He called the old keeper of the palace. Even the sound of his own voice echoing through the hills had an eerie quality.

The old man showed up in odd clothes, wearing a small, old-fashioned hat which covered his forehead. One of the monks asked him,

"Does a young lady live in this house? I mean...look at what we've found."

He pointed at the thing under the big tree. The keeper answered,

"It must be a trick being played by one of the foxes. They sometimes do odd things under this tree. In the autumn before last, they took a two-year-old boy away from the house and left him there, but since we were used to such occurrences, it was not at all surprising."

"Did the boy die?"

"No, he came back to life. Foxes often deceive us but rarely do anything truly harmful."

The old man spoke as if there were nothing special about the figure under the tree. He was not even concentrating on the conversation, worrying about how things were going in the kitchen. It seemed like preparing for dinner was of greater concern to him. Sozu said to the humble monk who had lead the way with the torch,

"Move in even closer, to see what kind of creature it is."

The monk approached it and said,

"Demon, god, fox or spirit, whatever you are, I don't think it's possible to hide who you are in the presence of a noble, high monk such as this man before you. So let me have your name. Just your name will suffice."

He tugged at its sleeve, and then it cried even harder, hiding its face in the collar of its kimono.

"What an ungrateful demon! Nothing will keep you hidden in the end."

In trying to see its face, he felt gripped by fear, wondering if it would resemble a female demon described in the old stories, without eyes or a nose. He was so desperate to show them his bravery that he attempted to pull its kimono off, but the unknown thing lay on its face and sobbed loudly. Since things so mysterious rarely occurred, whatever type of creature it truly was, people were going to watch to see what would happen. After a while, however, it started to rain heavily. One of the men said,

"It will die by itself if we leave it there."

Sozu induced them to treat it with respect.

"A true human being it is. It is sad to leave it there, knowing the life of a human could be lost in such a short space of time. Even a fish in the pond or a deer in the mountain should be released from a trap set by hunters, as a show of one's mercy. The life of a man lasts only for a brief while, so as long as we have a chance to extend a life even for just another day, we have to try with all sincerity. Maybe it is possessed by god or demon, or it was abandoned here by some evil man, or it was deceived as a result of some previous grudge. Anyway, since its death won't follow His decree, our Buddha would save its life. Although I'm not sure if we can keep it alive or not, why don't we at least try to take care of it to see what will happen? If it dies in the end, so be it, since it would be nothing but fate."

Sozu ordered the brave and humble monk to carry the creature into the house. Some of his followers spoke ill of him for his magnanimous gesture, saying things such as,

"This may not be my business, but I fear that bringing a mysterious creature close to someone struggling with a serious illness will only result in stirring up even more evil spirits and worsening the situation."

Others regarded it as a generous act of mercy.

"No matter what it really is, if it is still alive, leaving it here in the rain to die is not the way a man is supposed to act."

As humble people were prone to exaggerate and dramatize things unnecessarily, Sozu took her to an isolated room, in a shaded part of the house far from where most of the people were staying, and laid her down on the floor.

The carriage with the nuns arrived. When the mother disembarked, everyone was very worried about her and worked carefully, so as not to

142

create her any further stress, for she looked to be in a great deal of pain. After the situation had calmed down a little, Sozu asked one of his men how the woman in white was doing.

"She is still feeble and doesn't say a word. She doesn't seem to have fully returned to life. I think that she is a person whose soul has been stolen from her."

Sozu's sister overheard them talking and asked,

"What is going on, brother?"

Sozu told her what had happened and said,

"I have lived for more than sixty years, but I have never seen anything like it before."

On hearing that, the sister started crying and begged,

"Oh my, I had a dream when I stayed at a temple. What is she like? Let me see her, please."

"We have laid her down behind the door over there. You can see her now."

The sister rushed to the door. Behind it, she found a young, beautiful lady lying in a corner of the room all alone, who was in a kimono made of fine white silk and vermilion *hakama*.[1] The scent of the lady was strong and her figure was nothing but noble.

"I believe that my daughter who I have missed so much has come back to me."

The sister nun ordered her attendants to take the young lady into her room. Since they weren't aware of the odd way in which the lady was found, no one hesitated to do so. Although the young lady appeared far from fully conscious, when she looked up faintly the nun asked her,

"Speak to me, young lady. What in the world happened to you?"

The unknown lady kept silent, almost fainting away. The nun tried to give her warm water, but it didn't seem that her condition was improving.

"Was it for my watching her die again that I came to have this beautiful

1. Ladies' trousers.

lady here by my side?"

The nun asked Ajari to pray so as rid her of her ills.

"This is why I recommended not showing unnecessary mercy in vain."

Muttering so, Ajari started praying for the elimination of some evil spirit she seemed to have inside of her. Meanwhile, Sozu happened by.

"How is it going? You may be able to punish the evil spirit in order to force it to confess what brought her to this."

Upon saying so, it was becoming obvious to him that her life force was fading into darkness. Sozu's followers looked upon it all pessimistically.

"It doesn't look good. Now we are going to have to spend time here purifying ourselves after her death, just because we happened to find her. Besides, they say this lady is of noble birth, which means we cannot bury her body just anywhere. We have definitely been pulled into a very troublesome situation."

The nun dealt with them harshly.

"Keep your mouths shut and be quiet, please. No one can speak about this to anyone. I don't want any trouble."

The sister nun was so keen to help this lady, even more so than her own mother, that she stayed by the lady's side constantly, like a close relative. Although she was a total stranger to everyone in the house, even the female servants worked hard to save her, because they strongly felt that a lady of such beauty shouldn't die so young. Once in a while she awoke and looked up, but the only sign of her dimly lit life was the tears spilling out of her eyes.

"What a grievous situation!" cried the sister nun. "I have missed my daughter so much, but now I am very happy that I have met you, through God's will. If you leave me, however, I will suffer even more this time around. I'm sure that you and I must have had some strong bond in a previous life, because a miracle like this couldn't have happened by chance. Say something, please."

Upon hearing that, the ill lady finally replied to the nun in a low voice,

"Even if I survive, I'm not needed by anyone in this world. Please toss my body into the river so that no one is the wiser."

Regardless of its grave content, the nun was glad to finally hear her speak.

"Why do you say such things? What brought you here in the first place?"

The nun pressed her, but the lady didn't say another word. They checked to see if she had any bodily injuries. It impressed them how beautiful her body was, without even a scratch upon it. The nun felt deeply sorry for the lady. Then a doubt crept into her mind that the lady might be a supernatural being, as some had suggested, one which had appeared in a transformed figure so as to confuse others.

Sozu and his followers stayed there for two days, and the voices praying for the recovery of the old nun and the young, noble lady never fell silent. One day a local villager who had served Sozu in the past came to visit his former master. He passed along some local gossip, which included one interesting story.

"A daughter of the former Prince Hachi, who had a relationship with Commander Kaoru, died suddenly, but no one knows why or how. This story is the center of public attention at the moment. I couldn't visit you yesterday because I was busy helping them with the funeral preparations."

The nun thought that the ill lady might actually be the soul of the deceased lady which a demon had somehow stolen away and brought here. Even though she was visible to them, she might vanish without a trace at any moment. The nun was worried and scared of losing her. One of the ladies said,

"I saw the lights for her burial service last night but I didn't realize it was such a major event."

"The circumstances didn't allow them to hold a large funeral," he explained.

After they spoke, he was asked to depart without entering the house, since he had attended the funeral and was therefore capable of transferring an evil spirit to those within that were ill.

The ladies gossiped about this, saying things like,

"The Commander had a wife who was a daughter of the former Prince Hachi, but it has been a long time since she passed away. Who would it be this time? Having a daughter of the Emperor as his wife, it seems unlikely that he had another relationship with someone else."

When the nun's condition improved, they decided to return home, for they were afraid of encountering even more mysterious troubles in the house due to its strange atmosphere. The lady they had found there hadn't recovered yet, and they worried that she would not survive the trip back to Kyoto. Sozu and his mother rode in one carriage with two serving nuns, and his sister and the ill lady rode in another with one female servant. On the way, they tried to stop many times so that the ill woman could rest and take some medicine. Their house was located in a place called Ono, which was in the Sakamoto region of Hie. It was a long way home from Uji. Regretting not having organized a place to stay somewhere halfway, they arrived in Ono after midnight. Sozu and his sister helped his mother and the unknown lady into their respective rooms in order to lie down.

Although the mother would frequently become ill due to her old age, it took her quite a while to recover this time due to the long trip. When her condition seemed to have improved, Sozu left the house for the temple in Yokawa.

He didn't talk about the mysterious lady to anyone, as the fact that a noble monk had come back home with some unknown ill lady was more likely to cause gossip. His sister also ordered the people concerned to keep it secret, worrying that someone might show up searching for her. Wondering how a noble lady like this ended up wandering around in a remote village, the sister nun went so far as to imagine that she might have become ill on the way to pay homage at the shrine, and her stepmother, or someone else who despised her, may have tricked her and left her there to die. The nun worried so much about the young lady because she did nothing but lie in bed in a state of blank dejection and had yet to say anything, except for the time when she had asked them to throw her body in the river. Although the nun wished to adopt her after her recovery, her condition remained so critical that it seemed likely that the young lady would continue to waste away until she died. There was no possibility, however, that the nun would give up on the lady. She told Ajari about the dream she had one night in Hase Temple, so that he prayed for the young lady confidentially.

April and May passed by while they were praying and taking care of the lady. With no sign of improvement, the nun didn't know what to do any more. She wrote a letter to her brother.

"Please come down from the mountain one more time and help my sick lady. I think the fact she survived until today means that she is not destined to die yet at this stage of her life. Something evil must be causing her suffering. My great brother, since it is not necessary for you to go all the way down to Kyoto this time, simply coming to Ono won't be a problem, will it?"

The message made it clear to Sozu how desperate his sister was to help this lady. He thought,

"Life is such a mystery. This lady is still alive, although she would have died under the tree if we had left her there. It was no accident that I found her, but it must have been due to some bond we shared from a previous incarnation. Maybe I should at least try to help her in this life as much as I am able. If she dies after we have exerted all possible efforts, we can give up on her then, as we can never change fate."

He decided to descend the mountain once more.

His sister welcomed him with much gratitude and talked in detail about how she had been crying for the young lady for whom she felt genuine affection.

"One should look a fright when suffering from a serious illness for such a long time, but this is somehow not the case with this lady. She never looks haggard, but, surprisingly, rather beautiful. Her condition could have turned for the worse at any time, but it didn't. She is still alive."

"I remember how extraordinary she appeared at first sight. Let's see how she is."

Sozu stepped into her room.

"What a splendid figure she has. She must have been a person of great merit in her previous life to enjoy such magnificence. I cannot even imagine what she had done to ruin such a fortunate destiny. Did you catch wind of anything even remotely related to her identity or situation?"

"Not at all, but I know she is what the Goddess of Mercy brought to me."

"Even if that is true, there must be some reason for Her to have done that for you, wouldn't you agree? I don't believe that things like this happen simply by random chance."

Although the mystery still weighed on his mind, Sozu started to say a prayer.

The sister nun was worried that people outside would notice that Sozu, who would reject even the summons of the Imperial Court, had come down of his own accord to pray for some strange lady. His followers were also afraid of the resulting rumors which would tarnish his reputation. The nun, therefore, kept others out, so that no one could hear him praying. Sozu soothed his men.

"Silence please, my noble sons. Although I am a monk who has, on occasion, broken the commandments, I'm not ashamed of myself for that, and I have never been accused of nor committed a sin of a woman-related nature. I have lived for more than sixty years now. If there are still some people out there who blame me for this, I will take it as another of my fates."

One of them disagreed.

"If those who lack discretion exaggerate this into nasty and damaging gossip, the reputation of Buddhism itself is in jeopardy."

"If this endeavor fails, I will never pray again."

His decision was made with such finality that he staked his career as a noble monk on the recovery of the lady. The praying lasted all night long. At the break of dawn, he successfully transferred the evil spirit from the young lady onto another person who had agreed to accept it temporarily. Wanting to know what had caused her pain, he tried to force it to confess how all this trouble had begun. Some of his followers, including Ajari, continued to pray in turns. Then the spirit which had remained hidden for months suddenly revealed itself, screaming,

"I am not an evil to be examined by monks. Once I was a monk who practiced strict austerity, but I still had vengeance to take in this world, so that I was unable to find peace after death, wandering aimlessly around. It was then that I started to roam an area where many beautiful women lived. I took one of them away first, and I found this one next. This particular lady was holding a strong grudge against the world and was willing to die through any means possible, day or night. I carried her off in the darkness of the night when she was all alone. To my surprise, however, I discovered that this one was protected by the Goddess of Mercy, who kept interrupting my plans. In addition to her own resistance, your praying started and finally dragged me out. I will take my leave now."

Sozu asked him who he was, but the spirit wouldn't give his name, possibly because of the weakness of the possessed person.

In the freshness of the morning, the mysterious lady woke up to discover that she had regained full consciousness. She looked around to find many strange old monks with stooped backs. She became very sad, feeling like she had travelled far away to a foreign country. In searching through her memory, she found it impossible to recall where she had lived or even clearly remember her name.

"Although I remember that I threw myself into the river to be free of this world, I have no idea how I ended up here."

She tried hard to retrace her steps through the fragments of fading images in her mind.

"That night I somehow found myself caught up in a horrible state of depression, and then I opened a door to get out of the house after everyone had fallen asleep. The strong wind whipped my cheeks and the sound of the river assaulted my ears. I became so scared that I went into a panic. I stepped down from the porch, although I still didn't know which way to go: back to the room or forward toward the river. I was utterly lost. Then I made the decision to walk away from this world. I wished for anything, even a demon, to come and devour me so that I could die without the risk of being rescued. For a while, I prayed for that in the darkness of the night. Then a beautiful man approached me and I felt him actually take hold of me. I heard him say, 'Come to my side of the world, lady.' I thought he was a prince or some such nobleman, then...I lost consciousness. He disappeared and left me alone in some strange place. I cried and cried over my own misery, being unable even to end my own life.

"I cannot recall a thing after that. According to what the servants told me, it seems to have been many days since then. During my convalescence, this miserable husk that I inhabit must have been exposed to many strangers."

She felt even greater shame. Everything had gone against her intentions. The deep, interminable sadness refused to release her. She suffered from a constant sense of regret over her failure to depart this world. When she was hovering between life and death, she had eaten somewhat regularly as she would, on occasion, briefly pop back into a semi-conscious state. After her senses returned to normal, however, she resolutely refused to either eat or take medicine.

The nun nursed the young lady throughout the day without once leaving her side.

"Why do you look so unhappy? Now that the lingering fever has passed, I'm glad that your condition has significantly improved."

The ladies serving the sister nun also showed complete dedication when caring for the young lady, thinking that a woman of such distinguished beauty should enjoy her life for a much longer period of time. In spite of the fact that the young lady herself still couldn't give up her intention to commit suicide, her vitality, which brought her back into the realm of the living from her time on the edge, was so remarkable that she recovered enough to have her meals sitting up. As her condition improved, her face gradually became thinner as the swelling subsided. The nun was so glad and wished for her full recovery. One day, the lady asked the nun,

"Please let me become a nun. Otherwise I don't think I will survive."

"My poor lady, how could I allow you to do that?"

In an effort to appease her, the nun shaved the lady's hair only around the top of her head and gave her five of the basic commandments, which didn't satisfy the lady at all, but her tolerant nature didn't allow her to push the nun and ask for more. Sozu said to his sister,

"This will suffice for now. Your concern should be fully focused on her physical recovery."

He left the house and went back up to his temple.

The nun was so grateful for the opportunity to take care of someone in place of her departed daughter, that she often made the young lady sit up so that the nun could gently comb her hair. While she was ill, the lady had had her hair bound up roughly and untreated, yet once the comb went through her hair, it recovered its luster. Since the place was full of old ladies with white hair, the nun felt as if an angel from heaven had come down to live among them. At the same time, however, she became worried that she might lose the lady as suddenly and as magically as she had appeared.

"Although you know we care about you so deeply, why don't you put your trust in us and tell us more about yourself? Tell me, what was your name, from which family did you come, and how did you end up in such a strange place?"

The nun dared to ask these questions of the lady, who felt too ashamed to look up. She answered quietly,

"I have experienced a series of bizarre events. I may have permanently lost all of my memories because, at the moment, I don't remember anything about my past. The only thing that I can even vaguely recall is that I was idly looking out the window at dusk, wishing to part from this world. It was then that a man appeared from behind a large tree in the garden and took me away. Other than that, I'm not even sure who I am."

She continued pitifully,

"I dare not let anyone know that I am still alive. I sense that there will be grave consequences if anyone finds out about me."

As she burst into tears, people around understood it would be too cruel to ask her any further questions. Although there was an old tale in which an old man found a princess in a large, shining bamboo tree, she considered this lady's story to be even more mysterious. Her worry that the lady might disappear at any moment intensified and put her in a constant state of distress.

Sozu's mother was a nun of good status. His sister also used to enjoy her standing as a wife of a prince. After her husband had passed away, she had put all her love into raising her daughter so that she too could marry a great man. The daughter, however, passed away at a young age, which deprived the mother of her hope and joy for the future. In her grief, she decided to be a nun and live in a mountain village. Come rain or shine, the nun missed her daughter so much that she continually prayed to find someone in whom she could see her daughter's image, but her prayers had faded into oblivion a long time ago. Yet this young lady suddenly came into her life, a woman whose physical appearance and attitude seemed superior even to those of her deceased daughter. The nun was very happy, although it was hard to believe that it was all really happening, since they had met in such an unusual way. Despite her advanced age, the sister nun was also somewhat beautiful and exhibited an elegant character.

Here in Ono, the water flows more gently than it does in Uji where Ukifune used to live. The houses have a pleasing aesthetic quality, and the surrounding grove and its well-groomed border impart a sense of quaintness. As the autumn deepens, the more the sky touches the land. Many young female servants of the house work to harvest rice in a paddy nearby, singing some local folk songs for their amusement. The clappers rattled to scare away birds create a pleasing sound, which recalls to her the memory of a childhood spent in an eastern country.

This place is located a little closer to the heart of the mountains than the village where Lady Yugiri lived. Since one edge of this house is tucked against the mountain, the shade of the pine trees creates a gloomy darkness, and the wind blows fiercely, making a terrifying noise. The priority for the people there is to live the life of an austere Buddhist. Life just rolls slowly onward in a quiet and peaceful flow. On moonlit nights, the sister nun would play the *koto*, and a humble nun called Sho-sho would enjoy playing the traditional lute. The sister nun suggested to the lady,

"What would you say to amusing yourself by playing some kind of instrument? Otherwise you will be bored here."

Watching the elderly people gracefully and elegantly enjoying their favorite pastimes, the young lady couldn't help looking back over her past, when her unusually miserable situation wouldn't allow her to pursue any artistic accomplishments. She was so grieved and ashamed to be unable to enjoy any noble hobby because of the misfortune of her birth, that she wrote a sad poem about it.

"身を投げし　涙の川のはやき瀬を
　　しがらみかけて　誰かとどめし

(After the torrent of my tears met the river into which I threw myself, who plucked me from the current to keep me alive?)"

She blamed her fate for allowing her to be saved against her will. Being unsure about what she was going to do from this point forward, she felt tired of living, and her sense of desperation grew.

On brightly moonlit nights, old nuns happily composed poems and talked about things that had happened in their past, remembering good old days. The young lady, however, who couldn't join in the conversations, lost herself in her thoughts.

"われかくて　うき世の中にめぐるとも
　　　誰かはしらむ　月のみやこに

(Although I still inhabit this dismal world, Kyoto is none the wiser.)"

"When I decided to end my life, there were many people that I felt I would miss. Now, however, I don't think of others so often, although I worry whether my mother cries excessively over me and whether my nurse, who worked so hard to let me feel the happiness of a life felt by ordinary people, is filled with despair. I have no idea where she is, but she'll never know that I'm still alive. Once in a while, I also miss my best and only friend, Ukon. We used to talk about everything and share our darkest secrets."

Since it was hard for young women to live in the remote, quiet village, and give up worldly pleasures, there only were seven or eight very old nuns present. Sometimes, however, their daughters and grandchildren came to visit them, and some of these relatives worked in the Imperial Palace in Kyoto. The young lady took great efforts to hide herself from their eyes.

"When these people come here, I worry whether they have any contact with the people who knew me back in those days. I would feel greatly ashamed of myself if anyone should come to know about me being still alive. I'm sure they imagine that I was a person who lived the most miserable story ever."

Sozu's sister had sent two of her servants to take care of the lady. Both of them didn't look or behave anything like the ladies that she had known in the capital. She recognized, that in all aspects, that this place was far away from the world she used to live in. "It may be a good thing for me," she sighed. Seeing the young lady unwilling to meet people from Kyoto, the nun sensed her complicated history and wouldn't talk about her in detail even to those who worked in the house.

The former son-in-law of the sister nun was called Chu-sho, and one of his brothers lived on the mountain as a follower of Sozu in Yokawa. Chu-sho and his other brothers went up the mountain very often to visit their brother the monk. On the way there, Chu-sho stopped by the house for a visit. The young lady first heard the attendants of Chu-sho, and then saw the graceful man come in behind them. She remembered the figure and attitude of Commander Kaoru who used to come to Uji to visit her in secret. Although it was such a lonely place, like Uji, people here seemed to enjoy life in a simple and tasteful manner. The south side of their garden was filled with the colorful flowers of the season, into which many young men garbed in variously-hued clothes were led. Chu-sho was invited into the house. He sat down and gazed around thoughtfully. He looked to be about twenty-seven or twenty-eight years old, with a noble appearance and quite a mature attitude.

The nun met him from behind a screen placed between them. She couldn't hold back her tears.

"As time goes by, those days in the past seem so far away. While, at the same time, the strange thing is that somehow I still wait for you to visit this small village just like you did in the past."

Chu-sho said,

"Although I still feel an immense sadness and am unable to strike the memories of our time together from my mind, you live so far away from the world that I have been unable to contact you for quite a while. For that, I am deeply sorry. I visit my brother often, envying the life of a monk in the mountains, but when I have tried to visit here, there are always too many people in our party to make it possible. Today I left them all behind so that I could finally see you."

"You don't really envy the life of a monk, I think. You are just saying so because that's how young men talk these days, glorifying it. Anyway, all joking aside, I'm very proud that you are remaining resolutely true to yourself as time goes on. I also wish to thank you for continuing to value the things which happened in the past."

They served a light meal to Chu-sho and his men. Thanks to their hospitality, he felt so comfortable in the house where he used to come quite often to spend time with his wife. The rain outside made a good excuse for them to enjoy a long conversation after so many years. She had accepted that there was nothing she could do about her daughter, who had passed away at such a young age. It was rather sad for her that this great young man of such high spirits was no longer part of her family. She wished that her daughter had left some children behind as a remembrance of her. Since the nun had been secretly longing for that, she wanted to share with him all of her feelings on a rare occasion such as this.

Meanwhile, Lady Ukifune was musing over past memories, looking out the window in all her beauty and elegance. A simple white gown and dark brown trousers, which were typical garb for nuns but which she had never worn before, made her look even more tasteful in spite of their rough quality. Then she happened to overhear some ladies who worked for the sister nun.

"After feeling as if the deceased lady has come back to life, Chu-sho too came back to visit here again after many years. That makes my heart swell with happiness. It will be wonderful if he visits her here as often as he used to. I believe they will make a perfect match."

The young lady immediately dismissed such a notion to herself.

"What a silly idea! It's not even my will to be still alive, and how could I become involved in another relationship after all the troubles I've been through? If this were to happen, I would never be able to escape the past I want erased from my memory, and I would be haunted for the rest of my life."

While the sister nun was resting in her room, the guests were stuck in the house due to the unrelenting rain. While they were waiting to depart, Chu-sho recognized the voice of a nun from behind the screen, one named Sho-sho, and called her in.

"Although I have been wondering how people I knew here are, most of you may think it's ungrateful of me to have grown quite distant from this place."

Since Sho-sho had always been the one to take good care of him in days gone by, the memory of the past quietly crowded in on him, with a taste of sorrow. In the middle of their discussion, he asked her,

"When a wind blew strongly, swaying the screen, I caught a glimpse of long hair at the end of the hallway through a gap in the screens. It appeared to belong to someone quite distinguished. My eyes were affixed by the sight, which seemed very unusual to find in a place for those who had abandoned the world, and I wondered who it was."

Sho-sho was sure that he must have caught a glimpse of the young lady passing by the screen. She thought,

"If he looks at her more closely, he will certainly fall in love with her, for he has not wholly gotten over his deceased wife, who was much the inferior to this lady in terms of charm."

Upon realizing this she said to him,

"The mother of your deceased wife was still living in sorrowful memories and no one could save her from the depth of her sadness. Then recently this beautiful young lady appeared to us unexpectedly, and now we take care of her. I wonder how your eyes happened to catch sight of the lady in such a timely fashion."

Chu-sho felt delighted to hear this unexpected news. The beautiful figure of the lady that he had seen by chance flashed back clearly in his mind. He couldn't stop imagining what she would be like in person. Although he asked Sho-sho for further details, she wouldn't reveal anything and only said,

"You will find out about her sometime soon."

While he was wrestling with himself to avoid being too inquisitive, one of his men came to say that they should depart, since it had stopped raining and the sun was setting. They started organizing things so as to leave the house quickly.

Chu-sho picked up a beautiful flower in the garden and hummed an old poem to himself while standing alone in thought. He recited it in order to describe his wonder at a beautiful young lady living in a house of old nuns, as the first part of the poem expressed. The old nuns, however, translated it according to the second part, which deplored how thoughtlessly people speak, as in,

"He must be very aware of what they say."

The old nuns thought highly of him for his quaint way of putting it.

"He has grown up to be an even more flawless, sophisticated man, indeed. I hope the day will come when we welcome him to this house in marriage again."

The sister nun said to the young lady,

"Although he still visits his current wife so that he doesn't lose their connection, it seems obvious that he is not eager to see her, and in fact he often stays at his father's place instead."

The nun continued,

"To be honest with you, I feel very sad when you don't open your heart to us, still acting like a stranger. Accept the reality of your fate and enjoy it to the fullest. Even I, who have been depressed over my daughter's death for five or six years now, feel ready to get over it, thanks to the time I have spent taking care of you. There might be some people who worry about you greatly, but I'm sure they will be starting to accept that you have faded from their lives by now. Besides, whatever the situation, people don't hold onto their feelings forever."

Tears welled up in the lady's eyes.

"Although I've never meant to act like a stranger on purpose, since I survived in such a strange way, something doesn't seem right, and I feel like I'm living in a dream. I wonder if those who were reborn in another world feel like this. As you said, there may be some people out there who care about me, but I don't remember them. You are now the only person I can rely on."

The sister nun adored the lady for her innocent and lovable manner, and beamed at her in reply.

On Chu-sho's arrival at the temple, Sozu gladly welcomed him. Since it was the first time for Chu-sho to visit there in a long while, they talked at length. He stayed there that night and had a rather pleasant time listening to various forms of music being played and to the monks' beautiful voices as they read the sutras throughout the evening. He also enjoyed having an intimate conversation with his brother.

"I felt a strong sentimental attachment to Ono when I visited there early today. I have never met anyone more highly-cultured than the nun there, although she has already abandoned this world."

He continued,

"I saw a beautiful lady with long shiny hair when the wind blew through the house, disturbing a screen. Although she moved quickly away, perhaps because she was unwilling to be seen from outside, I could tell that she was someone very special. I don't think it's good to have such a beautiful young woman in that kind of place. All she sees there day and night are monks. She will get used to the situation and come to think that it is normal, and this will do her no good."

His brother told him what he knew.

"I've heard that she was found in some mysterious way when they went to Hase Temple this spring."

He couldn't speak about it in detail, though, for he was not present on that occasion. Chu-sho said,

"I feel sorry for her. I wonder what she is like. Did she grow weary of this world and move there to hide herself? It sounds like something out of an old fairy tale."

On the following day, since Chu-sho didn't want to pass by the house in Ono without saying a word, he stopped over again on the way back to Kyoto. People there had been expecting him. They welcomed him as they used to in days past. Sho-sho, took care of him as a proper nun should. He noticed that the color of her sleeves, which were refined, had become more elegant than they were in the past. The sister nun became even more emotional, looking at the two of them. Chu-sho asked her casually,

"Who is the person that seems to be living here, keeping out of others' sight?"

Although the sister nun thought it could cause some trouble, it didn't seem wise to keep hidden what he had seen with his own eyes, so she told him,

"We have been taking care of her here for several months now. She is a relief for me, to be free from a sense of guilt about the death of my daughter, from which, I'm sure you know, I have been suffering from for years. I'm not sure why, but she looks depressed, so full of troubles and afraid of letting anyone know that she is still alive. I have thought that in a place like this no one would be interested in searching for her. At any rate, I wonder how you found out about her."

"Maybe it was just a random thought, which occurred to me as I was traveling here this time, but since I passed over the mountains to reach your household, don't you think I deserve something for my effort? If you think of the lady as your daughter, you shouldn't keep me out of all of this, as if I have nothing to do with it. What made her hate this world so much? I'd like to ease her feelings somehow," said Chu-sho, being curious about her circumstances.

As he departed, he handed Sho-sho a message for the lady which read,

> "あだし野の風になびくな女郎花
>
> われしめ結はん道とほくとも
>
> (Do not ride on the wind to another's arms. No matter how far the capital, our ties are strong.)"

The sister nun read it and said to the lady,

"You should certainly reply. That man is highly refined and I'm sure that any response would be welcome."

The lady, however, refused to do so, claiming that her calligraphy was poor. The sister nun gave up and took up her pen instead, so as not to be impolite.

"As I have already told you, she is unworldly, unlike other ladies.

> うつし植えて思ひ乱れぬ女郎花
>
> うき世をそむく草の庵に
>
> (This flower that I have transplanted to our hermitage remains

unstable and hides itself away from the secular world.)"

Chu-sho understood and left the house.

The image of the lady was constantly on his mind, although it seemed a little embarrassing for him to write a love letter at his age. Not knowing what caused her suffering, he found himself helplessly attracted to her. He called at the house around the tenth of August, on the occasion of a falconry trip. He called in Sho-sho as he always did and said,

"My mind has not been at peace since I first saw that lady."

As it seemed most unlikely that the lady would reply to that type of sentiment, the sister nun spoke jokingly from behind the screen on her behalf.

"Just like an old story relates, 'Even when a woman refuses to get close to anyone, she will be someone else's in the autumn.'"

When he spoke with the sister nun face to face, he was unable to hide his utter infatuation.

"I'd like to know more about this lady and her depression. I, myself, also feel that nothing is right with this world and I wish I could live in the mountains, but thinking of my parents, who would never agree to such a course of action, I don't think it's realistically possible, so I'm still a man of the secular world. Whether due to my melancholic nature, I don't believe I am capable of getting along with those who are free of doubts about this world and enjoy it recklessly. I'd like a lady with a critical view toward life with whom to share my feelings."

The sister nun talked as if she had been her mother.

"If you want someone pessimistic, she may not be a bad match for you. However, she hates this world so much that she is completely unwilling to become intimate with anyone. Even an old lady like myself was very afraid when I abandoned my former life and became a nun. I worry about the young lady because she still has a lot of life to live."

The sister nun went back inside after her meeting with Chu-sho and spoke to the lady.

"You are acting too disrespectfully, young lady. Say something at least. As a person who lives with us in this kind of place, you have to learn to respect others' feelings, even when you think they aren't worthy of being heard. That's the way of life."

The lady answered in an abrupt manner while lying down,

"I don't know how to speak to others, and besides, I act clumsily with everything and everyone."

Chu-sho sighed wistfully.

What are you saying now? I'm very disappointed to know that what you promised me, citing the old story, was just a trick.

"松虫の声をたづねて来つれども
　　また荻原の露にまどひぬ

(Although I came here upon the voices of autumn insects, your rejection leaves me stranded here, soaked in the dew of the grass.)"

The sister nun laid the blame on the lady, feeling sorry for Chu-sho, and asking her to respond, even just this once. The lady, however, was reluctant to even feign interest in him. Besides, she knew this wouldn't be the last time she would be expected to attend to him kindly. If she uttered even a single word to him, it seemed quite probable that he would fabricate reasons to stop here regardless of the occasion and she would be forced to see him over and over. That was what had prevented her from responding from the outset. Although everyone else was very disappointed by her reaction, the sister nun, who used to enjoy modern life, answered for the lady with an impromptu poem of elegant taste.

"秋の野の露わけきたる狩衣
　　むぐらしげれる宿にかこつな

(Beating your way through the dewy undergrowth, you must have soaked your hunting gown through. Please don't blame this lodging for the surrounding brush.)

This is what the lady said. I believe she doesn't feel the same way as you."

Hearing that, the other nuns felt almost like pushing the lady out from behind the screen out of adoration for this man who had made the sister nun's deceased daughter so happy when they were together. The lady, for her part, was worried about how painful it would be to have it known that she was still alive, contrary to her will. Unaware of her concerns, they eagerly suggested to her,

"Even if you speak with him once or twice on a casual occasion like this, we are sure that he will respect your feelings and ask for nothing more if you show that you are not receptive to his advances. Don't be so obstinate, and make a show of goodwill by saying at least something to him in return."

Watching the old nuns, who had abandoned the secular world but were still victims of their old habits as they composed mundane poems and behaved like young girls, the lady found them untrustworthy. Although she had once decided to give up on this world, her life had unexpectedly been saved. Picturing how miserably she would live from this point forward, she lay in bed despairing of her future. She didn't want any attention from anyone, but just wanted to be forgotten. At the same time, Chu-sho also gave a deep sigh indicating that something was bothering him, and he began to softly play the flute. His atmosphere, which became even more apparent when he muttered a beautiful poem to himself, revealed to her his excellent character. The man lingeringly said,

"Although it still hurts to remember those days, there seems to be no one new to love me. Either way, I'm not wise enough to lose my hope for another love."

He then prepared to depart, but the sister nun tried to dissuade him.

"Why do you have to leave so early on this stunning night with the beautiful moon hanging high in the sky?"

"I should go. I now fully understand that the lady isn't interested," he said as he shook her off coldly, thinking,

"I don't think it's a good idea for me to play the role of a womanizer any longer. I came all this way to see the lady whom I merely caught a glimpse of the other day, hoping that she would heal my broken heart,

which is no one's responsibility but my own. However, I was greatly disappointed by her stiff, unfriendly attitude toward me, which was quite a shock to find in a mountain village such as this."

The sister nun didn't like to see him off, missing even the sound of his flute playing.

"ふかき夜の月をあはれと見ぬ人や
　　　　山の端ちかき宿にとまらぬ

(Do you not understand the beauty of the midnight moon? You choose not to rest here at the end of the mountains.)"

She composed this somewhat rough poem on the spur of the moment and told him that it was written by the lady. Chu-sho was delighted and answered,

"山の端に入るまで月を眺め見ん
　　　　閨の板間もしるしありやと

(I will gaze at the moon until it sinks beneath the mountains, wishing to get closer to you, like shafts of moonlight shining into a bedroom through gaps in the old roof.)"

The mother nun heard the sound of his flute and came out of her room.

The great nun's trembling speech was peppered with frequent coughs. She didn't discuss things from the past, as she probably couldn't even recall the name of the man in front of her.

"Play the *koto* for me please. The flute also sounds elegant on a moonlit night such as this. Come on, what's the matter? Prepare her instrument at once."

Although Chu-sho correctly discerned that she must be the grandmother of his ex-wife from the way she spoke to the others, he became emotionally overwhelmed by the unfairness of life, wondering why this very old lady could survive to this day while his ex-wife had to die so young. Chu-sho played the flute admirably, and then prompted the sister nun to play the *koto*. She was also quite an accomplished musician and would complement him perfectly.

"Even though my ears only hear the wind from the hills, this is not the only reason why your music sounds so beautiful tonight."

Then the sister nun started playing, worrying whether or not it would still be pleasing. The instrument she used had fallen out of fashion, which made it sound all the more exceptional and sentimental. The sound of the wind flowing through the trees accentuated the quality of the music. Since Chu-sho played so well alongside the sister nun's *koto*, it seemed like even the moonlight had taken up the melody in an affectionate embrace. The mother nun was so moved that she stayed up much later than her daily routine allowed.

"Although I was also a disciple of the eastern *koto* when I was young, they may view the instrument differently these days. My son once told me that it was not very pleasant to listen to my playing, and I subsequently abandoned my passion. Tonight, after so many years, I remembered how beautiful it sounds."

It could be clearly seen in her face that the great nun wanted to play it herself. Chu-sho smiled quietly.

"Well, your son must not have had any idea of what he was saying. They say that in a place called heaven, everyone from Bodhisattvas to the Gods plays music and enjoys dancing, which is considered most dignified behavior. It is not viewed as either a dereliction of your austerity or the committing of a sin. I'd love to have the honor of listening to your playing tonight."

His flattery lifted her spirits to such a degree that she asked a servant to fetch her *koto*, still coughing quite frequently. Although other people thought it was shameful of her to take the flattery seriously, they didn't interrupt her because they felt sorry for her situation, one in which she felt it necessary to even complain about her own son, Sozu. The eastern *koto* was brought to the mother nun and she started playing it; she didn't play in concert with Chu-sho's flute but enjoyed playing by herself as she liked. As the sounds of the other instruments faded away, the mother nun thought it was because they attended to her music too intensely to keep playing themselves. Her skill was surely impressive. She plucked the strings up and down fluidly, and all the lyrics she sang were sweet and traditional. Chu-sho applauded her.

"The song's lyrics are no longer popular, but you interpreted them marvelously."

As the great nun couldn't catch his words, she asked a person nearby what he said and answered,

"It seems that young people of today don't enjoy this kind of music at all. One young lady, though beautiful, has stayed here for a while, but she doesn't seem to enjoy any form of pleasure. All she does is hide herself in her room."

Sitting next to her mother, who was talking loudly, as if she knew everything in this world, the sister nun was feeling nervous. Thus Chu-sho's passion was spoiled, and he set off for home. While his party proceeded down the mountain road, people in the hermitage stayed up late, enjoying the superb notes of his flute floating down the hill with the wind.

The next morning, a message from Chu-sho arrived.

"I am sorry for leaving in such a hurry because of the great distraction within myself.

忘られぬむかしのことも笛竹の
　　つらきふしにも音ぞ泣かれける

(On top of my memories refusing to release me, the lady ignored my passion entrusted in the music and treated me coldly. I couldn't help but howl last night.)

Would you please talk to her and encourage her to understand my feelings, if only to be polite? You must know that there would be no way I could beg such a shameful favor of you if I were capable of restraining myself."

Having read it, the sister nun was left in a daze and replied to him,

"笛の音にむかしのこともしのばれて
　　かへりしほども袖ぞ濡れにし

(The sound of the flute reminded me of my deceased daughter.

Even after you departed, my sleeves were bathed in tears.)

I imagine that now you know how indifferent this lady is to others' feelings, as was expressed in our old nun's story."

Contrary to his expectations, he received another letter written by the sister nun, which was such a great disappointment to him that he could seem to do nothing but ignore it.

The lady was fed up with the letters from him coming in as often as the leaves made sounds in the yard. This reminded her afresh of how blindly men can be possessed by the idea of love, just like those times when she had learned about it for the first time. Rejecting more flashbacks of memories of the past, she prayed even while she learned the sutra with other nuns.

"Please make me a true nun, so that men will give up on me and stop all of this foolishness."

People saw her despairing of the world outside in every way and that she was not interested in things such as fashion, like normal young ladies were. Although they all thought that she was a person of a timid and gloomy nature, they overlooked all complaints about her because it was their pleasure to adore her flawless countenance. On the rare occasions when the young lady showed her smile, they felt very happy and grateful to witness it.

As it had turned to September, the sister nun traveled to Hase Temple to pay homage. After many years spent in deep despair over the loss of her daughter, her sorrow had finally been lifted by the arrival of the lady into her life, a lady who hadn't seemed like a stranger to the nun even during their first encounter. Thus, she was more thankful than ever to Kannon, the Goddess of Mercy, for her grace. Not surprisingly, she tried to persuade the lady to accompany her.

"Why don't you come with us? I'm sure that no one would catch even the slightest hint of this. Although there's no difference in that we pray to the same Buddha, they say that it will bring you more miraculous benefits and a more fruitful fortune to serve as an ascetic in a highly venerable place such as Hase Temple."

The lady rejected the invitation, for her mother and nurse used to say the same thing and often took her there, although all those wishes had resulted in nothing, and what was worse, she had even failed to end her own life and had to endure greater hardship as a result. Knowing that life would always treat her harshly no matter what she prayed for, she didn't think it was worth traveling with people she didn't know that well in order to wish for a better future. She turned down the nun's offer with a gentle excuse.

"Since I don't feel quite well these days, I'm not sure if I will be able to travel that far."

The sister nun instinctively sensed that she wasn't being sincere, but since she understood that the lady should be too afraid to pass by the mountain village where she had been possessed by some evil spirit, the nun didn't press the issue.

It was then that the nun found a poem composed by the lady lying among some waste papers she had left in the room after her calligraphy practice, which read,

"はかなくて世にふる川の浮き瀬には
たづねもゆかじ二本の杉

(Since I'm still alive simply because my will had wavered, I don't think visiting Hase River and its two standing cedars will do me any good.)"

The sister nun read it and joked about it.

"By 'two standing cedars,' you must be suggesting that you have someone whom you really want to see again. I remember that expression implies a situation where two lovers or longtime friends reunite with each other after a long absence in an old poem."

As the joke betrayed what she had insinuated correctly, she blushed, being startled, which showed them how hearty and lovable she was still. The sister nun expressed herself in a simple, indifferent poem, which went,

　"ふる川の杉のもとだち知らねども
　　　過ぎにし人によそへてぞみる

(Although I know nothing of your past, you carry me back to
better days when my daughter was with me like you are now.)"

She didn't anticipate finding many traveling companions from among
the residents of the village to accompany her to Hase Temple. Despite her
expectations, however, most of the people living there were quite willing
to travel with her. Since there was some worry about leaving the young
lady in the house alone, the sister nun asked Sho-sho, an old lady called
Saemon, and a young girl to stay and serve the lady in their absence.

Having seen them off, the lady felt totally lost without the only person
she had come to rely on by her side. Even when faced with her miserable
situation, she reluctantly accepted it, for it was obvious that there was
nothing she could do. Then Sho-sho brought her a letter from Chu-sho
which had just been delivered to the house. No matter how many times
Sho-sho recommended that she open it, she wouldn't do so. The house
was inert from the lack of liveliness, the atmosphere was sadly vacant, and
the lady was even more depressed, feeling dismay about her future. Sho-
sho tried to reinvigorate the lady.

"Seeing you like this, I feel like your sadness is crawling upon me too.
What do you say we play a game of *go* or something else, just for fun?"

Although the lady turned down her offer at first, saying that she was
not so skilled, she gradually changed her mind and finally agreed. Sho-
sho gave an early lead to the lady, in expectation of her advantage in skill,
yet the lady won a clear victory. She started another game, but with the
lead on her side this time.

"I wish the sister nun had already returned. We have to play it in her
presence because she has always been the best player. Once the great
Sozu loved *go* and also was very confident of his skill, admitting to himself
that he was a legendary virtuoso of the game. He boasted to the sister
nun, saying things like, 'Although it's not my intention to show off my

skills too much, I will never lose against you' and words to that effect. As a result, however, Sozu lost against her two times in a row. You must be a better player than the legendary Sozu. How brilliant, indeed."

As Sho-sho was greatly impressed, the lady grew regretful, watching the middle-age nun before her behaving like an uncultured person, dabbling in a troublesome situation where she would be matched up with the sister nun. Then she went to bed claiming to feel ill. Sho-sho was a little offended since the lady hadn't appreciated her effort to try and cheer her up.

"You should do something purely for fun sometimes, because I think it's such a shame that you stay depressed like this, making the least of being young. It seems that there is a fly in your ointment."

The lady composed a poem inspired by the sound of the evening wind, which triggered memories of the past.

"心には秋の夕をわかねども
　　　　ながむる袖に露ぞみだるる

(It is impossible in my heart to fully understand the melancholy of autumn evenings, although tears trickle down my sleeves, lost in thought.)"

In the splendid moonlight, Chu-sho visited the house on the same day his letter was received. The lady hid herself inside the house since she was quite reluctant to welcome him. Sho-sho tried to persuade her to come out and attend the man.

"That is too much of a discourtesy. You should at least understand the fact that he has made all this effort to come here just to see you. Give him a chance and listen to him for a minute. I think it's silly to fear that showing him the slightest favor would invariably result in an undesirable relationship."

The lady was still so alarmed that a messenger was sent to apologize to Chu-sho, saying that she had gone on a trip with the others. Chu-sho, however, knew that the lady had been left there alone, possibly from the messenger who delivered his letter in the afternoon. His displeasure was obvious, and he grumbled for quite a long while.

"If you don't care to, I won't force you to talk to me. I'd just like to speak to you once directly, and it is fine with me if you never wish to speak to me again. The decision is yours."

In spite of his persuasive messages, the lady didn't respond at all. He had no other path left to take, so he said,

"How cruel. I imagined a man would gain deep insight into emotions felt in various aspects of one's life. This is far from the way I expected to be treated here."

In leaving, he left a taunting letter.

"山里の秋の夜ふかきあはれをも
　　　　もの思ふ人は思ひこそ知れ

(A man sunk in thoughts would understand even emotions welling up from deep inside in the calm evening of a mountain village.)

Therefore you should have known how I feel about you already."

Sho-sho begged the lady to write him back.

"Now that the great nuns are away, no one can deal with the situation calmly like they do. If we let him go like this, we will seem to be hopelessly heartless and unkind."

The lady wrote a random line, not intending it as a response to Chu-sho.

"うきものと思ひも知らですぐす身を
　　　　もの思う人と人は知りけり

(How could you tell that I am one of those sunk in thoughts, when you know nothing of my past?)"

Sho-sho heard the lady mutter her poem out loud and relayed what she had heard to Chu-sho. On hearing it, he found it impossible to hold back his frustration and asked Sho-sho for a chance to see her immediately, in a manner so desperate that those who were around him were confused as to what to say.

"Her resistance towards re-entering the outside world is as unyielding as stone."

So said Sho-sho, and left the room to search for her. Then she found that the lady had shut herself in the mother nun's room, the door to which she had never even approached before. Sho-sho was completely taken aback by her rude behavior. She explained the situation to Chu-sho, her voice full of apology.

"Well, when I think about the fact that a young lady such as her has locked herself away in this isolated mountain village, I can get a sense of how sad she must be and I feel sorry for her. We can all see that she must originally have been an intelligent person capable of understanding others' feelings, although now she is acting like an ignorant girl or maybe worse, which is quite a shame. I wonder if this is because of some bitter experience from a previous relationship. Do you have any idea what caused these changes in her, what made her give up hope on others?"

Despite his intention to make the question sound as light as possible, a strong desire for digging further into her past could be seen in his eyes.

"All I know is that she had been separated from the sister nun, who had been in charge of taking care of her for some reason. They happened to find each other again when the nun traveled to Hase Temple and they decided to take the lady home with them."

Sho-sho spoke cautiously, recognizing that her answer was far from what his curiosity demanded.

The lady was lying face down in the room of the old mother nun, who she had been afraid of from the stories she had heard, being unable to sleep. Not only was the mother nun, who had been sleeping since early in the evening, snoring loudly, but her performance was accompanied by that of two other old nuns, as if there were some kind of bizarre competition taking place. The lady was terrified that they might eat her tonight if she fell asleep. In spite of her reluctance to linger in this world, she felt uneasy, like the man in the well-known tale who retraced his way back home because he couldn't cross the log bridge due to his cowardly nature.

Although a girl called Komoki had come with the lady to the room, as it was natural for a teenage girl to show interest in a rare male visitor, she had left to return to the part of the house where Chu-sho was currently waiting. The lady anxiously waited for the girl to return, knowing that it was all so uncertain.

No matter how hard Chu-sho tried, the lady wouldn't respond to his advances. Finally he gave up on meeting her and returned home in disappointment. Sho-sho complained about her behavior.

"She never considers the feelings of others or opens herself up to them. It's such a shame for a beautiful lady like her."

Almost all the people in the house slept in the same room that night for their own security.

Around midnight, the mother nun coughed herself into a half-waking state. Under the firelight, her white hair looked quite eerie, partially covered as it was by a black cowl. She found the lady lying on her belly, and asked, with a hand raised to her own forehead,

"How strange. Who is this?"

Her fixed gaze and way of speaking reminded Ukifune of a weasel and terrified her so much that her thoughts ran wild.

"When I was kidnapped by a demon, I felt no fear as I wasn't really conscious during the ordeal. What should I do this time? Since coming back to life from a rather ragged state, I have recovered a reasonably normal degree of health. Exactly for this reason, however, the peace I had finally achieved in my mind has started to be unraveled by past memories, and now this world forces me to devote myself to dealing with annoying and frightening things. Of course if I had died that day, I would be in hell with demons, which would be even more dreadful than this."

Staying awake all night, the lady looked back on her whole life, in which she could only see all the miseries she had gone through, thinking,

"I've never seen the face of the man I've been told is my father. Growing up, I lived in the far eastern region for years. I had an opportunity to become engaged to a great man and lead a new life not far from my father, although I was eventually forced to depart without uttering a word, even to my sister, due to an unexpected incident. Commander Kaoru was to take me as a wife, which would have helped me avoid many problems down the road, even though he was the one who had installed me in a quiet village. I was prepared to accept his kindness to make up for all the disgraces I had suffered before. It was then, however, that I became regrettably attracted to Prince Niou, which turned out to be the fatal mistake of my life. Looking back over this series of events, the reason why I am in the condition I am today is clearly due to the Prince and the fact that I thought I loved him once. Now I have no idea why I was so impressed by the Prince when he swore his eternal devotion by comparing his love for me to an evergreen island."

She hated herself for having taken the Prince's seduction for a form of love. Every time she came to think about the Commander who, in contrast, behaved serenely from the first, her appreciation of him and her reminiscence grew stronger than ever.

"If the Commander comes to know that I am still alive, that will be the greatest humiliation of all. A small but solid hope that one day I'll have the honor to see him again, even though I will stay out of his sight, still lingers somewhere in my mind. However, I understand that it is inappropriate to hold onto such a hope, and I shouldn't waste my time imagining things like this."

In her conflicted emotional state, she continued to think about him.

Finally, the lady felt such relief that the night had ended upon hearing a rooster crow loudly. The voices of the birds outside made her wonder how happy she would have been if they were instead the voice of her mother. Even the rays of the morning sun couldn't brighten up her gloom. She was hoping to return to her own room immediately, although she was stuck lying on her belly in the old nun's room because the young female servant who was to accompany her hadn't yet returned. The snorers woke up at dawn or possibly earlier, cooking a variety of unappetizing dishes like porridge made of rice. They recommended those dishes as if they were some kind of a feast, and moved in closer to offer breakfast to the lady, saying,

"Come on. You have to eat something."

Although she was frustrated by the officiousness of the elderly nuns and felt the worst ever inside, she politely refused their offer, by reason of feeling ill, which only resulted in showing how inconsiderate they were, for they still pushed her to eat even after hearing her excuse.

Then a number of lower-ranked monks came down to the house and told the people there that Sozu would descend the mountain that day. One of them asked,

"But why, all of a sudden?"

"Well, Princess Ippon was possessed by an evil spirit, and no matter how many times the great chief priest of Enryaku Temple has performed incantations and prayed, there seems to have been no sign of their efficacy. This is why they sent Sozu a second invitation, and the director general climbed up the mountain to visit us late last night to hand Sozu a letter from the Empress. As a result, he is planning to descend the mountain today."

The monks told the story in a quite dramatized way. The lady decided to meet Sozu, making herself as bold as she could be, to ask him for permission to become a real nun on this rare occasion when so few meddlesome people were about. She woke up and told the old mother nun,

"As I still feel very ill, I'd like to have Sozu give me all the commandments so that I may become a real nun. Could you please tell him that?"

The senile old nun only nodded while staring woodenly ahead.

Back in her room, the lady called on a servant to comb her hair like the sister nun always did. At first, she hesitated to ask someone else to do it, since delegating that type of task meant allowing someone to touch her hair, but she had to endure it, telling the servant to brush her hair as little as possible. The only regret she had was that she couldn't show her beautiful hair to her mother once again prior to becoming a nun. Although she was thinner than before because of her continual suffering, her nearly-two-meter-long hair still held a fine, beautiful sheen throughout its entire length. The flow of her hair was flawless and gorgeous to behold. The lady sat still while whispering old poems to herself, sayingthings like, "My mother never stroked my lustrous hair in the hope that I would become a nun."

In the evening, Sozu came down from the mountain. They had prepared a place for him to stay in the southern part of the compound. The atmosphere of the house had been drastically changed, with a number of shaven-headed priests here and there. It was somewhat frightening to see it in such an unusual state.

Sozu visited his mother's room.

"How have you been doing lately, mother? I've heard the sister nun is away to pay homage at the temple. Is the young lady from before still here?"

The mother nun replied,

"Yes, she is. Actually she expects you to confer the commandments on her to become a nun."

Sozu asked his mother's leave and went to the lady's room.

"Are you in?"

When he asked this, sitting right outside the room screen, the lady drew closer to the translucent rice paper and nervously responded that she was there. Sozu continued,

"Although we found each other in the least expected way, I did my best to pray for your recovery because I knew that an encounter of that kind couldn't have occurred without an extraordinary twist of fate stemming from a previous karmic relationship between us. I have been a stranger to you, but it was only because my position doesn't allow me to make contact with a woman without a specific reason. How goes your life spent with those unsightly old nuns?"

"Well, first of all, I am very grateful that you saved my life and took care of me throughout my ordeal. At the same time, however, since I had previously sworn to take my own life, I still feel ashamed of myself for lingering in this world. It is clear that I'll never be able to live like others. Could you please grant me the opportunity to spend the remainder of my days as a nun? No matter what happens, I can no longer continue to live the life of an ordinary woman."

Sozu tried to convince her otherwise by saying,

"How can you be so sure that becoming a nun at such an early age is the right choice? It will only lead you to a state of further confusion. I know that you hold your morals very firmly at the moment, and you will stick to them over time. In the case of female priests, however, their morals tend to collapse into decay with age."

The lady desperately insisted on the rightness of her decision.

"I have experienced such a string of unfortunate events since I was a child that my parents seriously considered leaving me in a convent. Sometimes they even told me that I should probably be a nun. Now that I understand things better, I have already given up on being happy like others in this world, but instead I hold a hope deep in my heart for a peaceful life in the next life. Possibly because of the approach of my death, I feel more and more fragile these days. I strongly believe that my time is coming."

She begged thus with tears in her eyes.

Sozu pondered her words carefully.

"I don't understand why this splendid lady blessed with such beauty came to despise her own life. Come to think of it, the evil spirit said something to that effect. In any case, there must be some reason behind her decision. In the first place, she wasn't meant to still be alive today. As the evil spirit found her so easily, something unfortunate could happen unless we take steps to protect her."

Sozu finally accepted her request and said,

"No matter what happened to you in the past, your decision has been made, which is a truly praiseworthy deed, and as a priest it is not my right to oppose it. Although I'm pleased to give you the commandments, today I descended the mountain due to urgent business. I must go to Princess Ippon before dawn, for incantations and prayers for her are starting tomorrow, and they will last for seven days. I promise that I will come back here after that, and we can have your ceremony then."

The lady could easily expect the sister nun's interference on her return. She needed to avoid such an incident.

"I have been ill for a long while. Now that my vigor is fading away, if I get any worse, even the commandments won't be able to keep me going. I thought today was really my only chance."

Watching her crying out thus, the warm-hearted monk felt very sorry for her.

"I guess it's getting late into the night. It didn't used to bother me to go down the mountain, but as the years pass, it's become quite an effort. That is why I came here, to take a break before heading out to the palace in Kyoto. But if you require it so urgently, I will perform the ceremony at once."

The lady felt a great wave of relief wash over her upon hearing that. Then she took out a pair of scissors and laid them on the lid of a box. Sozu called in a pair of monks. As the two who were the first to find her were in attendance, he let them in and ordered them to comb her hair out. The monks felt that it was no wonder that the lady was uncomfortable with living like everybody else since she had gone through such an unusual ordeal. They took her wish to be a nun as a natural course of affairs, although the hair they could see from around the end of the screen was too beautiful to cut without regret. Holding the scissors, they discovered that they were unable to proceed so easily.

Meanwhile, Sho-sho was in her room to see her brother, who had come down the mountains to accompany Sozu. As each of the nuns there attended to their guests as courteously as they could in the small village, the only attendant the lady had around her was Komoki, the young female servant. When she came to report what was happening, Sho-sho rushed into the lady's room. Sozu had let the lady wear some of his clothes to prepare for the sudden ceremony.

"Worship in the direction of your parents," he said.

The lady didn't know which direction to face and burst into tears. Sho-sho chided Sozu,

"How could you be so unreasonable as to do this? It's going to be a big problem when your sister returns."

He calmed Sho-sho down by telling her that once things had come this far, it was not wise to upset the lady in a vain attempt to stop the proceedings. She had to accept that it was impossible for her to get closer to the lady and put an end to the whole process.

While Sozu was reciting a sacred poem in the ceremony, the lady felt a deep sadness, remembering what she went through in her life, although she had already given up on the emotion of love. Ajari, a follower of Sozu, cut her hair, hesitating greatly while completing the job. He finally said,

"Please take the time to finish it off later with the help of other nuns."

The hair on her forehead was cut off by the hand of Sozu himself.

"Blessed with beautiful charms, do not regret your decision to be a nun."

Then he passed on to her the venerable teachings of Buddhism. The lady was so delighted to have finally become a nun, after hoping to for so many years. Everyone used to convince her to give up on the idea and there had seemed to be no chance for her to do it. Now, for the first time, she felt life was worth living indeed, bringing her so much joy.

Sozu and his men left the house for Kyoto, and silence once more held sway over the house. Hearing the sound of the night breeze, Sho-sho continued to try to convince the lady of the folly of her choice.

"I had been waiting for your recovery patiently, telling myself that you would be fine in time, and the day would soon arrive when true happiness would visit you. What in the world are you going to do with

your life from now on? Even old people feel very sad to give up everything when they become nuns."

The lady was happy, however, that she had finally achieved peace of mind. She was free from concern over how she could live in the secular world. She enjoyed the sense of thankfulness, and felt like a huge weight had been lifted off her shoulders.

The following morning, the lady hesitated to appear in front of others. Since the ceremony had taken place without anyone's permission, it seemed embarrassing for her to let them see her new appearance. Her hair splayed out at the end, being uneven in length. She wished to have someone organize the mess without scolding her for what she had done. All she could do was to dim the lights in the room, so that no one could see her clearly. Being the kind of person who didn't express herself to others, she had no one to talk with openly. When she tired from thinking too much, she escaped by devoting herself to calligraphy practice.

> "亡きものに身をも人をも思ひつつ
>
> 棄ててし世をぞさらに棄てつる

(Leaving who I was and the one I used to love behind, I again surrendered the world which I had once abandoned.)

Now I have finally tied up all the loose strands of my life," she wrote in one of her works. Reading it made her heart ache with sadness. Another poem read similarly,

> "限りぞと思ひなりにし世の中を
>
> かへすがへすもそむきぬるかな

(I once gave up on this world, and now am forever turning my back on it.)"

While the lady was creating these calligraphic poems, a letter from Chu-sho arrived. As the lady's unexpected conversion was still a shock to the people in the house, they relayed the details to him in their reply. Chu-sho was greatly disappointed to hear that.

"The reason why she wouldn't accept me in the first place must have been that she had already made up her mind to leave the secular world.

behind. Even so, how insipidly things have come to pass. The other night, when I asked her to let me see her beautiful hair more closely, Sho-sho answered instead, "Not tonight, but possibly on some more appropriate occasion."

He couldn't hide his dismay and replied at once.

"I don't really know what to say.

> 岸とほく漕ぎはなるらむあま舟に
> 　　　　乗り遅れじといそがるるかな

(As you are steering yourself so fast towards the other side of the water, I feel hastened to your side so as not to be left behind.)"

This time the lady read the letter word by word Then her sense of serenity reminded her that everything had ended. As usual, she expressed her feelings in verse.

> "心こそうき世の岸をはなるれど
> 　　　　行く方も知らぬあまのうき木を

(Even though my mind has floated far away from this tiresome world, my life still seems like a piece of directionless driftwood.)"

Sho-sho folded the lady's poetic response to send it to Chu-sho. Although the lady asked Sho-sho to copy her script more neatly, she mailed the original for fear of duplicating it incorrectly. Chu-sho received a proper reply from the lady for the first time. This brief happiness soon added more sadness to the fact that he had to give her up.

Those who had gone to Hase Temple returned. They were all shocked. The sister nun couldn't even stand due to her great dismay, and she cried out, writhing on the floor,

"I know that as a nun I should be happy for you now, but do you have any idea how you are going to get through the rest of your life which still stretches so far before you? Since I don't have much time left to live, I had been trying to figure out what I could do for you so that you could live in peace after my passing. In searching for an answer, I also prayed a lot to Buddha."

The lady thought of her mother, who must have cried like the sister nun when the lady disappeared without a trace, which made her feel sadder than ever. Sitting down with her back turned and not responding to others as usual, she seemed to be blooming with youth and loveliness. The sister nun started preparing clothes for the lady, although she couldn't help but express her discontent.

"You should learn how to appreciate others."

Since the sister nun was used to tailoring dark gray clothes for nuns, it didn't take much time for her to make a few new sets of clothing. The other nuns helped the sister nun sew the dresses and fit them for the lady. They didn't hide their disappointment, saying,

"We had faith that you would be our sunshine to lighten up this small mountain village. What a great shame."

They continued talking along these lines and eventually ended up complaining about Sozu.

With the participation of Sozu, the condition of Princess Ippon improved in all aspects. Just as one of his followers once said, the prayers of this monk must have contained something special as they were capable of curing illness completely. Owing to this achievement, his reputation rose greatly. Even after her dramatic recovery, the Princess was in need of attentive care. Since the incantations and prayers were to continue for a while, Sozu was unable to return back home and had to remain there for some time. One quiet rainy night, he was ordered by the Empress to stand watch over the condition of her daughter. The female servants were so tired from working around the clock for days that they all went back to their rooms to rest. There weren't many people with the Empress that night, and even fewer people were awake. The Empress was by the bed of Princess Ippon as she said,

"Although we have trusted you for so many years, my faith in you grew so much more this time that I swear I'll be counting on you for the rest of my life."

Sozu replied,

"These years Buddha has told me that there isn't much time left for me. So I was worried that I wouldn't be able to survive these last few years. That is why I decided to stay away from the world outside to concentrate on performing incantations. Although I have hidden myself deep in the mountains, I descended the mountain in response to your urgent request."

Sozu was telling the Empress how formidable the evil spirits were, about a case where a number of evil spirits appeared at one time, along with other similar stories. Then he started talking about what had happened recently.

"I happened across an unbelievably rare occurrence the other day. Last March, my aged mother finally realized her long-time dream of visiting Hase Temple to pay homage and pray. On the way back home, they dropped in on a place in Uji to stay for the night. Since a big palace which has been left empty for a long time always has some nasty spirits associated with it, I was worried that her serious illness might be worsened under their influence. Then, as I expected...."

He told her everything he had seen. The Empress became frightened upon hearing the story.

"That is quite unusual, indeed."

She realized that all the lady servants in the room had fallen asleep. Being terrified by Sozu's story, she woke them up immediately. Lady Kosaisho, a close friend of Commander Kaoru's, was also there listening to the story, yet the other ladies hadn't heard a word. Sozu saw in the face of the Empress that he had frightened her greatly and stopped short of supplying any more details.

"Actually, the lady had wished so desperately to become a nun that, when I stopped over in Ono on the way here, she tearfully begged me to give her the ten commandments. As she convincingly expressed her convictions, I accepted her request and cut her hair. But the problem is that my sister, who had been married to the late Emon-no-Kami, is now also a nun, and she has gladly taken good care of this lady as somewhat of a surrogate for her deceased daughter. She is angry at me by now for what I have done. This lady is so graceful, with such dignity and beauty that I often wonder about her origins."

Due to his chatty nature, the story never seemed to end. Lady Kosaisho asked him,

"Why was such a noble lady in a place like that? Well, you've discovered her identity by now, haven't you?"

"No, I haven't. But she might have told others by now. If she were originally high in status, how would it be possible to keep her background secret? There are certainly some beautiful ladies of her caliber in the countryside as well. If she is from an average family, she must have committed very little sin in a previous incarnation to deserve the beauty she's received in this one."

It reminded the Empress of a story of a lady who disappeared near Uji at around the same time. Lady Kosaisho was serving in the room and had also heard of a rumor from her sister that a young lady had died an unnatural death. Although she suspected the lady they were discussing was the missing one, she said nothing since there was no evidence to support her assumptions.

"The lady often says that she doesn't want anyone to know that she is alive, hiding herself in the house. It seems as if she is trying to avoid someone, like an enemy. I only mentioned her because she is still full of mystery."

Saying so, Sozu looked reluctant to talk further about the woman in question. Lady Kosaisho made no mention of her speculation over the lady's identity. The Empress said to Lady Kosaisho,

"I'd like to tell Commander Kaoru what Sozu talked about, for this mysterious lady could be the one he cared about so much."

Although it appeared quite probable that the lady was, in fact, Kaoru's missing love, they couldn't do or say anything, knowing that the lady had been unwilling to let Sozu or the Commander know the truth.

Princess Ippon was restored to health. Sozu went back to his mountain temple. On the way, he visited the house in Ono. The sister nun was indignant at what had happened in her absence.

"She could have committed a sin by converting herself to a nun. I think it was so unfair for you to give her the commandments without informing me beforehand. I cannot believe what you have done to me."

She couldn't help complaining, although she knew it would change nothing by blaming anyone. She turned to the lady and said,

"Now that you have achieved your wish, devote yourself fully to worship. People die sooner or later, young or old. All the misfortunes you have experienced were enough to make you despair of the future, isn't that right?"

The lady felt embarrassed when remembering that Sozu had seen her misery that day in Uji. He left behind some fabric, such as good silk and striped cloth to tailor new religious clothes for the lady. He said,

"As long as I live, I will take care of you. You don't have to worry about anything. For those who grew up in the world of today, being bound by chains to their lust for power and glory, I can imagine that it is not easy to abandon their secular values and desires. But when you spend most of your time praying hard in a place like this, surrounded by mountains and forests, what in the world could bother or embarrass you? As an old poem teaches us, every life is as frail as the thinness of a leaf." He added,

"The gate with large pine trees is illuminated by the wandering full moon."

Sozu preached to the heart of the lady. In spite of his being simply a priest, his modest, learned words impressed her to such a degree that she gratefully felt that they were exactly what she had been waiting so long to hear.

The sky above the castle surrounded by oak trees was filled all day with wind song. The wind roared without rest that day. It sounded so terrifying that Sozu said,

"Oh my, they say priests in the mountains cannot help crying out on days like this."

Then the lady fully realized that she was one of these priests he spoke of when she noticed the tears spilling out of her eyes. She walked out to the edge of the house to find many people in clothing typical of court nobles in the far distance. Usually there were few who passed through there on their way up the mountain. Besides, the few people who did pass this way were usually monks who came from the same temple. Thus she found it very unusual to see these worldly men nearby. The party was that of Chu-sho, the man who had persistently refused to accept the lady's spurning of his advances, which was why he had come all this way once more. Walking up the mountain, however, he was enchanted by the trees aflame with red and yellow leaves. They were colored even more vividly and beautifully than in any other place he had visited that autumn. Surrounded by the beauty of the season, he started to feel quiet and emotional at the same time. Chu-sho reconsidered, thinking that it would be rather strange to meet a lady without any secrets and thought better of complaining to her.

"I have much free time these days, although I feel uneasy. Today I took this trip expecting to be surrounded by beautifully colored leaves. It will give you a fine rest to sleep in the shade of a tree just like it used to do back in the old days," he said, looking out the window.

As usual, the sister nun was easily moved to tears.

"木枯の吹きにし山のふもとには

たち隠るべきかげだにぞなき

(Once the cold winter wind blows the tinted leaves from the trees, there is no shade in which to hide yourself.)

Now that the lady has become a nun, this is no longer a place for you to stay," the sister nun said tearfully and Chu-sho responded,

"待つ人もあらじと思ふ山里の

梢を見つつなほぞ過ぎうき

(Looking at the treetops in a mountain village, where I know no one is waiting for me, I still cannot pass it by.)"

He continued to speak of the lady in vain and proclaimed to Sho-sho,

"Though I understand that the lady is now a nun, could I gaze upon her for just a moment? You must permit me to do so, as you promised me the opportunity once before."

Sho-sho entered the room to check on the lady, who looked so splendid that it seemed a terrible pity to hide her, to make it impossible for the world outside to adore such beauty. Wearing muted clothes under a light gray coat, she was quite small but had a good figure, a fine-looking face and glossy, rich hair. The end of her bangs flared outward and looked like a beautiful fan unfolded. Her face, which was not only very attractive, but also as smooth as silk, appeared ruddy and shiny as if make-up had been applied. Her rosary was left hanging on a room screen nearby even while she was praying, so that she could concentrate her attention on her worship. How she surrendered herself to the sacred words was such a divine sight, a perfect model for paintings. Every time Sho-sho looked at the lady serving as a nun, it had been so hard for her to hold back her tears. Moreover, she had no idea how a man who had cared about her so much would feel when he viewed this sight. Since Sho-sho thought it was a good chance for the man to grasp the reality of the situation, she showed him an opening in the door and swept aside things in the room to ensure that his view would be clear. Looking into the room, Chu-sho was surprised that the lady so surpassed his expectations in beauty. He felt sorrow and regret, as if he himself had made a big mistake. The grief coming from deep in his heart was so overwhelming that he felt that he would lose control of himself. He left that part of the house at once, so as not to let others notice his distress. He pondered his thoughts of this mysterious lady over and over.

"When someone as extraordinary as her were to suddenly disappear, people would search high and low for her. Besides, if a daughter of some nobleman hides herself away without any information of her whereabouts, or turns her back on the world for a grudge against a man's betrayal, rumors would have been spread and I should have heard them."

But as far as he knew, none of this had occurred in this case.

"Even though she is a nun, having a relationship with such a beautiful lady won't bother me in the least. In fact, she looks all the more elegant now. I'm going to secretly make her mine."

He seriously discussed his idea with the sister nun.

"When she was a worldly person, there might have been some reason to keep her distance from me. But now that she has abandoned her old way of life, it will be much easier for her to talk with others. Could you tell her that? I have visited here because of the lingering memory of your deceased daughter, but recently, I must admit that it is also because of my feelings for the lady."

The sister nun replied,

"I'm very concerned about her future. If you are certain that you wish to continue to visit here, you don't know how glad that makes me. I feel sorry for her, just thinking of her life after I pass away."

She spoke while tears filled her eyes. Chu-sho couldn't fully understand the relationship between the sister nun and the lady, but it seemed that they had not always been strangers.

"Now that I have shared my decision with you, my will has hardened to the point where it is now unchangeable, although I also don't know how much time is left for me to take care of her in this world. Is it true that there is no one who has come looking for her? I'm not saying that this would change anything about my conviction to be with her, but as long as this point remains unclear, I don't quite feel right about it all."

The sister nun replied honestly,

"There might have been someone if she had lived in a more prominent way. But she has removed herself from the secular world, giving up an all greed and desire, which seems to have been nothing but her own decision."

Chu-sho went to greet the lady.

　　　"おほかたの世を背きける君なれど
　　　　　　厭ふによせて身こそつらけれ

(Although you became a nun on the pretext of despising your

life, if it were actually because of my persistent meddling, I could not forgive myself.)"

A female servant relayed what Chu-sho had said to the lady by repeating every single word of his passionate, long message. She continued,

"You can count on me as if I were your brother. We can have a pointless little chat to make you feel more at ease."

There the lady interrupted and said,

"I'm afraid I'm still too immature to know what is truly pointless. Even if someone tells me what is important, I won't realize it."

She didn't reply to the poem, which had asked her to disclose the true reason behind her decision.

After all the misery she experienced before, relationships with men seemed nothing but a disturbance. She wanted to live away from people, abandoned like a dead tree. Thus, she had spent months in a state of depression. Things had changed since her wish to be a nun was granted by Sozu. She learned to spend every day feeling better than before, laughing a lot with the sister nun and sometimes even playing *go* with her. She was also so dedicated to her religious services that she recited many sorts of sutras for herself, although when the snow covered the ground so deeply that it kept people away, her life seemed very boring with nothing pleasing to do.

The new year had begun. In this hidden quiet village in Ono, no sign of the coming season could yet be seen. The streams near the house were completely iced over, and their murmur had vanished. The lady felt so alone. It seemed impossible for her to leave her past behind, even though Prince Niou had once written her a poem saying,

"峰の雪みぎはの氷踏み分けて

君にぞまどふ道はまどはず

(The snowy peaks or the icy riverbanks cannot keep me at bay. Losing myself in my love for you, I will never lose my way to your side.)"

He was one of those that she wished to forget the most, but the memory of their time together still clung to her. As she always did, she created works of calligraphy to heal her sorrow in her spare time after her sutra sessions.

"かきくらす野山の雪をながめても
　　　ふりにしことぞ今日も悲しき

(When I see the snow falling down from the dark sky onto hills and fields, it reminds me of the old days, accompanied by so much pain and grief.)"

She often mused over her past memories, believing that, even though it had been almost a year since she had disappeared, there would still be someone who thought of her. The sister nun found a person who had come to bring young greens in a humble basket to revere the longevity of the nuns. She wrote to the lady,

"山里の雪間の若菜つみはやし
　　　なほ生ひさきの頼まるるかな

(Even the young greens that we picked in snow to celebrate your new life and our longevity remind me of your life which stretches far afield.)"

And the lady answered,

"雪深き野辺の若菜も今よりは
　　　君が為にぞ年もつむべき

(From now on, I will go and pick young greens for you even though the field is deeply covered with snow, which will give me reason to live longer.)"

The sister nun sadly understood that the lady truly meant what she said. Even more regrettably, it seemed to the sister nun that the lady had abandoned her life so easily. She cried, missing the times that they had spent together.

There was an apricot tree near the terrace of the lady's room, with its small red flowers in full bloom. Their color and scent were just like those she remembered from previous days. It might be because she couldn't forget the perfume of the man she had met secretly so many times that the apricot flowers captured her emotions more than any other bloom. On the following night, she put a out a tub of sacred water as an offering to Buddha. The lady then called on a young humble nun and asked her to pick a branch from the tree. The snapping of the twig wafted the scent of the flowers to the lady even more seductively.

“袖ふれし人こそ見えね花の香の

それかとにほふ春のあけぼの

(Although I can no longer find the man who used to leave his perfume on my sleeves with his touch, the scent of these young spring blossoms are easily confused with his fragrance.)”

A grandson of the mother nun, who was the Governor of Kii province, came to visit Kyoto. He was a handsome man of around thirty and filled with confidence from head to toe.

“How have you been, ma’am?” he asked her, but she didn’t respond to him due to her growing senility. Thus, he came to the sister nun’s room.

“It looks like she has gone senile after all these years. It’s sad for me to see her like this. I’m so sorry that I have lived so far away for so many years that I have been unable to take care of her when it seems she has not much time left to live. It pains me even more because when my parents passed away, she filled their role for both me and my sister. Does Lady Kita in Hitachi still often stay in touch?”

Lady Kita was his young sister, whose husband was the Governor of Hitachi province. The sister nun shook her head in disapproval.

“These years of life haven’t treated mother kindly. Your sister hardly ever writes to us. It seems apparent that mother won’t be able to last until Lady Kita returns after the duties of her husband in Hitachi are completed.”

The conversation reached the lady’s ears, and she became curious simply because Hitachi was the name of her mother. She listened to the man as he said,

"I'm sorry I couldn't come here sooner, but I have been kept very busy dealing with all of my troublesome official duties since I arrived in Kyoto several days ago. I even tried to visit yesterday, although it turned out that I had to accompany the Commander for the entire day. He decided to spend the day at a palace in Uji where the deceased Prince Hachi used to live. The Commander was once married to a daughter of Prince Hachi, but she passed away a few years ago. He then developed a secret relationship with a sister of his deceased wife, but again, that lady died last spring. Yesterday was the one-year anniversary of the lady's death, so the Commander organized a memorial service and instructed a monk from the temple in Uji as to what to do. I'm thinking to have a set of female clothes prepared for the ceremony. Would it be possible to ask you to tailor it for me? Of course, I can supply everything you will need to complete the task."

Having heard this, there was no way that the lady could stay calm. She was very touched to hear the story, sitting in a corner of the room facing the wall so that people wouldn't notice the disturbance in her mind. The sister nun asked, being confused,

"I thought the deceased Prince had only two daughters. Which was the one who married Prince Niou?"

"I guess the one who died last year was a daughter of a mistress. Although the Commander didn't make the relationship with this lady public while she was alive, now he grieves for her so much. The time when her sister died several years ago was worse though. Then he was so depressed that he almost abandoned the secular world to become a monk."

The lady grew scared to know that the Governor was one of the closest followers of Commander Kaoru.

"By a curious coincidence, both of the half-sisters who were loved by the Commander died nowhere else but in the same house in Uji. You cannot imagine how much he pined over them yesterday. He walked down to an open hallway to look over the river, and gazed into the current, breaking down into tears. When he came back up to the room, he left a poem on the wall:

'見しひとは影もとまらぬ水の上に
落ちそふ涙いとどせきあへず

(To the surface of the water, in which I cannot find a trace of those I have loved before, my tears flood down with no way to hold them back.)' "

The Governor said,

"He doesn't speak much, but it was so easy to see the depth of his sadness. I'm sure that any lady would admire him as a splendid man. I have served this respectable person since I was young, and I have never doubted his personality. That is why I have been a true admirer of the Commander without caring the least bit for anyone who says they are the greatest power in the world."

The lady was impressed that even a man who didn't appear to be so discreet could well grasp Commander Kaoru's worth. The sister nun said,

"I guess the Commander still cannot occupy the same class as his deceased father, his highness Hikaru, although it is a fact that only this family is prospering in the world of today. How does Commander Kaoru compare to Yugiri, the Great Minister of the Right?"

"The Great Minister is splendid-looking, sophisticated and very special. He has his own unique presence. But then, Prince Niou is also a great man indeed. Everyone would wish to be able to take care of him, especially the female servants who surround him."

He kept talking like this as if he was following the lines in some script written by another. The lady listened to the conversation with not only sadness, but also curiosity. In no way did what had happened to her seem real. The Governor spoke at length without once taking a break and then left the house.

The lady was glad to know that the Commander still remembered her, but at the same time she missed him deep inside. Although she was also worried about her mother, it seemed undesirable for her to let her mother look at her or even hear about her since she had crossed the point of no return. Watching people preparing and dyeing the cloth which was to be dedicated in her own memorial service was a distinctly odd experience that never happens twice in a lifetime, although she had to hide her feelings amidst all of this activity.

The sister nun asked the lady for some help as she handed her a piece of cloth.

"Could you help us please? Needlework is your specialty, right?"

Upon receiving the cloth, the lady was swept up by an enormous wave of anxiety. She refused by feigning sickness and went back to bed without even touching the fabric. The sister nun threw the cloth down and came to the lady's bed to see how she was, consumed as she was with worry, while the others chose a pink outer on a crimson layer of clothing. Some then said,

"Our wish was to let the young lady wear a nice dress like this, not the dark plain costume she now dons."

The lady composed a new poem.

> "尼衣かはれる身にやありし世の
>   かたみに袖をかけてしのばん
>
> (Although now I am cloaked in the plain costume of nuns, trying the gorgeous outer on, why do we so easily forget what it was like to live in the world outside?)"

Her confusion got her thinking.

"I am so sorry that I'm still hiding things from these nice people. If I die, they will know who I am because, in this world, no one can keep anything secret forever. Then they will understand why I stayed away from the outside world and hid my true identity."

She quietly said,

"Although I have almost forgotten how I used to live, when I see them preparing a kimono like this, it brings back old memories and makes me miss everyone so much."

The sister nun answered,

"I guess there are a lot of memories for you to remember. It's such a shame that you don't share any of them with me. I cannot tailor this garment particularly well since I have no awareness of the fashion in favor today, which makes me wonder what I would do if my daughter were still alive. I imagine that you also have someone who might be feeling the same way as I do right now. Even a mother like me, who lost her child before her eyes, wishes to know where her soul resides. I'm sure there will be someone desperate to know where you are, worrying so much about you."

"Yes, there was someone when I was just a layperson. She might have passed away by now."

The lady turned her back on the others so they couldn't see her crying.

"Every time I think of her, it just kills me inside, and this is why I cannot talk about it to others. Otherwise how could I keep a thing hidden from you?"

The words she spoke were few, but they were full of meaning.

After the ceremony of the one-year anniversary, Commander Kaoru was pondering the frailty of his relationship with the lady. As he promised before, he helped the adult half-brothers of Lady Ukifune to attain the status of Lieutenant of his division or of Chamberlain. Also, he was going to raise the station of some of her minor brothers and make them his men in the future.

On a quiet rainy night, he visited the Empress. Since there weren't many visitors that day, he was telling her some stories of himself.

"In one rustic mountain village, I had a woman with whom I was in a relationship for a few years, although some people said it brought me no good to visit such a remote place so often. I was sure that there had been some connection between us from the previous life. Generally, when a man falls in love with some woman, something had already started even before they were born into this world. Believing thus, the lady and I carried on a relationship in Uji. But after I lost this second lady as well, I began to think that the village itself might be the cause of all these tragedies. Once I became possessed by this idea, the place suddenly seemed so far away and I just stopped visiting there. The other day, after a long period of separation, I dropped in on my way to conducting some business. There I understood afresh the fleeting nature of people's lives. At the same time I came to realize that I needed to reconsider the place as that which the sacred Prince Hachi left behind so as to raise a greater sense of morality in me."

The Empress remembered the story of a mysterious lady she had heard before from Sozu. She felt sorry for the Commander and asked,

"There may be some demons in that place, indeed. How did the lady die?"

Commander Kaoru supposed that Prince Niou worried about him for losing two ladies in a row.

"I guess that's what it is. An isolated village is always bound to be haunted by some kind of evil spirits. Even the way they passed away was such a mystery."

He responded so without further explanation. The Empress sensed that he still didn't want others to know what happened. If she had told him that Prince Niou had known everything then, the Commander might have been greatly humiliated. Knowing how strongly the truth of the lady's death devastated the Prince, ending in depression, she didn't ask anything more about the lady. She understood that it must be hard for both of the broken young men to mention their loss.

The Empress called on Lady Kosaisho and told her secretly,

"The Commander talked about the ladies' deaths with so much sadness between the lines, that I started wondering if I should tell him the story or not. But since it is still unclear whether the mysterious lady that Sozu mentioned and the ex-fiancé of the Commander are the same person, I hesitated to tell him. You have heard the whole story, haven't you? Setting aside the things the Commander doesn't seem to want to know, tell him roughly what Sozu told us about the unknown lady, just as part of a chat between close friends."

Lady Kosaisho held back from committing to the idea, saying,

"Even Your Highness hesitated to tell him. How could someone like me do this?"

The Empress gently convinced her by replying,

"This sort of things wholly depends on the situation. I know that you can understand the reason why I am not the one to tell this to him, can't you?"

Lady Kosaisho understood what she really meant, and respected the Empress for her deep consideration of the Commander.

On an occasion when the Commander stopped by to visit Lady Kosaisho in her room, she mentioned the story to him in passing. It was no wonder that he couldn't stay calm to hear of such an unbelievably strange happening. Then he realized what was going on behind the Empress's words.

"She must have asked me how the lady died because she was vaguely aware of this fact. Why didn't she just say so in my presence?" he thought to himself.

He also understood his own fault in the matter.

"Well, I didn't honestly tell her how the lady and I had been together either, so the fault might partially be mine. Hearing what I have done from others' mouths, what surprised me the most was my own foolishness. Although I didn't tell our story to anyone, it seems clear that there must be some rumors going around, for even the secrets of the living cannot be kept in the world of today."

Recognizing this, he still didn't dare to easily confess what had really happened between them, even to Lady Kosaisho.

"The lady in the story sounds quite similar to someone I know, whose actual death was never truly confirmed. Is she still doing fine, by the way?"

Lady Kosaisho answered,

"When the monk came down from the mountains, he made the mysterious lady a nun. Although even while she had been seriously ill, those who took care of her tried to stop her from taking the commandments. Sozu said her will to abandon this world was so strong that he couldn't turn her down."

In addition to the fact that the strange lady had appeared in Uji, considering all the circumstances at that time, there wasn't a single reason to contradict his assumption about her identity.

"If I come to find that this nun is the same lady I thought I'd lost, then I will feel like such a fool. How can I find out for sure? If I go out to look for her myself, some shameful rumors will be spread, that a nobleman like me is searching desperately for a young lady of humble origin. Besides, if Prince Niou happens to catch wind of it, he will remember his feelings for her and try to get in the way of the religious life into which she just has taken her first steps. Or, he may have known about it already and told the Empress not to tell anyone else. That's possibly the reason why she didn't mention the story to me. If the Prince has already started pulling some strings behind my back, I'd rather tell myself that the lady has been dead and give up on her completely, no matter how much I love her and miss being with her. Since she is potentially alive, there will be a chance only in the distant future to meet her and have a talk in private after this life. I would certainly never attempt to make her mine again."

His groundless thoughts raced so far ahead that he became confused. Expecting that the Empress wouldn't give him any further information, he couldn't help trying to figure out why she didn't tell him about the lady. Thus he made a point of visiting her the next day.

This time Commander Kaoru tried to speak in more detail than he did the day before.

"Someone told me that a lady whom I thought I had lost in a lamentable way was still alive, living an incognito existence. I cannot believe it yet, but I have always been sure that considering her modest personality, there was no way that she had willingly committed such a horrible deed and left me behind. But if the story is accurate and she had become possessed by an evil spirit, then I think it all makes sense."

Although when the topic turned to Prince Niou, the Empress' son, he avoided direct expressions and instead said,

"If the Prince realized that I've found out the lady is alive, he will think that I'm a miserably amorous man. So I'm going to pretend like I have no idea of what happened to the lady."

The Empress apologized for her son's selfishness.

"I know only what Sozu told me, but I didn't hear the whole story because it was such a horrible night and I was so scared. Besides, my son doesn't know about this. I don't know what to say, but as I've heard the situation among the three of you was quite complicated in those days, I understand there will be a bit of trouble if he comes to find out about this. I'm terribly sorry about that. He always gets in trouble when it comes to love affairs, and some people don't care for that aspect of his nature."

The Commander was very impressed by her noble discretion. He was certain that she would never utter a word of what he had said, even when making small talk with her closest people.

The Commander couldn't escape his constant thoughts about the lady.

"Where is the village where she lives? How can I visit there without damaging my reputation? It would be better to go there directly and meet with Sozu beforehand to discuss the details.

On the eighth of every month, Commander Kaoru visited the central hall of the famous Enryaku Temple to pay homage and make contributions to the temple. This time, Ukifune's younger brother accompanied him, and the Commander planned on stopping in Yokawa on the way back home. He didn't tell her family that the lady had been found alive because it was too soon to be certain, he said to himself. But the truth seemed to be that he wanted their reunion to be as romantic as possible, just like a fairy tale. Even if the lady was Ukifune, if she looked unhappy living with other nuns, or some sad rumors about her came to his ears, he wouldn't be able to bear his inevitable sense of regret.

10. A Floating Bridge in a Dream

A Floating Bridge in a Dream

CHARACTERS

Ukifune

Commander Kaoru

Sozu, a high-ranking monk

The sister nun, Sozu's younger sister

Ukifune's younger half brother

As he did every month, the Commander went to pray in the temple at the top of Mt. Hiei. The following day, he visited Yokawa Temple, surprising Sozu, who was honored to have him as a guest. Although the Commander had known the monk for years through their shared prayer sessions, they had never been particularly close. Yet now Commander Kaoru felt great respect for Sozu, since he had seen with his own eyes Sozu's remarkable capabilities in curing Princess Ippon's illness, and thus their relationship had grown. It seemed quite odd to Sozu that a man of such considerable status had come to this most isolated area of the temple to visit him in person. The people there treated the Commander with warm hospitality. They offered him a bowl of rice cooked in tea while the two men engaged in a lively conversation.

As their discussion eventually wound down, the Commander offhandedly asked Sozu if he owned a house in Ono.

"Yes, I certainly do. It is just a crude one though. My mother is an old nun and she lives there since I couldn't find her a proper place in Kyoto. Besides, the house provides a convenient place for me to visit her at any time of day or night during my retreats from the outside world."

The Commander said,

"I've heard that there were formerly many houses around there, but it seems the area has fallen on hard times recently."

He drew a little closer to Sozu and said quietly,

"It may be just a false rumor, and I know that you may think ill of me for asking this, but I've heard that a lady whom I had once taken care of lives in that house of yours, hiding herself away from the outside world. I was thinking to tell you what had transpired between us, once I confirmed that this story was true. But I also heard that you had already given her her vows and that she is now one of your disciples. Is this true? Since most believe her to have perished, it has been said that I am the one responsible for bringing about the death of such a lovely young creature."

Upon hearing that, Sozu regretfully thought,

"I had felt that she couldn't be just an ordinary lady. Considering the

Commander's attitude, it's clear that he cared about her deeply."

Sozu had no idea what to say, feeling quite distressed that he had given in so easily to the lady's plaintive requests to become a nun, without first having given any truly thoughtful consideration to the matter.

"He seems quite certain that the story is true. Now that he has come to ask me in person, knowing as much as he does, I must in no way try to keep it secret. If I don't tell him the truth now, trouble will certainly follow."

Thus he considered his position carefully, and said,

"I still don't completely understand the situation, but are you talking about the mysterious lady who came under our care recently? The nuns who live there went to Hase Temple one day on a pilgrimage. On the way back, they stopped over at a palace in Uji. A messenger came to let me know that my mother's condition had suddenly worsened and she was suffering greatly. I came down from the mountain to see her. But immediately after my arrival, I witnessed a quite unusual series of events."

He lowered his voice.

"While our own mother was in danger of dying at any moment, my sister put ever more energy into taking care of the lady. She was near death as well, but clung to her last breath. I thought of an old story, in which a dead body laid in the Palace of Souls[1] somehow came back to life. Wondering if what was happening was a similar type of occurrence, I called for the best prayers of my followers and commanded them to perform an uninterrupted series of incantations. Although my mother had already lived long enough to dissolve her lingering attachment to this world, it seemed she had chosen to end her life on the road. I worked so hard, wanting to help her concentrate on her prayers undisturbed, so that she could rest in peace. Therefore, I know little of the lady's state at that time. They told me that they assumed a goblin or a tree spirit had possessed

---

1. A place to lay body before a funeral.

her and kidnapped her, taking her to the forest. Even after we had all returned to Kyoto, the lady's condition showed no improvement for the first three months or so. My sister used to be called Lady Kita, the wife of a deceased captain of the outer palace guards. She became a nun after losing her only daughter many years ago. No matter how much time had passed, her grief refused to set her free. Then this mysterious lady came into her life, and she was around the same age that my sister's deceased daughter had been, looking absolutely beautiful, as you know. For my sister, the lady was like a gift from God. She was so happy and, at the same time, filled with a sense of obligation to save her life that she begged me desperately to do something to help her, with tears in her eyes. Watching her trying her utmost, I had little choice but to assent, so I went down to the house in Ono and prayed for the protection of the lady, which, fortunately, turned out to be very effective. Little by little her condition improved and she eventually recovered. But even after that, the lady mournfully claimed that she sensed that what had initially possessed her still clung tightly to her soul, and that she wanted to escape from its disturbing influence to pursue peace in her next life. As a monk, I am unwilling to prevent someone from entering Buddhism, so I allowed her to become a nun. Well, with no outside information, how could I have realized that this lady was anyone you would have been concerned with? This was such a strange incident that I wanted very badly to talk with someone about it, but I have kept it a secret because the older nuns who live there were opposed, fearing that the rumor might spread and cause trouble."

The Commander was struck speechless to learn that the lady actually lived. Even though he was the one who had sought to confirm her existence, what Sozu just told him was hard to believe, as if it had come to him in a dream. He was so stunned that, for a few moments, tears flowed down his cheeks. When the Commander regained his senses, he felt suddenly ashamed for having shown so much emotion in front of Sozu, and tried to behave as if nothing had happened. It was then that Sozu fully understood the extent of the Commander's feelings for the lady. Having permitted her to become a nun, Sozu was left with a deep sense of guilt.

He asked the Commander,

"I assumed that she had been taken away by some evil spirit. This kind of thing often happens because of a karmic debt from a previous life. She was evidently born the child of a nobleman. How could she possibly have gone so wrong? What was it that ruined her life?"

"Her father was from the royal family, but she herself was modestly born. We met by chance and began a relationship, but I never planned to take her as one of my official wives. Of course, I didn't intend to destroy her life either. Anyway, one day she unexpectedly disappeared. They said she had thrown herself into the river, but nobody was actually sure what had happened because there was no body and there were so many questions left unanswered. I was relieved to hear that she became a nun in an effort to make up for her sins, but since her mother is devastated and still terribly misses her daughter, I'm thinking of telling her the truth, although I understand that it has been kept secret for a reason. My actions may run counter to the effort you made, but do you still think it will actually cause you any serious problems? Since the bond between the mother and child cannot be broken, her mother would certainly come visit her here."

He continued,

"This will quite possibly cause you a great deal of trouble, but could I have a chance to visit the house in Ono? Can we go down the mountain together? Knowing the truth now in such detail, I can feign ignorance no longer. Now that she has become a nun, a woman beyond this world, I hope we can have an honest talk about the things we have been through."

The expression on the Commander's face revealed his inner pain. Feeling sorry for him, Sozu was unsure as to what the right course of action could be. He thought,

"We abandon worldliness by changing our appearance. Nevertheless,

I've heard that some monks who have shaved their hair and beards off still have difficulties in transcending earthly desires. I cannot even imagine how hard it would be for a woman to become a nun. I'm afraid that this meeting would only cause her further suffering."

Thinking thus, he hesitated to make any immediate decision and said,

"I don't think the situation allows for me to visit there in the coming days, but I promise that I will contact you about your request next month."

The Commander was irritated by Sozu's reply because he wanted the meeting to take place as soon as possible, although any show of desperate begging would bring his dignity into question. He had no choice but to accept Sozu's promise, and left it at that.

Kaoru returned several days later with the most handsome of the lady's younger brothers in tow. Kaoru said to Sozu,

"This boy is a relative of the lady, and I'm going to send him for her now. Could you write her a message? You don't have to give her my name. Please just tell her that there's someone who's looking for her."

Sozu was unsure about the wisdom of this plan and said,

"I fear that telling her about it myself may provoke a sinful consequence. I've already shared all of the details with you already. Why don't you visit there yourself? I don't see any inconvenience in that."

The Commander laughed, and he shared with Sozu some of his religious inclinations.

"I am truly sorry that you think of this as a trouble of such a nature. I view a religious life so highly that I wonder why I still live in the secular world. Since my childhood, I've always wanted to be a priest. My mother, Princess Sanjo, however, has relied on me to such a degree that I couldn't abandon her, or her expectations of me. So I started my career as she hoped, and now here I am. When I look inward, I find myself a man of unexpectedly high status, one who cannot move freely, being bound by duties and responsibilities. While I was waiting for the chance to become a monk, I acquired some relationships which still cling to me, ones that will never let me be. I won't do anything that runs counter to how the Buddha taught us to live, unless I have some reason to violate these precepts out of a sense of duty. Even when faced with temptations, I try my utmost to calm myself and follow my principles. My resolution is as firm as that of a saint. Why do I want to break from my ethics and commit such a great sin over such a foolish impulse? Think about it. It's an impossibility. I simply feel guilty for not telling her mother about this, since she is the one who has suffered the most. All I want is to relieve the mother's sorrow by letting her know how her daughter is doing and to set myself free from this sense of guilt. Only then can I enjoy a truly calm and peaceful mind."

Sozu finally nodded in agreement and commended the Commander for his pious attitude. Since the sun had set by the end of their talk, it seemed best for them to stay overnight in Ono on their way back to Kyoto. After careful consideration, however, he decided not to do so, for their visit would be bothersome to those residing with the lady, since nothing had been settled ahead of time. Before the men left for Kyoto, Sozu noticed the brother of the lady and made a complimentary comment about him. The Commander said,

"Please leave your message with this boy informing her of my intentions."

Sozu wrote a letter and handed it to the boy.

"You should come and visit here sometimes. I am not a total stranger to you."

Although the young man didn't fully understand what Sozu meant, he accepted the letter and left the temple with the Commander. When they arrived in Ono, those at the front of the party were ordered to spread themselves out a bit and to proceed quietly.

In the village of Ono, the lady was losing herself in melancholic thoughts, looking back upon the past as she faced the deep mountains covered in dense green forests. Her eyes traced the paths of the fireflies twinkling in the air around the stream of the garden. No matter what she did, it seemed impossible to escape her feelings of depression. She noticed some nuns sitting on the veranda of the house peering far down the valley. They could hear the subdued voices of men emanating from both the front and rear of a procession which was winding its way through the mountains toward the uphill village, and a large number of torches could be seen dancing amongst the green. The nuns started chatting about the unusual sight.

"Who is approaching? There are so many people in the vanguard of that procession."

"This afternoon, when I went up the mountains to dedicate dried seaweed to the temple, they were very appreciative because they were in the middle of preparations for the Commander's sudden visit."

"The Commander? Who? Is he the husband of Princess Ninomiya?"

Their conversation reminded the lady of how far removed this place was from the capital. The local culture here was so distant from that of the world outside that some were not even sure who the Commander was. It must be him, the lady thought. From the conversations echoing below, she recognized some of the voices of the Commander's followers from the times when he had traveled all the mountain trails to come visit her in Uji. Then she realized that the memories she had tried to forget would never fade away, regardless of time's flow. There was already nothing she could do. To avoid her feelings of misery, she closed herself off more tightly than usual and devoted herself to praying so as to cast away her thoughts of helplessness. In a place as isolated as Ono, the only conduit to the secular world was through those who visited the temple in Yokawa.

The Commander was thinking to send the boy back to Ono, but he hesitated to do so out of fear that some of the others traveling with him would notice. He returned directly home and sent the boy to Ono on the following day. A few of Kaoru's mid-ranking followers accompanied the boy, including one who had been sent to Uji many times. The Commander called on the boy when no one was around.

"Do you remember what your deceased sister looked like? Though we believed that she had passed away, I've found out that she is, in fact, still alive. I don't want anyone else to know about this, so I'm asking you to go there to see how she is doing. Just don't tell your mother about this yet. If she gets upset after hearing about your sister's fate and makes a big fuss, those who shouldn't be in the know may also discover the truth. I am making considerable effort to search for your sister on your mother's behalf so as to help pull her out of her deep sorrow."

The Commander placed the boy under strict orders to speak about this matter to no one. Although the boy had been very young at the time, he had thought his deceased sister had been the most beautiful of all his siblings. He had been feeling very sorry for her since he learned of the tragedy. But what the Commander had just revealed to him filled him with joy and happiness. He couldn't hold his tears back, even though he knew that it was shameful for boys to cry. He tried very hard to act like a man.

A letter from Sozu arrived in Ono early in the morning.

"Did a boy arrive last night to deliver a message from the Commander? I've come to learn what transpired between him and the lady before her sudden appearance in our lives. As the one who permitted her to become a nun, I regret my lack of deliberation. Please relay this message to her. Since there are some other matters still to discuss, I'll visit there in a few days time."

The sister nun had no idea what was going on. She rushed into the lady's room and showed her the letter. The lady blushed slightly upon seeing what the sister nun held in her hand. She became filled with anxiety, worrying whether some rumor about her was already making its rounds. She thought that the sister nun would be angry at her for concealing her past. The lady struggled to find something to say, her mind racing. The sister nun became upset and said,

"Now I need to know what really happened to you. You make me feel worthless by continuing to act like a stranger."

Since she didn't fully understand the situation, she waited for the lady's response.

At that very moment, a messenger from Sozu arrived.

The sister nun found it strange to receive another message from Sozu on the same day, but expecting that this time the truth would be revealed, she showed him in. A beautiful, elegant boy in lovely attire entered her room. She offered the boy a cushion to sit on behind a room screen.

"Since this occasion is not so official, this screen will be unnecessary."

Then the sister nun reorganized things and met the boy face to face. The letter was addressed to the lady from Sozu himself. Ukifune found herself no longer able to dodge questions related to her identity. She felt so uneasy that she hid herself further inside the house in an effort to avoid contact with anyone.

"You have always been very shy, but this time your attitude is shameful."

She showed the letter to the lady, which read,

"This morning the Commander came here and asked me how you had been. So I told him everything I knew about you from the day we met until now. I was very surprised to learn that you turned your back on such a great man, one who cared so deeply about you, and that you abandoned the world outside in this poor village. I'm afraid you might have committed a sin by doing so, although there's nothing we can do about it now. Try not to disturb your destiny by rekindling a relationship with the Commander, and do your utmost to make his sin of fixation on your love fade away. Since deciding to follow the life of a priest so early in life means so much to you, you should keep relying on the mercy of Buddha. I will provide you with more details during my next visit. For now, the boy I sent will answer your questions."

Reading the message, the lady could see that it was unmistakably clear that Sozu knew the whole story, although others didn't have a clue as to what it meant. The sister nun blamed the lady for not bringing it all out herself and said,

"I wonder who this boy is. What I cannot believe is that you are still trying to conceal these facts from me. I feel very sorry about this whole affair."

Tired of listening to the sister nun's words, the lady redirected her gaze outside. There she noticed the boy, whom she had missed so much, even on that fateful night when she decided to end her life. When they had lived together, she hated him because he seemed very arrogant and mean. Her mother, however, cherished him so much that he often accompanied her to Uji. As they both became a little older, they started to get along. She felt like she was dreaming, remembering her childhood. Above all, she wanted to ask him how her mother was doing. She had learned that most of those who were involved in her life had been getting on, but no rumors informed her of her mother's present state. Looking at her brother, her sense of sorrow seeped out in her tears.

The sister nun saw an image of the lady in the cute face of the boy and said,

"You are the lady's brother, aren't you? She must have questions to ask you. Come inside."

The lady didn't care for the sister nun's decision, however. Since her younger brother wouldn't have expected her to still be alive, it would confuse him all the more if she showed up before him as she now looked, completely changed from the sister he had known. The lady was too nervous to face him right away, so she took some time to gather her thoughts and said calmly,

"I don't want to say anything now, because it hurts me that you don't trust me, thinking that I've been hiding something from you. As you know, I was a pile of misery when you first found me. I must have been a horrible sight. I had possibly lost my sanity and my soul may have been altered at that time. No matter how hard I try, I cannot recall anything of what happened to me before then. But when I happened to hear the Governor of Kii Province chatting with someone, I had the slightest inkling that they might be talking about the place I used to live. Afterwards, I kept trying to recall small pieces of memories, but I was unsuccessful. The only person I remember is my mother, who tried her best to raise me to adulthood. My concern is whether she is even still alive. I worry about it so much that I can't shake the overwhelming sense of sorrow that clouds my mind. Now that I have seen the boy and have recognized his face, I remember him when he was much younger, which makes me feel like the lady I used to be, and I really miss that feeling. But at the same time, I want to leave everything in this world behind, without informing my relatives that I'm still alive. If possible, I'd love to meet my mother, but nobody else can change my mind, especially not the man Sozu wrote about in the letter. Please tell him that there was a misunderstanding and let me continue to hide myself away."

The lady begged so, but the sister nun was unrelenting.

"How can I say such a thing to him? Sozu is naturally such a man of integrity, even among priests, that I'm quite sure that he has already told the Commander everything. Glossing over the fact won't cover it up for much longer. Besides, no one should ever prevaricate before a man as great as the Commander."

"She is too stubborn to accept the will of others. I've never met anyone like her."

Grumbling thus, the nuns decided to invite the boy into one of the rooms at the end of the main house with screens obstructing his view of the inside.

Although this boy also knew the lady living there was his sister, being an adolescent, he was, at first, too shy to talk to her in a familiar manner. He said to the sister nun with downcast eyes,

"I'd like to hand her another letter. I believe what Sozu told us was sincere. I don't understand why she hides the truth so desperately."

The sister nun smiled to see him so baffled.

"Relax, young man. How sweet you are. It looks like the person to whom you are going to hand over the message is here. Even those serving around her are quite confused at her obstinate attitude. Please talk to her like you just did to us. I assume that there should be some reason for you to have come here despite your young age."

"But what can I say to her when she is upset with me and won't talk about anything in specific terms? If she takes me for a stranger, I have nothing further to say. I just wish to fulfill my obligation by passing this letter on directly to the lady."

The sister nun returned behind the screen and tried once more to convince the lady.

"I totally concur with him. Please stop acting so deplorably. I am almost frightened by your stubbornness."

The lady was pushed out into the room and sat down with a screen separating her from the boy. The situation was so unexpected to her that she felt as if she were dreaming. As soon as the boy recognized the outline of his sister in the shadow behind the screen, he came closer and handed her the letter from the Commander.

"I will leave immediately upon receiving your reply to my lord."

Since it was shocking to the boy that the sister he had looked up to the most was treating him so coldly, he had no desire to linger there any longer than was absolutely necessary.

The sister nun opened the envelope and showed the letter to the lady. She recognized the handwriting and the fragrance of incense which saturated the paper. His high level of sophistication had gone unchanged. Glancing at the letter, the lady felt it was as elegant as his previous writings She must have been enjoying this rare, curiosity-kindling event.

"I want you to know that I am capable of sincerely forgiving your previous sinful decisions through the aid of Sozu's mercy shown you. I simply wish to talk with you to learn how it all came about, since it has affected me like a nightmare, although I understand that having a private meeting with you might be inappropriate, considering your present status. I am also afraid of what others might imagine about our relationship."

It seemed that the Commander couldn't fully express his feelings even in his prose. Thus he wrote politely,

"法の師とたづぬる道をしるべにて
　　思はぬ山にふみまどふかな

(Although I traversed the mountains to visit a Buddhist master, the same path led me to you, where I became unexpectedly lost in love.)

Do you still remember this boy whom I sent to deliver this letter? He is the one who keeps me connected to the memory of us, and that's why I keep him at my side."

She sensed his truly delicate sentiments in the words, and thus she understood that she could in no way brush them aside with insincere correspondence. At the same time, however, she felt greatly humiliated just thinking what he would say to see her now, so different from the woman that he had known. Without a clear path before her, her mind seemed cloudier than ever and there was absolutely no way she could think of by which to explain herself. The lady finally started to cry out of confusion and fell prostrate on the floor. The other nuns didn't know what to do or say when faced with this degree of naiveté.

The sister nun asked the lady to tell her how she should respond.

"For now, I'm too confused and distracted to reply to him properly. I need to rest until this heartache subsides, and so I will reply to him sometime later. No matter how hard I try to remember the old times, nothing at all comes to mind. He mentioned that this situation was like a nightmare, but I have no idea what he is talking about. I may find some clue from what was written there, but only after my mind sorts everything out. At any rate, please take the letter back today. Besides, it will be inconvenient for you as well if this turns out to be a case of mistaken identity."

The lady pushed the unfolded letter across the floor to the sister nun.

"What kind of disrespectful attitude is this? We will also be held to blame for your rude behavior."

The sister nun began yelling. Feeling tired of the noise, the lady hid her face behind her sleeves and lay face down.

As she was the landlady of the house, the sister nun talked a bit with the young boy.

"Probably because of evil spirits, she seems to have lost her wits and suffers constantly from a bad disposition. Besides, becoming a nun has completely transformed her appearance. Although we have been anticipating the development of a complicated, problematic situation like this if someone were to find her here, which has kept me quite worried, now that I see you here in search of the lady, I am truly sorry to know the heart-breaking history behind her disappearance. Her emotional state has never stabilized, but this time, she looks even more distraught than usual."

After explaining this to the boy, the sister nun served him a proper, country-style dinner, taking pity on him for not being able to complete his duty. He dropped his shoulders and said,

"What do you think I should tell my lord, since it is clear that I have failed to meet his high expectations? Please tell me something that I could bring back to him, even a few words would be of great help."

The sister nun was moved and went to talk with the lady about what the boy had requested, trying to persuade her to write something back to the Commander. In spite of this, she wouldn't write even a single line. Having no idea what to do, the sister nun said to the boy,

"Well, apparently what you can do is to tell your lord honestly that no clear answer could be dragged out of the lady. Since we are not so far from Ono, please come again sometime in the future, in spite of the strong wind that blows through the mountains."

In the end, the boy thought it somewhat strange to stay there until sunset without a particular purpose, so he prepared himself to retrace his way home. The boy was greatly disappointed that he was unable to see the face of his sister after such a long time apart. He went home filled with a sense of disconsolation.

The Commander had been waiting expectedly for the arrival of the lady's response. When the boy returned with no obvious resolution, however, he regretted having sent a messenger at all. His delusion drove him so far as to suspect that someone might be keeping her there as a mistress, away from people's curious eyes. His mind raced uncontrollably through all of the possibilities generated from his past experiences.

Epilogue

When I finished this work in Ichijoji, in north Kyoto, the autumn season was coming to an end. The wind was blowing along Mt. Hiei and traveling down the hillside, causing the tree branches to sway in response. Colored leaves danced in the blue sky.

Kyoto has quietly observed the passage of people's lives during these some fifty years since I first entered Kyoto University. If you were to visit this ancient city, you too may feel that certain qualities of Murasaki's age linger in the city's atmosphere even today. The city of Uji, where the love triangle played itself out, also seems to have retained aspects of its original atmosphere.

During the course of translation, I often experienced the feeling that I was actually talking directly with Murasaki beyond the veil. Reading through the original work with the aid of copious notes, and then reconstructing the sentences in English, I came to grasp the real meaning of what Murasaki intended. I think to experience this type of satisfaction would be impossible in a project of this nature which involved only a single language. This feeling is somewhat similar to that of a composer who is rewriting a piece of Bach's music in a jazz arrangement.

Her subtle sense of humor made me feel as if we were sharing a private joke between friends. By the time I had completed the translation, however, it was lonesomeness rather than satisfaction which awaited me. But I have no time left to revisit these chapters as I must once again cross the Uji river and return to Kyoto.

This work would not have been possible without the aid of many individuals. Nahoko Toyota, age 24, who collaborated on this project, is almost the same age as Ukifune, and she injected into this work her vibrant and passionate interpretation of the poetry. I would especially like to thank Bruce Hall who generously donated his time in the evening hours after his workday had ended. I also want to express my gratitude to Mark Lucas who initially joined this project as a proofreader but eventually became the de facto editor after I discovered that our discussions on the story had helped to elevate the quality of the project and had deepened my own understanding of the tale. I am also indebted to Saori Yamaguchi for agreeing to create numerous original paintings to be used in this project. I am thankful to the Tale of Genji Museum in Uji for granting me permission to reprint several of the works from their collection. Finally, I wish to acknowledge Mayumi Yamamoto and Harumi Takemura for their assistance in the preparation of the manuscript.

Kazuyuki Hijiya

Kazuyuki Hijiya

Graduated from Kyoto University School of
Medicine, where he received a PhD in 1979
Board certified gastroenterologist
President of Higashiyodogawa Medical
Association (Osaka)
Translator of Japanese classical literature
Author of "Intelligent Rugby," published by
Yamaguchi Shoten

The Tale of Genji
The Uji Chapters Part II

by Murasaki Shikibu

translated by Kazuyuki Hijiya, Nahoko Toyota

Company：Yamaguchi Shoten
Address：72 Tsukuda-cho Ichijoji Sakyo-ku Kyoto 606-8175 Japan
Tel. +81-75-781-6121
Fax. +81-75-705-2003
URL：http://www.yamaguchi-shoten.co.jp
E-mail：yamakyoto-606@jade.dti.ne.jp

The Tale of Genji
The Uji Chapters Part II　　　　　　定価 本体 1,000 円（税別）

2012年1月20日 初　版

著　者　紫　　　式　部
訳　者　土 屋 和 之
　　　　豊 田 菜 保 子
発行者　山 口 冠 弥
印刷所　大村印刷株式会社
発行所　株式会社　山口書店
〒606-8175 京都市左京区一乗寺築田町72
TEL：075-781-6121　FAX：075-705-2003
出張所電話
　　東京03-5690-0051　　中部058-275-4024
　　福岡092-713-8575

ISBN 978-4-8411-0914-6　C0093　　　　　イラスト　山 口 紗 織